BROKEN
rules

ALSO BY I. A. DICE

Broken Promises

The Sound of Salvation
The Taste of Redemption

Edited by: Kylie Ryan at Final Cut Editing

Connect with I. A. Dice:
Instagram
Facebook
Reader Group

To my husband,
my very own
knight in shining armor

I. A. DICE

CHAPTER ONE

Layla

Cool droplets drip from my hair thanks to the fall thunderstorm, and a twenty-minute wait before I reach the bouncer stationed at the club's entrance.

Six feet tall, with an eagle tattoo on his neck, he looks me over slowly. A self-indulgent smirk twists his lips as eyes rove my legs longer than appropriate.

"Enjoy your night," he says, pushing the door open.

I'm two years shy of legally entering a club, but my surname poses a much bigger issue than my underage status.

Harston.

The Harston.

Daughter of Frank Harston, the man Chicago fears.

With a heavy sigh, I step inside the club, surprised that the bouncer didn't check my ID. He should have. His mistake will probably cost him the job, if not his head.

A hostess stamps my wrist with a Greek letter, Delta, the club's name, then points at a glass tunnel bathed in a red LED light hue. It leads to a room playing pop music, where sweet smoke hangs thickly above the crowd, the fragrant scent a mixture of summer berries and vanilla. Colorful strobe lights cut the air, bouncing off the walls, matching the rhythm of "Single Ladies" by Beyoncé, while hundreds of sweaty bodies dance to the beat.

POP room is nice enough but not quite what I'm after. I need a different music tonight, louder and with more bass to drown out my tormented, screaming mind. Clutching my bag, I push through the crowd, searching for the next room. A red, backless dress and neon-yellow heels work wonders for my self-esteem. I'm not shy but not overly confident either. At least not usually.

Tonight, anger bubbles inside me, rushing to the surface like diet Coke when you throw a Mentos in the bottle. I cross the room as if I own the goddamn place. As if I'm ready to set it alight and watch it burn.

I might be...

I have two valid reasons why jittery fear courses through my veins and why anger boils my blood, masking my unease. My face must reflect my emotions because people step out of my way, awe tinged with respect shining in their eyes, but one guy blocks my path, rooted to the floor. He's either blind or ignores me as I sail across the dance floor in a whirlwind of fiery annoyance, red fabric, and wet hair. I shove him aside, harder than intended... he trips over his legs, landing on his butt.

He glances at me with wide eyes before his head snaps to the beer in his hand. He holds the glass up like a trophy, grinning at his friends. "Yay!"

I keep walking. "Single Ladies" changes to "Umbrella" when I disappear behind another door. Heavy bass vibrations give the impression of the ground shaking beneath my feet. Fewer sweaty bodies crowd the dance floor here, but that's not surprising. Ten o'clock hasn't struck yet. People are only starting to arrive.

In need of a drink, I scan the room, searching for the least crowded bar. The one in the VIP section upstairs looks deserted compared to the two downstairs. Here, at least twenty people wait in line, impatiently stepping from one foot to another.

I make a pit stop in the ladies' room to pat myself dry with hand towels, wiping away the two tiny mascara rivers off my cheeks. I do my best to tame my dark brown, dripping locks, wringing a bit of water out over the sink. Satisfied with the reflection staring back at me in the mirror, I leave for the bar. My two sidekicks tonight, anger and disappointment, follow suit.

Empty stools at the far end of the long wooden counter catch my eye as I pass a short line of men waiting to be served. I sit down by the wall, away from other people. Not that anyone's looking to join my pity party. They grab their orders, rushing back downstairs, eager to spend the night dancing. I might be the only loser who arrived here alone.

I rest my elbows against the sticky counter and hide my face in my hands, willing my annoyance to ease up.

When I closed the door behind Chase two hours ago, I ignored the compulsive need to lock myself in my bedroom with ice cream. It doesn't help the heartbreak. Although, heartbreak might not be the correct word. I'm not mad at Chase, per se. I'm mad at my father. It's his fault, his idea, and his sick execution. Chase was a tool in his hands, just like my two previous boyfriends.

You'd think I'd learn the lesson by now, that I'd expect the same old bullshit my daddy put me through twice before, but I believed him when he promised he wouldn't do that again. Yeah, right!

Instead of moping or confronting my father, I slipped into the sexiest dress I found in my closet, snuck out of the house through the window in my bedroom, hailed a cab, and came straight to Delta.

Chase is the last guy who fooled me.

Again, not his fault, per se. Who wouldn't fake-date me for fifty grand? Correction: who'd have the guts to say *no* to my father? No one. Frankie Harston gets what he wants.

Always.

And so, for the third time in a row, my new relationship ended after exactly three months with the same line the previous two boyfriends used: *Layla honey, I'm gay, sorry.*

He can shove his sorry where the sun doesn't shine.

Three men, three disappointments. No one but daddy to blame or thank for this mess. I wouldn't mind it half as much if they weren't the *only* three men I've ever dated, but they are. Why did Chase choose tonight to break the news? Couldn't he have waited just two days? He told me his truth the day before my birthday.

Some gift.

"Hey, are you alright there?" The bartender eyes me with curious, albeit slightly apprehensive eyes.

I bet he expects me to burst out crying. Or maybe he's afraid I'll whine about the reason for my solo club outing... I'm not that cruel. No one in their right mind would willingly listen to the messed-up thoughts polluting my head. "Yes, I'm okay. Can I have a mojito, please?"

"Put it on my tab," someone behind me says.

Thanks, but no, thanks.

I roll my eyes, which makes the bartender smirk under his nose. Delta is *not* the place where I should politely subject myself to some idiots' wooing. I'm alone here. No one will come with a rescue mission if I get in trouble. No one from my side is welcome inside the hottest club in Chicago.

"Thanks, but I pay for my own drinks." Irritation, sticky like honey, covers the words shooting out of my mouth.

The man takes the stool beside mine, the corners of his lips curled into a coy smile.

He's not a drunk idiot.

No, he's sober.

He's *lethal.*

A black leather jacket hugs his broad shoulders, hiding a thin, grey t-shirt. It works well with his short, dark hair and sharp features. My cheeks heat when emerald-green eyes meet mine briefly before traveling south to take me in.

I glance at the ceiling, swearing quietly.

Of course. The one heterosexual man who ever chatted me up out of his unforced will has to be the enemy.

Not mine, my father's, but it doesn't change much.

"I wasn't asking for permission," he says, his voice rough like that of an old rocker.

I click my tongue, making a show of rolling my eyes again in case he missed it the first time. The cold, harsh truth is that inside I'm shaking like a cornered baby deer. I didn't expect him *to* approach me. I didn't expect to see him tonight, yet here he is in all his merciless, unforgiving, arrogant glory. The bartender sets a tall glass before me. I hold out a twenty, adamant about paying, but before he accepts the cash, he glances at the man on my left, awaiting his call. He nods once, an enigmatic response worthy of a powerful man like him.

"Will you introduce yourself, or would you rather stare at me all night?" I ask, closing my lips on a twirly straw. The alcohol should ease the tremble of my hands and the erratic rhythm of my pounding heart.

There's no need for an introduction. I know exactly who he is. I'm actually having a hard time believing he casually took a seat beside me. All things considered, he should know who I am too. He should also throw me out of his club, but no. By the look of him, he has no idea that here sits beside him, the daughter of the man who'd sacrifice almost everything to see him dead.

Careful not to get caught, I check him out, flinching at the sight of a gun strapped in the holster by his belt. That might end up pressed against my temple a few minutes from now, once he learns my name. I move my gaze back to his eyes and then, like a cheap detective, to his left hand. The signet ring adorning his finger betrays his surname better than a birth certificate could.

He turns my way, eyebrow raised, eyes sliding up my body to meet mine. "Dante."

"Dante Carrow," I scoff, straightening my spine.

"Same one."

My impudent behavior has a different effect than antici-pated. Matching his arrogance won't work. I'm not nearly good enough at this game. Instead of the desired reaction—a muscle ticking on his square jaw, betraying annoyance, he presses his together, fighting a smile. He's enjoying this.

Nobody within a ten-mile radius would dare snap at him as I just did, yet he finds me amusing. If not for the volcano of emotions erupting inside my head every few seconds, maybe I wouldn't hiss either. Then again, if not for the volcano, I wouldn't have entered Delta.

Dante is the mafia boss ruling the South of Chicago. My father commands the North. Two biggest enemies in the history of this city scrambling for power.

Dante can easily use me as bait. He can threaten my father's business by holding me hostage. He can throw me in the trunk and take me somewhere no one will ever find my body, no matter how long they'd look. Daddy may keep me away from his work, but I'm not daft. I hear things not meant for my ears. I have some confidential information Dante could force out of me with. I'm sure he's very persuasive when the mood takes him.

Thankfully, I'm still raging after Chase's confession, or rather my father's blatant broken promise, so I don't care.

I glance back into his hypnotizing eyes. "So, *Dante*, I sug-gest you find another girl who'll entertain you. If it's not too much trouble, don't summon your pawns. I'll let myself out once I finish." I point at my drink when two lines crease his forehead. "I'm Layla. Layla Harston."

"Layla Harston," he echoes. My name on his lips sounds like a sexual innuendo. "My, my. What are you doing here?"

I raise my glass. "I'm drinking."

"So, I see. I'm asking why *here*. You know it's my club."

Everyone knows, hence my choice. "Thank you for not doubting my intelligence," I clip. "Delta's the only place in the city where my daddy's vultures won't look when they realize I'm gone. Even if they figure out with their limited brain cells that this is where I am, they're not allowed inside."

Dante waves his hand at the bartender. Half a minute later, the bartender hands him a drink and an ashtray.

Looks like he's not going anywhere.

He lights a cigarette ignoring the *No Smoking* sign above the bar. "You're hiding on my territory. Why?"

"You're not the brightest bulb in the box, are you?" I flip my hair over one shoulder, pinching the straw between my fingers. "I told you. No one will find me here."

He smirks, all brazen arrogance. He takes a long, delicious drag, disappearing briefly in a cloud of smoke. "Are you always this pissy?"

"Always."

Cruelty is a part of my character after living under the same roof with Frankie Harston. I developed a sharp tongue and sure take after my daddy where sarcasm is concerned.

"*Why* are you hiding? What did you do?"

Oh, I'm not hiding.

If I wanted to hide, I'd crawl under my bed the way I did when I was a child. Why the hell is he still here? He should've thrown me out the door the moment he learned my name. So important, yet so careless.

"Bad day." I shrug, pushing the empty glass aside.

"I assume you're also always this vague?"

"No, I just don't feel like entertaining you with a chat."

Someone taps my shoulder, forcing me to spin in my seat. A reasonably handsome guy smiles wide, swaying to the beat reverberating throughout the club. "Let's dance."

"I didn't come here to dance."

"Come on, please. Consider it compensation for how you manhandled me in the other room."

I look at him again—blond hair, tall, no neck. "Are you the guy who tripped?"

He nods, taking a step closer. "Please. Just one dance. I've been looking for you all over the place."

I'm not in the mood to dance, but I'm also not in the mood for Dante's company. I've not mentally prepared for such a turn of events. Who knew he actually spends time in his club? Not me.

And so, the lesser of two evils wins.

I stand, adjusting my dress. "I hope you can dance..."

"Jake," he offers, taking my hand.

"Layla."

He flashes me another broad smile before he leads me downstairs. We squeeze our way through the dancing crowd, and Jake whirls me around, pressing my back against his chest, his arms around my middle. He's not just a good dancer but a well-behaved one too. He's not seizing the opportunity, not trying to grope me.

We dance through one song, and, a man of his word, Jake's ready to take me back upstairs when "Cool Girl" by Tove Lo blasts from the speakers. I hold him in place, resuming our dance. Two more songs pass before I approach the upstairs bar again. I promised Dante I'd leave, and leave I will.

Rule number one when dealing with mafia men: Don't test their patience. They don't have any.

"Still here?" I ask, finding him right where I left him.

"If I remember right, you were the one leaving."

"That's what I'm doing," I fling my bag over my shoulder.

"Sit down." He clinks his glass to a fresh mojito waiting on the counter. "You wanted to have a few drinks somewhere Frankie's vultures won't find you. You're safe here."

Arguably.

"I wanted to have a few drinks *alone*." I take a seat, silencing the voice of reason urging me to lose my heels and sprint out of here. Instead, I give in to the plea of a different voice, one that'll probably get me killed. "Spiked my drink, did you?" I raise the glass to my lips, my muscles relaxing with every sip.

"Obviously. You're very snappy, Layla... nothing a good drug cocktail won't fix." His face's impassive, but his voice lacks credibility.

"You should've popped a few sleeping pills in here too. I only shut up when I'm asleep."

He smirks again. "I'll keep that in mind."

"What will you do when I'm all drugged up? Will you lock me in a golden cage? Send for ransom?" I set the glass aside, tilting my head toward him. "Sorry to clip your wings, but my father won't pay a dime."

Dante leans closer, one elbow on the bar, eyes boring into mine. "Will you tell me why you're here?"

The smell of his heady, spicy cologne fans my face, captivating my senses better than any drug he undoubtedly has in his arsenal. Hiding the reason why I'm here makes little sense. Maybe the truth will scare him off? Although, I'm not sure I want him to leave.

"My boyfriend dumped me."

"His loss, not yours, but I'm intrigued," he says in a low voice I can barely hear over the growing background noise. "Why did he dump you?"

"I'll make you a deal. You ask all your questions, I answer, and then you move on. Okay?" Getting rid of him is the wiser choice, rather than entertaining us both.

"Are you in a hurry, or are you afraid of me?"

"He's gay," I counter.

I *should* be afraid. I also should leave, but fear is absent.

Dante's intriguing. He emanates ruthless confidence, but when his eyes meet mine, I notice more in those alluring emeralds of his... kind of softness.

"Your boyfriend is gay? How have you not realized? You're not very clever, are you?"

"*Ex*-boyfriend. If you want to laugh more, I'll tell you this, he's the third one. Well, the second gay, but boyfriend number one preferred boys too. The difference is that he wanted to be a she. It's no longer Sam; it's Samantha. I'm secretly jealous of her boobs."

Dante's gaze roves my chest. "Yours aren't bad."

"Could be better."

A mixture of great music, alcohol, and surprisingly enjoyable company helps me relax. Once I get home, I'll have to deal with being used in my father's puppet show again. Deal with my life being controlled at every turn. I'm two hours shy of turning nineteen, but no one has ever kissed me because Frank keeps all heterosexual men away from me.

My bag vibrates on the counter, the incoming call from Frank's right-hand man, Adam.

Ah, so it begins...

I slide my thumb across the screen. "I report, I've not been kidnapped by aliens or the opposition."

A nervous laugh is his first answer. "Where are you?"

Lying is an option, though I'm not a good liar. I'm sure there's a reason why Adam's calling—my father's orders. I left an hour ago without a word, and that's enough for Frank to raise the alarm. He keeps tabs on me, controlling my life to ensure I won't cause him trouble. He plans my every move and watches me chase the carrot dangling from the stick.

I glance at Dante, my nerve endings firing with sudden bravery. "I'm in Delta."

Adam inhales sharply, holding his breath as if I just admitted I murdered Elmo. "Voluntarily?"

"Didn't I mention I wasn't kidnapped?" My mouth turns dry when Dante takes a drag of a cigarette, holding my gaze. His cheeks puff out before he parts his full lips, letting out a thick, gray cloud.

How can smoking look so sexy?

"Frankie will go nuts."

That he might. I'm going rogue here. Acting on impulse. "Then don't tell him. You're crafty. I'm sure you'll come up with an interesting lie. Bye-bye for now. I'm busy." I cut the call, rising from my seat.

I need a break from Dante, his green eyes, and his effect on me. I also need to stop looking at him like I usually look at a chocolate cake. The club is busier now. The line to the upstairs bar starts halfway down the stairs. Thankfully, the restroom is quieter. I wash my hands, squeeze my neck, and count down from ten.

Time to go home before Dante permanently damages my not-so-perfect mind.

"Running away, are you?" He asks when I return.

I finish my drink and grab my bag. "I'm not running. I'm leaving. There's a difference.."

"Is Daddy's *baby girl* afraid she'll be punished?" He crosses his arms, leaning back with another smug smile.

Every time his eyes travel down my body in a heated once-over, I feel exposed as if he sees right through me... as if he knows my deepest secrets.

"Of course. Can't you see my legs shaking?" I fling the crossbody bag over my head. "Your company's not that great, you know?"

"It's better than you're willing to admit."

"Let's agree to disagree."

He cuffs my wrist, yanking me closer until I stand between his legs, my thighs touching his knees. "Sit."

I cock an eyebrow, staring him down. "Oh, you think I take orders, baby? Sorry, I don't."

His grip tightens, and he pulls me closer again, gentle but demanding when his free hand caresses the soft spot at the back of my knee. "It's been an hour since we met, but this is the third time I've wanted to shut your mouth with mine, Star." His gaze stops at my lips, eyes dark like green velvet. "Can you sit down?" Again, he tugs on my hand, his warm breath fanning my face. "We're not done, *baby*."

Maintaining an impassive expression while my body feels like I've been dipped in a Jacuzzi is not easy. No way I'll let my face tell him how much I enjoy his touch.

And his words.

"Fine, but keep your mouth away from me." I wiggle out of his grip, taking a seat. An unpleasant chill slides along my spine once I'm no longer in his personal space. "If I'm staying, you must make my birthday wish come true."

"Is it your birthday today?"

I take his hand, dizzy when the same electric pulse washes over me at the touch of his warm skin. I roll the sleeve of his biker jacket, revealing a silver watch. "In ninety-three minutes, I'll be nineteen. One wish, Dante. Don't worry, it's not complicated. The biggest one is reserved for someone else."

"Do I look like a genie, Star?"

"No, you don't." I tilt my head, ignoring the unusual pet name. I ignore it even though an anemic butterfly flaps one wing in my belly. "You look a bit like a fairy, though."

A one-sided smile curls his lips. "Fine. I might regret this but do go on. What is it that you wish for?"

"Get me drunk. It's been a long day, and the morning isn't looking up. A small hangover will hopefully drown out the earful I'll get from Frank."

"Done. I'll get you drunk. Now, raise the bar." His hands brush against my knee. It looks like an accident; however, it isn't. "There must be something else I can do."

"You're not fit to fulfill my other wishes."

He's not appeased but leaves it without comment. "I'll make sure your douche of an *ex*-boyfriend is the last thing on your mind tonight."

CHAPTER TWO

Dante

Frank Harston's daughter is an enemy.

Not as big as Frankie, but still an enemy. Alarms blared, and red lights flashed in my head when she introduced herself. If she hadn't grown up so beautiful, my bouncers would've escorted her out, no questions asked. But she's fucking spellbinding.

I can't peel my eyes off her to save my life.

She shouldn't be anywhere within my reach. The mere thought of entering Delta should make her all kinds of scared, but there's no fear tainting her steel-gray, almost silver eyes, just a blazing fire. Not only did she have the courage to show her beautiful face on my territory, but like a true pussycat, she hissed, showing off her claws. My surname didn't change her attitude.

It pissed her off more.

She's fucking irresistible with that sharp tongue, disdain painted over her doll-like face, and the abhorrent disrespect. Six years have passed since anyone spoke to me the way Layla does, and it was her father.

She inherited the nasty personality I hate most about him, yet I find it utterly impressive on Layla.

I spotted her on the many screens in my office displaying live feed from inside the club. A small commotion started in the POP music room where a petite girl dressed in red pushed her way through the crowd as if pushing through a jungle. I liked how she walked: head high, shoulders back.

People stepped out of her way, awestruck.

No wonder. She's a sight to behold. Dark brown hair fell to her hips, hidden under a flared dress. Most girls who greet Delta with their presence just about cover their asses, but Layla doesn't show her thighs, fascinating me that much more. She's outrageously sassy and utterly unfazed by me, my money, position, and reputation. Everyone else is, but Layla doesn't give a shit, showing no respect, fear, or interest.

Another novelty. Indifference isn't a reaction I'm treated with often. I like her more than any other woman who crossed my path, even though I should stay away from her.

What a shame I don't want to.

The vodka bottle we started over an hour ago is half-empty, but Layla hardly looks tipsy. Jake comes by every twenty minutes to take her dancing, so she's burning the alcohol, moving in sync with that asshole's arms around her middle.

"That's it," I say when she comes back with Jake's hand holding hers. "No more dancing. Sit and drink."

The guy can't stand straight without assistance anymore. He'll likely fall down the stairs if he takes her dancing again. He'll trip, or I'll push him. Either way, he won't leave the club without at least two broken bones; jaw and nose.

Layla raises a shot glass, throwing the vodka at the back of her throat. "Sir, yes, sir," she salutes. "Favorite color?"

I push a Marlboro between my lips, pinching the filter with my teeth. "Is this a game, or are you curious?"

"You shouldn't answer a question with a question."

"Red." Since two hours ago. "You want to play twenty questions? How old are you? Five?"

She wags her finger. "That's three questions right there. Are you afraid I'll ask something inappropriate?"

We just met. Two hours ago, but she already knows how to get by me. Accusing me of fear does the job. There's no fucking way I'll pass on the game now. Besides, with the right questions, it might get interesting.

"Favorite song?"

She catches her bottom lip between her fingers, pulling gently. I imagine my teeth in their place, biting, sucking, consuming her sweet mouth. "I think "One Way or Another" wins it at the moment."

"You're kidding, right?"

"No. I'm not talking about the original, though." She pulls her phone out, tapping the screen.

"Don't tell me you're a One Direction fan."

"Nope. Until the Ribbon Breaks." Standing on her stiletto heels, she presses the phone against my right ear, covering the left with her tiny hand.

I stare at her mere inches away from me, her hands cupping my face. Jesus wept. What the fuck is this spark between us? I grasp the stool, digging my fingers into the leather to contain the urge to touch her. It's too loud around to enjoy the song playing from her phone's speaker, but I focus on the melody, dark and slow, the words a husky whisper loaded with emotion.

My stomach ties itself into a double knot when Layla bites her lip. I think it's her tic. A tell of sorts. Some people crack their knuckles, some play with their hair, but Layla... of course, she'd have the sexiest tic out there.

Just my fucking luck.

The song isn't over when she steps away, brushing her hand along my cheek, the touch delicate, feather-light. Intentional or not, my cock hardens in response. I make a note to take a cold shower later and check out that song again. The bartender pushes the ashtray closer as I keep flicking the ash across the counter, too busy watching Layla.

"Nice, isn't it?" she asks, tucking her phone away. "They're great but not mainstream. What about you? What are you into right now?"

You, baby. So into you.

"Ellie Goulding is my go-to CD."

Layla relaxes with every shot until worry no longer taints her pretty face. We've been sitting at the bar for almost four hours when the club closes at two a.m. Half an hour later, once the staff tidies up, the last person exits the building, leaving us alone. If I were a fucker... fine, if I were a bigger fucker than I am, I'd pull out my gun, aim it at the pretty bug, and call Frank to set up a trade.

Technically speaking, I *am* a big enough fucker to pull this off, but looking at Layla, scaring her feels like a felony. She's softer outside and tougher inside than women I've encountered in my life. Not a docile wannabe like *"The Princess and the Pea."* More like a stunning witch. Using her against Franks is out of the question because I *see* her beauty. That, coupled with the invisible pull, the odd spark between us, makes kidnapping for ransom a big no-no.

We start a second bottle once it's just Layla and me. She drank as many shots as I have but still acts as if she stopped after the second mojito.

"Why didn't you go home earlier?" I ask.

She sits up, shoulders back, her spine suddenly rigid. "You asked me to stay."

"And that's why you did?"

"I'm not sure what you're getting at. I came here to clear my head. I was going to leave because I thought I'd be carried out by security if I didn't, but I stayed because you didn't mind me being here."

Her presence should've bothered me. She could've been trying to separate me from my people and succeeded when the last person left Delta so Frankie could barge in with his troops. I don't find my own theories plausible, though. Just as I don't believe Layla stayed because I asked.

Attraction sprouted between us the moment I offered to buy her a drink. One look at her gorgeous face and my brain short-circuited. Changing all the wires won't help. Desire is saved on the hard drive, and I can't do shit about it. Especially, that said desire grows stronger with every minute.

I grip her stool, dragging it closer.

Instead of flushed cheeks or shallow breaths, she cocks an eyebrow. "You're staring at me again, Dante."

"And what a sight it is."

Her lips twitch, curling into a ghost of a smile, but she contains it quickly, arranging her face back into an impassive expression. 'Impassive' is a euphemism here because Layla looks cold, cruel, and calculated. Resting bitch face in all its glory. So fucking beautiful.

"You're not too bad either."

Years have passed since the last time I flirted. Nowadays, I don't make an effort. The women I fuck don't require wooing. They crawl out of their skin trying to impress *me*, not the other way around. A stuffed wallet summons all sorts of bitches. Yes, bitches, not women.

Real women don't care about money.

They all say they don't, but one trait makes the gold-diggers easily noticeable in a crowd: dollar signs in their eyes. Layla doesn't give a damn about my money. She doesn't give a damn about *me*.

A challenge at last.

"Are you comfortable?" she glances at my knee touching her thigh.

I grip her stool again, pulling it closer until her shoulder brushes against my chest, and I regret the decision. It's damn near impossible to keep my hands off her when she's this close, when her sweet, flowery perfume fans my face, making me feel oddly peaceful. "Better now," I say. "What do you dream of?"

"A little shooting star." She ridicules, tilting her head back to swallow the contents of her shot glass. "I don't know. I don't have dreams. Just a few wishes."

"Like...?"

"That's another question. It's my turn. Why *star*?" Her eyes shine, curiosity pouring off her.

"Quid pro quo. Tell me your biggest unfulfilled wish."

"I'm not that curious."

"Will you tell me if I promise I won't act on it?"

She bites the inside of her cheek. "Promise."

I hold two fingers up, hoping that her wish isn't something

I can, or more importantly, might want to do. "Scout's honor."

She inhales deeply, bracing for whatever she's about to tell me. "I wanted to... I *want to* be kissed."

The cigarette smoke enters the wrong pipe, setting my lungs ablaze.

What the fuck?

I stare at her, searching for mockery or amusement, but she's dead fucking serious. Someone designed her for me. She's got all the qualities I find attractive: sassy, feisty, intelligent, stunning... *and* she's a virgin.

How the hell am I supposed to stay away from her now? Even the fact she's Frankie's daughter no longer means shit. "Are you saying you've never been kissed?"

"Why are you surprised? I told you I've only dated boys who like boys."

"You said you dated three guys who like guys, not that you dated three guys total." I size her up, double-checking if maybe I imagined how perfect she is, but no, she's flawless. "Jesus, Star. Have you seen yourself?"

She shrugs, indicating that it's not a big deal. Yeah, sure. I mean, beautiful, nineteen-year-old virgins crowd every street corner in Chicago.

"You tell me. I'm not a man. I don't know what's so fundamentally repulsive about me."

"Frankie." Nothing else is an option. "Men won't touch you because they're afraid of your father."

Her dress rolls up a few inches when she readjusts her position exposing more skin. A beauty mark halfway up her thigh comes into view as if to taunt me as if to say, *this marks the spot where you kiss*. And, fuck if that's not all I want to do right now.

I move in, resting my elbows on my knees, and place my hands on her legs, stroking the small dark spot with my thumb, my mind filled with indecent images. Images that shouldn't pop into my head while I'm touching a virgin.

Gut-wrenching desire mixes with a cruel, compelling need to taste her lips. The intensity of my lust quadruples because *no one* has kissed her yet. *No one* has had her between the sheets. I feel like Neil Armstrong the day he boarded Apollo 11 with the moon in his sight.

I have Layla, my star, right here. At an arm's length. I want to be the first man that'll do everything with her that she should've done by now.

"You're not afraid." She utters, breathing on the shallow side as she eyes my hands caressing her smooth, silky thighs.

I push my fingertips into her flesh, my blood like red, hot soda water. "I'm not afraid of Frank, Layla."

Acting as if my touch doesn't affect her, she spins an empty shot glass on the counter, but her cheeks tell the truth, warming up. That pale rose shade sends an electric pulse deep inside me.

I retreat my hands.

Controlling myself is easier when I'm not touching her.

"I don't think my daddy is the problem. He's not protective. He has no time for nonsense."

Once he finds out you spent the night with me, he'll have all the time in the world to care and voice an opinion.

"It doesn't matter." I clench my fists, itching to touch her again. "Everyone knows who Frank is. That's enough. No one will take the risk."

Layla rests her forehead against the countertop with a heavy sigh. "I'll die a virgin."

Not if I get a say in this.

She turns toward me, eyes sparkling. "Your turn. Why *star*?"

"Because you're like a movie star. Stylish, unattainable, annoying, and so fucking feisty."

"I'm not that feisty. Well, not always. You just get on my nerves, Dante."

I smirk, enjoying the quips. "And vice-versa. Cheers."

"It's almost four o'clock in the morning, but I'm still not drunk. Still thinking clearly."

"You're a tough one."

"Or your pace is off." She finishes her shot, grabbing her bag. "Thank you for a surprisingly pleasant evening."

If I could, I'd press replay to relive it all over again. "Hold on. I'll call my driver. He'll take you home."

"No need. I'm sure Adam is waiting outside." She leans over, pressing a soft kiss on my cheek. "Goodnight. Let's hope I won't see you again."

"Don't hold your breath," I clip, fighting the urge to sit her on my lap, cage her in my arms and deflower those plump lips.

She teeters on her stilettoes toward the staircase, hips swaying. "Don't stare at my ass." She chuckles, not bothering to turn around.

"Stop swaying your hips."

Now, she does turn around, gracing me with a broad smile that makes me feel fluffy inside. "Goodnight, Dante."

"Goodnight, Star."

The happy clicking of her heels echoes throughout the empty space for the next two minutes until the door closes behind her. I reach over the bar, snatching a bottle of whiskey. With a cigarette pinched between my lips, and a drink in hand, I head downstairs to the DJ's station.

The song Layla regards as her favorite seeps from the speakers a short while later. Atmospheric music fills the club while I rest my back against the wall, staring straight ahead, captivated. There's no trace of the funky rhythm.

The hairs on my neck rise while I listen to the familiar words. The new arrangement somehow changes the meaning of the lyrics. Both the melody and words mirror how I feel when Layla's around. A bit like a psycho.

A fascinated psycho.

CHAPTER THREE

Layla

"Explain why you left last night without a word and why you chose the last place you should find yourself in," my father says the second I show my face downstairs in the morning.

No birthday wishes.

Not even *hello*.

He sits at the kitchen table in a three-piece gray suit, eyes narrowed, nostrils flared. Fetching a cup from the cupboard,

I start the coffee maker choosing cappuccino on the touch screen. Ever since I was a child, a peculiar dread—an itching fear of sorts, has been my companion whenever I'm alone with Frank. He never physically hurt me, but his commanding personality hits the most vulnerable parts of me with a sniper's precision.

When I was a little girl, he sent me to the naughty corner whenever I crossed him. The curt tone and disappointment gleaming in his eyes hurt more than a belt could. Now that he can turn my life into a living hell, I miss the naughty corner.

I glance over my shoulder at the open patio door, checking whether we're alone or if I should watch every word coming out of my mouth.

October is almost over, no more than fifty-five degrees outside, yet my mother, Jessica, sunbathes outside, sprawled across the sun lounger by the pool, a vintage sun tan reflector in hand. Her ears perk up like those of a dog that heard another dog bark. Eavesdropping is her second favorite pastime. Doing nothing productive is number one.

"I had an awful evening. I wanted to clear my head," I say with a theatrical sigh. "We both know I can't do that with your pawns breathing down my neck."

Frank peers at me from the morning paper. We have similar eye and hair colors, but I inherited my looks from my mother. People mistake us for sisters, and Jess never bothers to correct them. No wonder, she was two months shy of turning sixteen when I was born, so it's not surprising that people don't see me as her daughter. Especially that Jess looks twenty-eight tops, not her almost thirty-five.

"Then why did you make such a secret out of it?" Frank asks, sounding like a judge pounding a gavel.

"I didn't. I told Adam where I was. I didn't tell *you* where I was going because you wouldn't let me leave."

"Of course not!"

Of course not. That's not how my father operates. He's a control freak, and when I left home without asking for his opinion or permission, I took control out of his hands.

He throws the paper aside, stroking his goatee. "However, you could've taken Adam, Allie, and whomever else to any other club in Chicago. I wouldn't oppose."

"Adam bows low enough to kiss your shoes, and Allie would've invited me out with her plastic-fantastic friends. I wanted to be alone. Chase dumped me."

As you already know, Dad.

Frank regards Allie, Adam's girlfriend, as my best friend because he introduced us two years ago. We get along well, I guess, but I wouldn't call it friendship. She's the embodiment of a mafia woman. Always immaculate, always smiling, always lacking twenty IQ points. She overuses *like,* and *oh my God* to the point it drives me crazy.

"Why?"

"He's gay."

That's not news to him, but I play along, aware of the eavesdropper drinking in our every word. There's a reason why Frank controls my life; why he chooses who I date, who I'm friends with, and what I look like.

"Another one?" He chuckles, playing his part too. "You only need a transvestite then you'll have them all."

What the hell are they? Pokémon?

"You should've thought twice before choosing Delta last night," he snaps, morphing back into a heartless bastard. "From now on, you'll have a full-time bodyguard."

28

"Frank!" Jess opposes from the garden, her high-pitched shrill like needles prickling my eardrums. "You're overreacting. Layla's an adult. You can't watch over her like she's still your sweet little girl."

Sweet little girl? Try nuisance*, Mom.*

Frank raises his hand, breathing the air through his nose like an enraged bull ready to charge. "Dante's not stupid, Layla. I'm sure by now, he knows you were there. I won't risk that he'll use you against me."

I could try until I'd turn blue, but I know there's no changing Frank's mind about the bodyguard idea. He doesn't do negotiations. If he says the sky is pink, then the sky is pink, end of story. He's spiteful, stubborn, irrational... like father, like daughter.

"I'd be surprised if he didn't know I was there," I say, ready to make him bleed. Metaphorically, but still. He deserves a bit of pain after all the shit he put me through and still puts me through. I want him wounded. I want chaos in his head. His own blood, his only daughter, fraternizing with the enemy. "He joined me for a drink. We talked all night. As you can see, he didn't torture me. He's quite nice."

His lips form a thin line. He grips his cup tighter, turning red in the face, then snatches his phone off the table, probably to call Adam or some other goon to babysit me. I don't need to hear it. I take my coffee, joining my mother in the garden. The chilly fall wind whips at my clothes, swatting my hair as it forms tiny waves on the pool's surface.

So not the weather for sunbathing.

"Don't worry." Jess peers at me from above her designer shades. "He'll get over it. Oh, I almost forgot. Happy Birthday."

That's my mom and her motherly affection at its highest point. I cringe, unsure whether the lump lodged in my throat is the start of bubbling laughter or a sob.

"Thanks, Jess. I'm surprised you remembered."

"You were awfully bitchy last year when I forgot, so I set a reminder on my phone." She beams, pleased with her doubtful cleverness.

My parents have treated me with reserve my whole life, but there's no denying their indifference hurts. I can only dream about a hug, even if it is my birthday. They were never loving or caring... never proud of me. I can count how often I heard them say, "I love you." It made me self-sufficient. I don't need them or anyone else. I'm resilient and deal with problems on my own, but I'm not made of stone.

I crave their closeness. I wish they'd take care of me at least a little bit. I wish they'd worry about my safety, not how much trouble I can bring upon my father or how my actions can threaten his business.

I sit on an oversized daybed under a natural canopy of grapevines. They're dry now, leaves falling to the ground, but this place looks like a postcard from an exotic location during summer. Too bad grapes attract colonies of wasps.

"What do you want for your birthday?" Jess sets the sun reflector aside. Short, blonde hair frames her petite face, the disproportionately large eyes surrounded by too much eyeliner. "A shopping trip? A week in Bali? Spa weekend?"

Frank joins us, dropping a car key with a pink ribbon attached to the loop on the table. "Happy Birthday. You'll find your gift parked outside."

"You bought me a car?"

"If I knew what you planned on doing last night, I would've thought twice about it."

He'd fall ill if he'd just answer with a *yes*.

"Thank you."

"Don't get too excited." He checks the time on his watch. "Burly will be here in ten minutes. He'll be your shadow which means he'll be driving you around everywhere."

"Burly?" He's probably thinner than a rake. Most of Frank's men have unfitting nicknames like in the movies where Shaggy is bald and Speedy is slow. "Is he new?"

"Yes, he's Adam's cousin."

"Don't you think you're overreacting?" I hiss, pinning him down with a pointed stare that he hopefully understands because I can't speak my mind when Jess is around. "If Dante wanted to use me, he wouldn't have let me go home last night, don't you think?"

Frank ignores my words in his usual style, heading inside, and slides the patio door shut behind him. Blood boils in my veins whenever he dismisses me, but I learned that arguing is pointless. Besides, I understand his reasoning. I should act according to his instructions...

A babysitter isn't necessary, though.

At nine o'clock sharp, I enter a small restaurant in the city center. Allie gave me the silent treatment all day, busy hating my guts for keeping Adam outside Delta until dawn. She surrendered before seven p.m. and invited me out for a birthday drink. Burly follows me inside like a thin, starved shadow. The moment he started the job as my nanny, he made it a point to fulfill my father's orders in great detail. He even followed me to the restroom and waited outside the door.

"So... I heard you spent last night with Dante Carrow," Allie says, toying with a strand of platinum-blonde hair. She's naturally a redhead but claims it doesn't suit her. She bleaches the beautiful auburn locks every couple of weeks, so it's a miracle she still has hair.

"Did your small birdy tell you all about it?" I emphasize *small*, glancing at Adam. Burly almost chokes on his soda, swallowing his laughter. "He joined me at the bar, but I'm still alive."

"Layla, do you know why Dante and Frank hate each other?" Adam ignores my remark, running his hand through his short, dark hair.

He's used to me by now and deals with my snappishness by meticulously ignoring it. He crosses his arms, ready to deliver another lecture. It's our ritual. I annoy him, and he gives me vital life lessons. Not that he can teach me much, being four years older, but it doesn't stop him from trying.

I never gave much thought to Frank's and Dante's hatred. They fight over territory. That much is obvious. I'm as interested in Frankie's business activities as I am in a leech's respiratory system. I grew up among criminals. Frank's occupation isn't odd. Quite the opposite. Being a mafia boss's daughter is probably as natural to me as being a lawyer's daughter is to Allie.

A few years back, in a spur of hormonal rebellion, I tried to draw a line between my parents and myself. I was ready to run, but the idea lost its appeal quickly. I doubt there's a place in America I could hide from my father. Besides, deep down, I don't mind Frank earning his money the way he does. I only hate when people stare or stop their conversations mid-sentence when I enter the corner shop.

Frank's skating on thin ice. He could get busted any day, but nothing comes out of the many accusations despite having FBI, CIA, DEA, and a few other abbreviations hot on his tail.

"Six years ago, your father became the boss." Adam starts in a news presenter's voice.

"Call a spade a spade," I snap. "Six years ago, Frank drowned Dino in Lake Michigan."

Everyone knows the story. The whole city... God, the entire *state* was buzzing when the police fished out Dino. He was the boss before Frank took over. Italians ruled Chicago back then, and everyone, be it a lawyer, a cop, or a criminal, worked with them. After Dino's death, Frank's pawns guarded our house for months. My mother and I became prisoners because Frank was sure the Italians would retaliate.

It never happened.

"Dante was your father's right-hand man," Adam clips, glaring at me. "Frankie introduced him to our way of life twelve years ago. He taught him the craft. When Dino died, Frank and Carrow took over *together*."

"Wait a minute, how come Dante never showed up at our house all these years?"

Adam scoffs, narrowing his baby-blue eyes. "He did. You just don't remember. Frank barricaded himself away until the Dino backlash stopped being a problem, waiting for the Italians to take revenge. I'm sure you remember that." He takes a swig of his drink, tapping his signet ring on the glass. "Dante stayed put too. When everyone forgot about Dino, he recruited his own people."

I'm not the only one drinking Adam's words as if he's unraveling ancient secrets. Burly listens with flushed cheeks, mouth hanging open. I usually let Adam's lectures in one ear and out the other, but this is different.

This is interesting.

"If it was Dante who left Frank, why do you all think he wants to take Frank's place?"

"They both want to see each other dead." Allie clicks her tongue while rolling her eyes, the same baby-blue color as Adam's. If I didn't know better, I'd think they were related. "Can we like *change* the subject? Why do you even care? You always avoid Frank's business like the plague!"

Good question. I'm not sure why. Maybe because Dante doesn't fit Frank's description.

"Can you get us more drinks, babes?" Allie asks Adam, resting her hands on the table once he's out of earshot. "Better tell me why Chase dumped you!"

"He's gay."

"Oh my God! Another one? What's wrong with you?! Did your gay radar not develop in the womb?"

"Does your radar work?"

"Well, yeah... of course, it does!"

"Then a heads-up would've been nice."

She giggles, accepting a colorful drink from Adam. "Did you hear that, sweetie? Chase is gay."

"I know." Adam's eyes widen as if he slipped up. That's new. I didn't realize Frankie trusted him this much. "I mean, I heard."

My phone informs me of a new text message, interrupting our gravely exciting conversation.

Thank God for small favors.

Unknown number: Have you told Daddy who you spent the night with, Star?

Aware of everyone's eyes on me, I smile.

Me: Of course. I got a car for being such a good girl. Who gave you my number?

Dante: You are a good girl. A good girl that'll join me for a drink.

A certain zestful excitement grows swiftly in my stomach at the thought of seeing him.

Me: Orders might work on your men but not on me. Say please.

Dante: You're asking for trouble.

Dante: Please.

Me: Tempting, but I'm celebrating with a friend. With the car came a 24/7 nanny.

I stare at the screen, waiting for the three dots to start dancing, but after a few seconds, I tuck the phone back into my bag. Adam watches me for a while longer with creases marking his forehead. I'm sure he's curious who texted me since everyone who usually does is here. He chooses not to ask, though. Good, I wouldn't tell him anyhow.

It's half-past eleven when Allie decides to hit the club. Her friends will probably join us there, and I'm not in the mood to bite my refrain from saying something their tiny brains wouldn't grasp. They're living proof that evolution can go backward.

"I'll get going," I say, flinging my bag over my head.

Adam looks past me toward the entrance, his face twisted into an ominous scowl. Muscles in his jaw tense and a vein on his neck starts pulsing when he shoves his right hand under the suit jacket, reaching for a gun. "Get Layla out of here." He pins Burly with a pointed stare.

Burly glances over his shoulder, then leaps to his feet as

if his butt caught fire. He grips my arm, tearing me out of the chair, delicate and careful as a brute. I glance behind me, catching a glimpse of two men entering the restaurant. I don't recognize either, and within three seconds, I no longer see them when Burly drags me down a "Personnel Only" corridor, aiming for the emergency exit.

He shoves the metal door open, pulling me behind him like a dog on a leash. He stops abruptly three steps outside. I slam into his bony back, mentally tearing Frank's head off. Couldn't he hire *Skinny* to babysit me?

As he shoves me back against the wall, he draws his gun, his stance wide. My head bounces off the stonework with such force my vision blurs for a few seconds before I can refocus on the unfolding scene.

Burly shields me with his frail frame, aiming his gun at the man resting against a black Dodge Charger.

My stomach somersaults back, the sensation intense enough to balance between pleasure and pain when my eyes lock with Dante's. His jaw works in tight, furious circles as he looks me over before taking a moment to acknowledge my bodyguard.

He pushes away from the car, closing the distance between him and the gun, each step measured. He knocks the pistol out of Burly's weak grasp, aiming it at his head.

"Next time, don't hesitate. Now, turn around," he says, his tone controlled but dripping with malice. His eyes hint at none of that as they shift to me briefly while Burly spins on his elegant shoes. "It says *handle with care* all over her. Apologize."

The emergency exit door flies open again, hitting the concrete wall and missing me by an inch.

Adam bursts outside with Allie close behind him. The sound of the safety being flipped on a gun clicks in the silent night. "Don't fucking move, Carrow."

Dante smirks, ignoring Adam when he nudges the back of Burly's skull with the gun. "*Apologize.*"

Shame washes over Burly's cheeks, painting his skin red, but he doesn't dare act tough while a single twitch of Dante's finger could end his life. "I'm sorry, Layla."

Dante leans closer . "Touch her again, and I won't be so fucking altruistic." He takes the clip out before handing the gun back. His features soften when he looks at me. "Ready, star?"

I push away from the wall, ignoring Allie's quiet whimper when Adam lowers his gun the second I walk into his line of fire. I kiss Dante's cheek, holding my lips there longer than a simple greeting requires.

It isn't a simple greeting.

Nothing about us is simple.

"What took you so long?" The fear his presence evoked last night is absent tonight. I'm at ease. It didn't cross my mind he'd look for me; that he'd find me but teasing him might be my new favorite game.

He drapes one arm over my shoulders, pulling me to his side, and his lips brush against my ear. "Stop sassing, or I'll gag you," he whispers, then looks over his shoulder. "Relax, Adam. She's in good hands."

He opens the passenger's side door, letting me in his car. I get comfortable while Adam steps from one foot to the other, eyes jumping between Dante and me.

"You know I can't let you take her, Carrow. Frank will lose his shit when he finds out. Layla, get back here."

"She wants to come, so she's coming. You can try to force her out of the car if you're ready to bleed."

Adam takes a few steps forward, and Allie's hands fly to her mouth, fear etched in her eyes.

"You're stalling," I say, summoning Dante's attention. "It's my birthday. I expect a drink before the day ends."

He checks the time on his wristwatch, and thirty seconds later, Adam's only visible in the rear-view mirror.

CHAPTER FOUR

Dante

We're only half a mile from the restaurant, but running out of time, I slam the brake, stopping the car in the middle of the road despite the lights turning green at the junction ahead. I'm about to break a promise for the first time in my fucking life, but my word is the last thing on my mind as I round the car. I open the passenger's side door, dragging Layla outside, no longer an ounce of patience left in me. There's only feral, uncontainable anticipation writhing inside me. I don't give her the time to push me away.

I cup her face, dip my head, and catch her lips with mine. Fuck... she tastes like everything that's right with this world. Like sunshine, rainbows, and candy.

Adrenaline throbs in my limbs, sending a fit of shivers down my back. I slip my tongue inside the silk of her mouth, tasting her sweetness, fucking drunk on her already. The delicate touch of tiny hands grasping my neck titillates my nerve-endings like a live wire.

This isn't cute or tender. Not how I imagined it'd be. Not how I wanted Layla's first kiss to be, but there's nothing I can do about the burning, primal need that consumes us both. Her floral scent, sweet lips, and the soft whimper escaping her strip me of any inhibitions I hoped to have.

I fucking devour her, pulling her closer. She grips a handful of my jacket, pressing herself to my chest; enough power in her kiss to light up downtown.

The cool evening air fills with blaring horns, but I can't stop. I don't want to stop. Fulfilling her wish is the most gratifying moment of my twenty-eight years. Merciless desire churns in the pit of my stomach when her fingertips ghost across my jaw. With that delicate touch, the kiss evolves... slows... deepens.

And I want more.

So much more.

Layla trembles in my arms, her body frail, hinting at the reaction I can expect when she'll lay naked, spread-eagled on my bed, moaning, gasping, coming on my lips.

A deafening blare of a truck's horn pierces the air, towering above other sounds. Layla flinches, moving away, but I'm not ready to let her go. Not yet.

Pulling out my gun, I aim at the incessant noise. It stops immediately, and all the other horns with it. We're blocking the largest junction within a few blocks, so the drivers have every right to be pissed off.

Too bad I only care about the hungry-for-my-lips pretty little bug clinging to me for dear life. She's not acting cool. Not by a long shot. She seizes the moment, taking handfuls of what I offer.

It's fucking adorable.

I pull away, close her lips, peck her nose, and step back, loving how flustered she looks. "Happy Birthday, Star."

She blinks twice, coming out of the haze, lips opening and closing as if too many words pile into a traffic jam on the tip of her tongue. There's no escaping the ache shining in her eyes.

I kiss her again, groaning when I finally bite her lower lip. I've thought about it since last night, but imagination can't compare to reality. Layla drapes one hand over my neck, forcing me closer. She's on me like duct tape. I'd need to tug hard to break away, but a moment later, she inches back with a quiet, satisfied sigh.

Thank fuck for that. We'd be here until the police would arrive to have us removed because I sure wouldn't find it in me to push her away.

"I won't ever trust you again." She fails at sounding irritated. "You promised."

"You're officially deflowered, Star. Well... your lips are."

For now.

"Are you done?" She crosses her arms, gracing me with a pointed stare even though her eyes sparkle with fulfilled dreams. "Can we go now?"

As I take the wheel, joining the traffic, I can't stop smirking. "How about *thank you?*"

"Thank you? What for? For invading my personal space? The tinnitus from all the horns? Or should I thank you for not keeping your promise?" She touches her lips with her index finger to check what changed.

"Stop sassing, or we won't get far. Kissing keeps you happy and quiet."

"So, you'll keep kissing me if I keep talking back? We sure won't get far."

I oversteer, stopping the car by the curb. Layla bursts out laughing, the sound gentle, melodic, fucking hypnotizing. "Shut up, Star," I mutter. "Shut up, or I won't stop kissing you till dawn."

She holds her breath, amusement tugging at the corner of her lips, but she doesn't stay quiet long, giggling again when I drive away. I could listen to her for hours. It'd be best if she'd take turns laughing, hissing, and whimpering while I wring out an orgasm out of her.

She calms down a few blocks later, readjusts her dress, and brushes the long dark hair behind her ears. "Judging by the route, I'm guessing we're not heading to Delta."

"No. Why? Do you want to dance?"

A flashback takes me back to last night when she danced with Jake. She's not like most girls her age I've come across. She didn't writhe around the guy as if he were her pole. Her moves were soft, delicate, calm... I couldn't tear my eyes off her. I have a hard time looking anywhere else when she's close. To my surprise, I'm not staring at her ass or boobs.

That doll-like face is far more alluring. I'm doing my best to decipher Layla's expressions, gestures, and the tone of her voice as if learning the meaning behind every frown and smile means I'll be worthy of her.

"I wanted to hide from my nanny. I'm not sure if you've noticed, but we're being followed. They probably wouldn't have caught up with us if not for the quick kiss."

"*Quick* kiss?" I grasp her thigh, spreading my fingers as they sink into the smooth skin. "Stop teasing. It doesn't take me much to snap. If you ask nicely, we'll lose them."

She folds her arms, seemingly unaffected by my touch. I call bullshit. Her cheeks grow pinker by the second.

"I'd think you wouldn't want Frank to know where you're taking me."

What the hell is wrong with me? Layla's attractive—pretty face, petite, curvy body, decent boobs. She's sexy, but that doesn't mean shit because her personality is far more arousing—the sass, the talking back, the godawful attitude. I don't care about Frank, but I don't want Adam or Burly standing outside the gate all night long. I change lanes, break traffic regulations, and take shortcuts, but Adam stays on my tail as if I'm towing him.

"Why are you doing this?" Layla asks.

"Be precise, Star. What am I doing?"

She turns to face me. "Why did you find me tonight? If you hope you'll get something out of this, think twice. I don't know much about Frank's work, and as I've already mentioned, I'm not the light of his life. He won't trade me for North."

My intentions are clear. I'm not hiding how Layla makes me feel, and I sure hope to get something out of this, although not what she thinks.

A few turns later, my patience runs dry. I press a few buttons on the touchscreen, calling my right-hand man.

"What's up?" Spades asks, laidback but curious.

"You and Nate take the beauties, Meet me on the corner of eighteenth and Ashland in ten minutes."

A small commotion ensues in the background.

My entourage is in the VIP section at the club like every Saturday evening. We gather there for a few drinks and wind-down time after a busy week. Tonight's not an exception... but it is *exceptional*. When Layla texted that she won't come over for a drink, I ordered my people to find her.

Ten minutes later, two Chargers identical to mine pull out from the side street once we reach the meeting point.

"Beauties?" Layla asks.

"Get down, baby. Hold on."

I switch places with Spades and Nate when Layla slides off her seat, bracing against the floor to stop herself from flying around the car like a corpse.

Adam's not as stupid as he looks. He stays close behind me, but once my number one driver, Rookie, joins the party, drifting around Adam's car in a tight circle, he has no choice but to stop.

I don't slow down until we reach my estate.

Layla sits back in the seat while I park in the garage and kill the engine. She doesn't move when I open the passenger door for her, clearly uncertain. I rest against the side of the car, lighting a cigarette.

"What about you? Why did you get in my car? You could've told me to leave you alone."

"I tried that yesterday." She toys with a few bracelets adorning her wrist. "You didn't listen then. I doubt you'd listen today. Besides, thanks to you, I have a new way of annoying Frank."

"Don't you think if I wanted information out of you, I would've forced them out of you by now?"

She doesn't look convinced but steps out of the car, stopping before me, her heels an inch from my shoes. "Maybe you're waiting until I'll trust you? Until I'll let my guard down?"

"You said you won't trust me again, Star, and I doubt you're easily outmaneuvered." I take her hand, leading her upstairs to the living room, our fingers laced together. Amazing how her tiny palm fits in mine.

She scans the vast space, dark décor, and the large, long bar taking the entire right wall. "I like this." She points at the car parked in the corner.

"Nineteen sixty-seven Shelby. An eighteenth birthday gift from Dino."

She drags her fingers across the bonnet while inspecting the room more as if she wants to learn more about me without asking questions.

"What do you want to drink? Mojito? Wine?"

"Mojito, please." She admires my music collection with a soft smile before she comes to sit at the bar, legs crossed, elbows on the counter. "Why did you kiss me in the middle of the road?"

"I thought you'd ask why I kissed you, period."

"That's obvious."

"Obvious?" I smirk, reaching for the shaker.

"You like me. You like being the first guy who kissed me. You as a species strive to be first."

Yes, yes, and hell yes.

"It was almost midnight. The kiss was a birthday wish come true, so I had limited choice of scenery." I sit beside her, itching to drag her stool closer. "I still can't believe no one had kissed you before."

"Was my inexperience not that obvious?"

I had no time to rate her skills, too busy with the emotions coursing through me like a quickly progressing disease. "You'll get the hang of it." Under *my* wing, it won't take long. "Put the music on."

She cocks an eyebrow, looking away nonchalantly. "Either change your tone or say *please*."

Whenever she talks back, I forget how innocent she is. All I think about is ripping off her dress and thrusting deep inside her sweet, tight, virgin pussy. "Put the music on, Star. *Please*." The word feels foreign, forgotten, unused for so many years it almost tastes bitter.

I tuck a Marlboro between my lips as the living room fills with a familiar melody. Sam Smith? I ask, recognizing the first notes of "Nirvana."

"You have his CD; you can't not like him."

"I didn't expect bedroom music."

Her cheeks flush pink, and being two steps away from me, she spins on her heel.

I grab her hand. "Leave it, and don't flatter yourself. I kissed you, but that doesn't mean I want to sleep with you."

"You do. We already established you like the idea of being my first."

I will be your first, little bug. I let go of her hand to squeeze the glass. I'm fucking lost in her mindset. As the layers of her personality shine through, the physical attraction proves less significant.

"It was a surprise kiss," she says. "You can't pull off surprise sex. Consciously, I won't let you touch me."

I refrain from laughing. As if her personality and body aren't enough of a turn-on, she has to show her rebellious nature too.

Fucking perfection.

Her phone starts ringing in her bag. "I'm sorry, it must be Adam." She slides her thumb across the screen, pressing the phone to her ear. "I'm fine. I'll be back home alive in a couple of hours. Tell Frank I said so—" Her lips fall open, eyebrows know in the middle. She glances between me and the screen, chewing on her lip. "It's for you," she whispers, handing over the phone and showing me the screen.

Frank Harston

It's been two years since we talked, but I expected a chat the moment I decided to find Layla tonight. "Frank. What do you need?"

"Stay away from my daughter," he snaps through gritted teeth. "Let her go."

"She's not tied to a chair."

"Send her home. She's young and fucking stupid. She only sees you to piss me off. Leave her be."

"That's the one thing I can't do for you."

Or anyone else.

"She's a fucking kid, Dante!" A loud bang suggests he slammed his fist on a table or some other flat surface. "You'll let the snotty brat use you?"

You have no idea.

There's not a single reason that would make me forget about Layla. In the brimming inventory of my flaws, one stops me from giving up—territoriality. Kissing me back, Layla showed me that she wants more than a drinking buddy for one evening. I'm a bit worried that I'm so possessive of her, but it's also refreshing. I want her, and only she can tell me to leave her alone. Until then, she's mine—a fantasy I hope to turn into reality.

"Like I said, she's not tied to a chair. She can leave at any time." I hand Layla the phone.

"Yes, *Dad.*" The disdain in her voice takes me by surprise. I don't know why, but I expected her to be a Daddy's girl. "He didn't do anything!" she wails, her skin turning ashen. "You can't boss me around! I'm all grown up!" She listens for a short while, then tosses the phone aside and storms out through the sliding patio doors.

Whatever Frank said, he hit a soft spot. He's the most skilled manipulator I know. He can make anyone dance to his tune. He's clever enough to fool his prey that they don't even realize they're being worked. My brainwashing skills can't rival Frank's, but I'd never manipulate Layla even if they did. I want her to, *want* to be mine. That's not to say I'll just wave a white flag. Especially now when she's torn between reason and emotions.

I finish my drink and, determined to get ahead, join her on the terrace.

CHAPTER
FIVE

Layla

"Daddy told you to head home?" Dante rests his hands on the railing surrounding the terrace.

Chills slip down my spine, but the gusty wind is not the one to blame. It's his closeness and the emotions he awakens inside me. It's Frank's words and his contradicting behavior. I'm confused. Unsure what to do. Unsure whether Frank meant what he said over the phone or if he's scaring me into obedience.

The dark sky, speckled with bright stars, hangs above, the vast lake in the distance calm, the air saturated with Dante's cologne. I tear my gaze from the black canvas to look at him, his cheekbones like hewn in stone, expression emotionless.

"No," I admit with a sigh. "He promised that Burly will end up in a body bag if I decide to see you again."

"He won't kill his man because you're rebelling. Without my help, you wouldn't escape Burly long enough to use the toilet." Dante pulls me closer, nestling his face in the crook of my neck. "He's bluffing."

My eyes close when he moves his hands to my hips. A jab of fear comes first, but a wave of heat radiating off him calms me down. I've been treated with harsh, cold restraint for years. Dante's tenderness is addictive. He's a plaster for my neglected, bruised heart. I crave his attention, ignoring the inevitable consequences. I can't fall for him, no matter how alluring the idea of what he offers—the closeness, concern, and wonder in his eyes. At the end of the day, he's Frank's enemy.

"Maybe, but I'd rather not test that theory or his patience. I don't want Burly to get hurt because of me." I turn my back on the majestic view, slipping out of Dante's embrace. It's hard to trust my reason when he's close. "You haven't answered my question. Why did you find me tonight?"

"Stop playing the fool, Star. You know why. I made myself quite clear in the middle of fucking Chicago."

I am playing the fool.

One look at him is enough of an explanation. He enjoys both my company and me. "I know, but I don't understand."

"What don't you understand?" He rests his back against the railing. "Why do I like you? Show me one man who doesn't."

"Don't belittle yourself. You're not shallow. And I know I'm not ugly, but, as you said, I'm sassy, feisty, and inexperienced. That's even before I mention who my father is."

He peers at the sky as if praying for patience. "I don't care about Frank, Layla. You haven't listed a single flaw."

With every passing minute, I'm digging myself a deeper hole. This is harder than I imagined for an entirely different reason. Dante's intriguing... his looks, the way he carries himself, the tone of his voice, and the unpredictable, volatile nature he tries to contain when I'm around. The more time we spend together, the deeper the hole becomes. If I don't want to be buried alive, I have to put down the shovel and separate my mind from my heart.

"Call me a cab."

He grips the railing on both sides of my waist, caging me in his arms. "What happened to annoying Frank?"

"Mission accomplished." I bite my lip. It's a nervous gesture I can't control despite trying to rid the tic.

He lets out a heavy sigh as his gaze darts to the floor. "You're such a fucking tease, baby." His lips catch mine, gently at first, greedier when his hands touch my back.

I'm feverish. Hundreds of colors light up my mind like fireworks light up the sky on the fourth of July. The world brightens with his presence as if I was *Sleeping Beauty* for nineteen years, and his kiss woke me up, introducing a different, better reality. One in which I matter; one in which I'm wanted.

"Didn't you say you won't let me touch you again?" His nose grazes my cheek before he nips my earlobe. "Liar, liar."

"It's almost impossible to speak when you kiss me."

"I'll remember that. C'mon, We'll have another drink and call Rookie. He'll take you home."

I can't say *no* when he holds me. Five minutes later, we're comfortable on the leather couch in his living room, drinks in hand. "Adam told me why you and Frank hate each other," I say, trying to change the course of my thoughts because not one is unrelated to Dante's lips.

"A wild guess, he told you that when Frank killed Dino, I started doing business on the side."

"More or less, yes."

Dante drapes his arm over the back of the couch, his fingers an inch away from my head. "But he didn't tell you that after taking Dino's place, Frank introduced the *Ten Commandments* of Cosa Nostra among his people."

I read about the Ten Commandments—*never look at the wives of friends, never be seen with cops, wives must be treated with respect*—all rather obvious.

"I thought those only apply to Italians."

"Yes, but Frank was fascinated with Cosa Nostra. He breathed their culture long before he became the boss. Even though the Italians gave up on the idea that no one with an illegitimate partner could join the ranks, Frank married your mother when they were just sixteen."

That explains the lack of love in their marriage. They're strangers living under one roof. They spend less time together than they do with me, which says a lot.

"What does that have to do with your work?" I ask, once again interested in a subject I never cared about.

Now it interests me too much. Dante's side of the story shouldn't matter, but after twenty-four hours of knowing him, I realize my father and Adam's rendition of their hatred is one-sided and influenced by Frank's hurt ego.

Dante tucks a loose strand of hair behind my ear. "Frank wanted to implement the rules of Cosa Nostra in his ranks. He was so busy cleansing his ranks that he neglected business. Once he realized old bulls no longer want to join the mafia, I was dealing on my own account."

Being a mafia man became a profession ruled by the younger generation. The oldest boss I met during the many parties in our house is Mauricio, who is sixty-odd. Next in line is Nikolaj, but he's still a few years short of his fiftieth birthday. Dante isn't the youngest at twenty-eight. The boss from Orlando is twenty-five, while the head of San Francisco is just a year older.

"Why does Frank think you want to take over North?"

"Because I do. He wants South, I want North, but we respect each other too much to shoot. Why do you think he's scared now? Even if you don't think he cares about you, he won't let me hurt you."

I'm sure if push came to shove, he would let Dante put a bullet through my head. Frank's not scared. He's furious. But maybe Dante has a point. "His pawns would think less of him," I mutter, adding two and two together. Who'd deal with a man who doesn't care about his family? "Why won't you use me?"

"I've got boundaries." His fingers brush against my neck, sending waves of shivers through my body in a series of faint vibrations. Who knew a simple touch like this could be so pleasant? "This isn't your war. You always were and always will be Switzerland no matter what happens." He laces our fingers, lifting my hand to his lips. "I won't ever hurt you, and I sure won't let anyone else do it either."

I slide across the sofa, away from his touch. "You've no idea how quickly I'll get addicted to you."

"Is that supposed to stop me?"

I hide my face behind a curtain of hair, searching for the right words to convey the chaos ruling my mind. "You said I haven't listed a single flaw yet."

"I'm sure you have some." He drinks the last of his whiskey, setting the glass aside. "No one's made up of only good qualities."

Either the mojito, the atmosphere provided by the music, or Dante himself breaks a dam inside me. Words roll off my tongue of their own accord. "When I was a child, I had toys other kids could only dream about." I fiddle with the hem of my dress, watching the fabric crease. "Then came the gadgets. Now it's clothes, shoes, and jewelry. We spent our holidays in the most luxurious hotels. I took singing lessons, ballet, and horse riding. Whatever I wanted was mine because my parents tried to compensate for not loving me."

"Every parent loves their child."

I find the courage to look at him, and he holds my gaze, waiting for more. "Not every parent. I lacked warmth for so long that..." I scoff, shaking my head. "My first boyfriend wasn't affectionate, but I took the scraps he offered with open arms. I used to hold so still whenever he hugged me. He always moved away first because I was too hungry for closeness to let go."

That's not normal.

I'm not 'normal.'

"Sam was next, then Chase. Both as cold and distant as Michael. And here we are. Now, it's you. I want to believe I'm Switzerland, but I can't trust you, Dante. There's too much hatred between you and my father."

Dante's silent for what feels like an eternity. I get up to change the music. Slow, emotional songs aren't doing me any good, considering how much information escaped my lips. John Newman's CD catches my attention when I stop in front of the shelf. I can't resist.

Dante grabs my arm when I approach the couch, his touch urgent as he pulls me in, and grips my waist, sitting me on his lap. His warm mouth closes my parted lips with an eager, demanding kiss. I want to melt into him and bask in the unrestrained attention, but I jerk away when an unpleasant thought hijacks my confused mind.

"I don't want your pity."

He grips my jaw. "You're talking back again."

With a sigh, I link my hands around his neck and take the initiative, pressing my lips to his, dictating my own rhythm as I deepen the kiss. The slow, passionate battle raises the temperature around us by a few degrees. I'm not in control for long. I might be sitting astride him, but he takes over, dictating a lustful pace.

I want to say that giving me hope, then taking it away in a few days is vile, but I can't reject the closeness. I abuse the protective bubble of his arms, praying it'll never burst. This won't last, but a moment of affection I've been denied all my life is worth the river that I'll inevitably cry.

The sound of the alarm being disarmed brings me back to reality. I flinch to slide off Dante's lap, but he holds me firmly in place, his strong hands on my hips.

"I'm here." A tall man enters the living room, catching us in an intimate position.

I wiggle out of Dante's embrace, my cheeks burning, eyes avoiding the guy who just walked in.

"You're the most adorable little bug I ever saw," Dante utters, eyeing my lips before he looks over his shoulder. "Rookie, this is Layla. You're taking her home."

"Sure, Boss." If my presence at Dante's side surprises him, he doesn't let it show.

Dante holds my hand until I'm tucked in the back seat of Rookie's Camaro. "Good night, Star," his hot lips press against my forehead before he closes the door, moving over to the driver's window.

"I'll keep her safe, Boss," Rookie says.

"Yes, you will. Make sure she gets inside before you leave. Call me when you're done."

CHAPTER
SIX

Layla

Frank waits in the kitchen with a glass of neat vodka. He's not alone. Jess sits beside him, painting her nails hot pink despite the clock showing two-thirty in the morning. I've had enough excitement for one night, but one look at Frank, and I know I'm not allowed to go upstairs before he tells me off. He's too fixated on maintaining his image in front of Jess.

"Explain because I'm having a hard time understanding," he says, drilling a hole in my face with a piercing, hateful stare. Nothing new. "Why are you suddenly willing to risk everything I worked for all my life?"

Translation: Why aren't you listening to what I say? Follow the orders like everyone else.

I glance at Jess, who pretends she's not listening, but this conversation will be relayed to her friends early in the morning. Her inquisitive nature means we have to watch what we say, even in our own house.

Especially in our own house.

"I'm not trying to endanger your business. I tried to get rid of Dante," I say. I did try, I think... or maybe not. "He's persistent, but he won't use me against you." I match his pointed stare with my own, nonverbally asking him to trust me this once.

I enjoy the panic flashing in his eyes; the hint of uncertainty on his face. I wish I were cruel enough to openly admit I *like* Dante. That spending time with him is the best thing that has happened to me in a long time.

"Why are you taking his word for it? You don't know him, Layla. You've no idea what he's capable of."

"He's the same as you, I guess. You taught him all he knows, right?"

He ignores the mockery ringing in my voice, proud like a peacock when he nods, glancing at Jess, whose cheeks match the color of her nail varnish. "That's why I know he won't hesitate. I won't repeat myself again. Do as you're told. Don't engage."

He treats me the same way he treats his pawns, as if he pays me to follow his orders. As if I'm his errand boy.

"I'm not sure if Adam told you, but I wasn't looking for Dante tonight. *He* found *me*."

Two wrinkles mark Frank's forehead, his worldview shifting for a second. "How did he know where you were?"

"How do you? You both have your ways."

"The mere fact he was looking for you should make you pause, Layla. Stop being so fucking naïve. Start acting like the adult you claim to be."

"Dante didn't ask me about your business, *Frank...*"

I trail off, suddenly enlightened.

Irritation replaces hormonal dizziness. The lustful fog clouding my mind dissipates, sharpening the scene as if a picture came back into focus. Of course, Dante hadn't tried to dig for information. I took the ace out of the hole when I told him that I don't know much. What if he wanted to corner me last night but needs to alter his game plan?

Jesus... I actually told him how to deceive me. I gave him the gun and showed him how to pull the trigger.

I should've been smarter.

Dante's devious, and I... I'm short-sighted. Blinded by the novelty of his attention. The attention my father wants to give me but can't while Dante's around.

Frank leans back in his chair. "You'll fall in love with him, and you'll soon beg him not to hurt you. He won't listen. He doesn't understand what mercy is, Layla."

"*I'll* fall in love with *him*?" I raise my eyebrow. "I think you're forgetting—"

"Layla," he snaps, casting a sideways glance at Jess. "I know Dante. I know how charming he can be when it matters. He already has you wrapped around his finger."

Jess clears her throat, waving her hands to dry the nail varnish. "Oh yes, he's charming as all hell. I can't blame you for liking him." She winks, driving Frank up the wall. His nostrils flare, and anger almost froths at the corners of his mouth. "The heart wants what it wants, Layla. If you trust Dante, don't back down, or you'll regret it forever."

She's an incurable romantic who never experienced true love. I'm not surprised she's siding with me despite knowing little about what's happening. All Jess sees is a movie-worthy relationship looming in the distance. She will push past Frank to see me in Dante's arms.

Frank shuts his eyes briefly, taking a deep, calming breath. "I don't stick my nose in your life, but I won't calmly watch while you endanger yourself and me. You need to *listen* to me, or we'll end up six feet under."

"Since the day I turned fifteen, all you do is stick your nose in my life. *You* introduced me to my boyfriends. *You* introduced me to Allie. *You* told me to grow my hair and chose my degree, so don't tell me you don't dictate my life!" My voice shakes, the words bitter on my tongue.

I follow his orders, no whining or objecting. Even now, I'm ready to bow out *again*, but not so fast.

This time I'm in control.

I dictate the rules of my relationship with Dante. Maybe if I stand my ground for once, I'll earn Frank's respect. Perhaps proving him wrong will help him realize that I'm more important than his lowest-ranking soldiers, smarter than them, too.

"Burly will remain your shadow until I say otherwise. You don't move unless he's around. Dante will be looking for another chance to see you."

"He found me once. Do you really think he won't do it again?" I jump to my feet. "Do you think I'll discourage him?"

Frank grips the edge of the table, anchoring himself in place. "Do *you* think if you follow him around like a lovesick puppy, he won't question your intentions?!"

"I'll take the risk."

Frank turns purple, but one glance at Jess reminds him that he needs to remain in control no matter how difficult that may be. "Trust me, Layla. Trust me for once in your fucking life. Stop taking offense! If he finds you again, get rid of him. Do you honestly think he's falling in love with you? After *two* evenings?!" He bangs his fist on the table so hard the nail varnish tips over, splattering the white oak tabletop with hot-pink stains. "You might be pretty, but stop and *really* think about this! It's fucking ridiculous!"

He hits the soft spot, and my arguments fly out the window. I can't deny it all smells a bit fishy. Dante started to care about me fast. *Too* fast. Frank's not the father-of-the-year type, but he knows Dante well. He understands his way of thinking better than anyone.

I bow my head low, fresh tears prickling my eyes as I retreat upstairs. I'd give a lot to erase this weekend from my mind, or at least the emotions Dante awoke. Not in my wildest dreams did I expect him to be so caring. Frank made him out to be a monster, a ruthless, vicious killer.

That may be true, but he's much more than that. And that *more*, will be the death of me if I'm not careful.

Curled in an almost fetal position, I hug the pillow to my chest, fighting the tears, but I smell like Dante's spicy cologne, and when I touch my lips, the memories of his kisses bring me undone.

CHAPTER SEVEN

Dante

A sleepless night. That's what I get after Layla leaves my house. I can't stop replaying her words, trying to understand why her parents don't treat her like the light of their lives.

She sure as fuck is mine already.

It's painful to imagine the little girl with big gray eyes who was denied affection by her parents. What kind of monster doesn't hug their child?

I knew Layla before she entered Delta on Friday, but twelve years have passed since the last time I saw her. She's hardly the child I remember. A smile plays on my lips when I recall the good old times. I spent most of my time at Frank's house during the first six months of my career as a mafia man. Layla was a few months away from her seventh birthday at the time and the biggest pain in my ass.

Once. Only once had I asked her what she was up to while she sat at the kitchen table, drawing. From then on, she clung to me whenever I entered the house. Luckily, she never enjoyed playing with toys. As a sixteen-year-old fucker I wouldn't have been keen on dressing up Barbies with her, but I didn't have to.

Layla loved crayons, paints, and everything she could mess up my clothes with. I left their house with playdough stuck to my jeans more than I could count.

The one thing that hadn't changed over the years is Layla's eyes. Large, steel-gray irises watched me with admiration back then and now watch me with curiosity. Back then, I thought she was simply taking advantage of my weakness and inability to say *no* when she pleaded quietly, almost begging me to look at what she had drawn the day before. Like any other kid, she wanted someone to play with.

Now, I wonder if she craved attention back then as she does now. And how much does she need it now, exactly?

The question kept me awake most of the night. I'm not an emotional man. The few women I dated in my early twenties complained about my lack of attention outside the bedroom. Things are different with Layla, though. I hold her hand and touch her whenever she's within my reach. I kissed her in the middle of the road and kissed her forehead more than once—something I'd never done before. My mother once told me that a man who kisses a girl's head cares about her deeply. I'd forgotten all about it until the first time my lips touched Layla's head.

Two evenings.

Three kisses...

I'm way over my fucking head with this girl.

But in a way, I'm put off by her desperate need for attention. I can't imagine dealing with her monopolizing my time. I also can't imagine dealing with her unsatisfied craving for adoration. There's no way I can or even want to live up to her expectations.

I know me. If she tries to cling to me all day, it'll start pissing me off real soon. There's something undeniable forming between us, sure, but it's fresh and based mostly on hormones. We just fucking met, but my mind is preoccupied with the petite cutie non-stop.

Another reason behind the sleepless night is my newfound ability to trust at the snap of my fingers. I didn't question Layla's appearance in my life. At least not how I should have. Not how I question everything else. It crossed my mind that our relationship might be built on ill intentions, but I pushed the idea aside before it sprouted roots.

Layla wasn't trying to seduce me; she wasn't even trying to act friendly. If anything, she tried to push me away. On the other hand, her attitude is what intrigues me most.

A battle raged in my head all night. Despite not reaching any conclusions, I text her the moment I wake up, then check my phone every ten seconds like an infatuated teenager. Half an hour goes by while I wait for a reply, to no avail. When I try calling, it goes straight to voice mail.

Frank got his way.

Either he brainwashed her or pulled out the big guns,

reverting to sabotage. Relief washes over me like a cleansing shower, relaxing my muscles and silencing the infuriating train of thoughts—the problem solved itself. There's no longer any need to debate whether Layla's worth the trouble.

Rejection doesn't *feel* good, but it *is* a good thing.

At least, that's how I choose to think of it for the first half an hour or so until the initial relief evaporates like rain puddles on a hot summer day. My mood deteriorates with every hour of her silence. I drive around the city, busying my mind with *anything* other than Layla, but nothing works. She's dancing at the back of my mind, smiling adorable smiles, and kissing me with an aroused kind of urgency.

And then comes another sleepless night. At least I made up my mind. I wake up, determined to find out why she's ignoring me. If it's Frank's doing, then maybe it's fixable, but if *she* made the decision, I could forget about her. Given how quickly she got me to where I am—losing my fucking mind—forgetting may be the safer choice.

After a quick shower, I call Spades, ignoring the ungodly hour: six a.m.

"Why the hell are you up?" he mumbles.

"I need to know when Layla starts classes. Call everyone who might know."

"Wouldn't it be easier to ask her?"

"Call me back by eight. You better have an answer."

"Okay, okay." The bed creaks on his side of the line. "I'll call you when I find out."

He cuts the call, and I dial another number. This time it's Rookie. His girlfriend, Jane, studies at the same college as Layla. After dragging two of my men out of bed, I call the rest too. What a good fucking idea that was. Neither Spades nor Rookie comes back with an answer.

Luca's the only one who rose to my expectations within half an hour of receiving the order. "She starts at ten."

"How do you know?"

"I've got my ways. She's usually there early. Burly's with her at all times now. She drives a blue BMW M1."

She got the car on Saturday, but he already knows what make and model. Looks like he has a spy up North he didn't mention. I call Rookie again, so he'll pick me up at nine, then drive to the nearby cafe for my morning caffeine fix.

At half nine, we park in the college parking lot. Time ticks by, but Layla's car is nowhere to be seen. I light one cigarette after another, losing my patience at ten o'clock sharp. Either she slipped by me unnoticed or decided to skip classes today.

Luca calls when I'm about to do the same. "Boss, Layla's in the dance studio on Michigan Avenue. She just walked in."

How the hell does he know that?

"Thanks," I say, looking at Rookie while shoving my cell back in my jacket pocket. "Dance studio on Michigan Avenue."

He starts the engine, pulling out of the parking space. It takes eight minutes to arrive at the destination. I walk inside the building with Rookie following suit. "One Way Or Another" resonates throughout the small reception area, sending a pleasant chill down my spine. I lean over the large desk, towering above a young girl wearing rimless glasses.

She glances up from a stack of papers on her desk. "Good morning. Would you like to sign up for dance classes? Modern Jazz, maybe?"

"Boss?" Rookie says behind me.

I shush him, raising my hand, focused on the snarky receptionist. "I'm looking for Layla Harston."

"Oh... um, follow the corridor down, but—"

"Boss," Rookie clips again. I turn to find him at the mouth

of the corridor. "Burly's here."

"Exactly." The receptionist folds her arms over the busty chest. "Layla came in with a bodyguard."

I didn't expect anything else. To be perfectly fucking honest, I'm glad she has security even if the idiot Frank chose is not fully equipped to take care of my star. I'm calmer knowing someone's always watching over her. The music grows louder as we enter the long corridor.

I hope Layla's not pole dancing.

Burly stands at the far end, but I stop once we reach a glass section of the wall.

Dance floor.

Mirrors.

Layla.

She looks like an angel in a white, loose dress. Closed in her own bubble, unavailable to the outside world, she glides across the dance floor, lighter than a feather, as if gravity doesn't apply to her. Together with a tall, blonde guy, they dance something that resembles ballet, but it's not standard ballet. It's a game of seduction. Their movements; *her* movements ooze sexuality. He touches her, pulls her in, and pushes her away in a slow, flawless rhythm; a couple of lovers fighting for dominance. I let out all the air from my lungs. She's captivating. Even though her dance partner is close, even though he's touching her, I hope the song will never end. I could stay here for fucking ever, watching her dance. I like how my chest tightens every time she jumps, so graceful it's almost like she's flying for a second before he catches her with undeniable ease.

"You're not getting in there, Carrow," Burly says, his tone hinting unease, but he takes a broad, artificially confident stance. "You're supposed to stay away from Layla."

"Is that right?" I move closer, every step calculated, muscles in my back harder than stone. "Try and stop me."

"I've got orders to shoot." He reaches behind him, feeling the belt of his trousers to retrieve his gun.

Rookie's faster. He pulls out his pistol with a laid-back, almost bored expression. He's the youngest one in my main entourage, just three years Layla's senior, but he's the best driver I've ever had. I hired him a few years back when I attended an illegal race organized by one of our many clients. He wasn't just way ahead of the competition, winning the race by a landslide, but he was also completely relaxed. No signs of stress on his face. He's a natural.

"I'll give you a valuable piece of advice, so try and keep up," he says. "Don't ever stand between him," he nods in my direction, "and anything he wants."

Burly stumbles back a few steps, pressing his back against the door leading to the dance room.

Determination worth applause.

Stupidity worth pity.

I glance back at Layla when the song's about to end. She takes to the air, wrapping her arms and legs around her partner, and hides her face in his neck. A jab of envy pokes me right in the gut. He lets her go only to catch her thigh and arm, stopping her pretty face mere inches off the floor as the room falls silent. He lays her down, then offers a hand, helping her up. That's when she sees me.

Her cheeks blush, and her body freezes in surprise. It takes one heartbeat before she regains her composure, gesturing to the door Burly protects with his life. I stand there, completely frozen, waiting for my legs to start working again. Layla's dance partner drapes a small towel over her neck and hands her a water bottle.

Using a second of my inattention, Burly takes a chance at getting to Layla before me. He stops at the sound of safety being flipped on a gun.

My gun.

"You think you can take her away from me?" I hiss, aiming at the back of his head. "Don't fucking touch her, or I'll skin you alive."

Two sleepless nights and the long hours spent thinking about Layla kicked my possessiveness up a notch. There's no way I'll let him anywhere near her right now. I'll kill him, risking the silent war between Frank and me turning into something much more sinister.

Burly steps aside, resting against the wall, hands in the air and the gun pointed at the ceiling.

Layla's partner exits the room when I enter. I cross the dance floor to where she stands, cheeks heated, breathing on the quick side. My hands disappear in her hair, and I close the distance that parted our lips too long. She slips her tongue in my mouth with a quiet sigh, clasping her hands over my nape. Warmth radiates off her when our mouths work in sync, mimicking the rhythm of their dance.

"Good morning to you too," she says, stepping away. "How did you find me here?"

"There's no place in this city where you can hide from me, Star. Your phone's switched off."

She takes another step back, so I can't reach her. The desperate need to feel connected to another person, satisfied by my touch, means she doesn't trust her reason when I'm close. "You should stop stalking me, Dante."

The last thing I expect after she just fucking kissed me like there'll be no tomorrow is rejection. I push away the surprise, watching the tone of my voice. "I want you to trust your gut, not listen to your father."

"That's what I'm doing."

"No. You're not. You're doing what Frank wants."

She hugs her frail frame, lifting her head in a fake display of courage. "And I should do what you want? I don't trust either of you, but if I take someone's word, it won't be yours." She's not shouting. She's calm, and that scares me most because I know she means every word. "You have too many reasons to hurt me. Frank has none."

In theory, it's true. Mercy was a foreign concept to me until recently. I used all means available to get my way, but Layla's an exception. She's untouchable. Off-limits. Swapping her for North would take less than half an hour. It would eliminate Frank from the picture without killing him. The flaw in the otherwise perfect plan is that there's no way I'd use Layla as bait. I'm not sure what I want from her, but I crave her like a starving man craves food. Still, imagining our relationship with her constant need for closeness is beyond my capability.

"You should do what you feel is right. It's not quantum physics, Star. You either want me, or you don't."

She stands there, silent, eyes on me but not seeing me at all. My hands grow damp for the first time in years.

"It was the best weekend of my life..." She inhales deeply, biting her lip, "...and we'll leave it at that."

Thirty seconds ago, I wasn't sure what I wanted from her. Now I only want *her*.

My jaw ticks while I fight paranoia.

She crosses her arms over her chest, the feistiness acting as a defense mechanism. "I don't trust you. I want to, but I have no reason to. I don't believe you could be interested in *me*. Not so fast. You don't even know me."

I expected many things, but this? This is fucking bullshit. What does time have to do with any of this? Since when does attraction have a set timeline? Why do people think '*too soon*'? Why? Because it's not socially acceptable? Because people won't approve?

Fuck people.

Fuck caution and scavenger hunts.

Fuck the three-date rule.

Five minutes talking to Layla, and I wanted us to talk for hours. One kiss and I wanted to kiss her every day. One missed call, and she's all I can think about. I want her. I want to know what she likes, what makes her smile, and what makes her frown. I want to find out if there's a *best before* date on the intense attraction. Who cares that we met three days ago? If I haven't gotten bored yet... she's extraordinary.

"Your self-esteem is too low. I know you well enough to have a dozen reasons why I want you close."

Layla moves her weight from one foot to another, toying with her bracelets. "One of those reasons might be my father."

"No." I curl my fingers under her chin, tipping her head so she'll look at me. Her eyes swim with uncertainty laced with sadness that bothers me more than I care to admit. I dip my head, stealing a short, sweet kiss. "Baby, I wasn't looking for you. *You* came over to Delta."

Her face tells me everything I don't want to know—my words won't change anything. Frank brainwashed her like the pro he is. The manipulative bastard stops at nothing. He knows Layla, so he knows exactly where to push for the desired result.

And even though she's strong, she's fragile.

"I don't trust you," she utters, her voice small, defeated. "Don't make this harder than it is."

There's no changing her mind. At least she answered the question that kept me awake for two nights. She doesn't need attention as much as I thought she did.

Otherwise, Frank's arguments would've hit a wall.

And now I can't care less if she wants to be kissed and hugged all the time. I *want* to do it but can't because she won't give me a chance. She won't take the risk.

Human nature is fucking ridiculous.

When she was mine to take, I hesitated... and that hesitation possibly cost me the only thing I ever wanted this badly.

CHAPTER EIGHT

Layla

"I'll be at yours in like half an hour." Allie's voice sounds loud and clear through my phone's speaker.

"Did I forget about something?"

Wardrobe doors slam on her side. "We're going out on a double date. I found the perfect guy for you. Don't even think about refusing. You've been absent-minded for two weeks because of Carrow. Enough is enough."

True. Two weeks is a long time to lust after someone I spent two evenings with. Unfortunately, evicting Dante from my mind is a Sisyphean task. I can't stop thinking about his lips, firm touch, and rough voice.

After I asked him to leave me alone, I checked my phone every few minutes, hoping he'd call. I also searched the crowds outside my college, hoping to see him, but he stopped seeking me out just as I asked.

So why am I disappointed?

Oh, that's right. *I* didn't want him to leave. Frank did, and I hoped Dante wouldn't listen. But he's proud, decent, and apparently a man of his word. At least sometimes.

Too bad he started listening to me *after* the first kiss.

We're two ends of a magnet. I'm North, he's South, but we pull each other in against all odds. He won't stop invading my thoughts, so maybe it truly is the right time for drastic measures. A blind date isn't the brightest idea, but knowing Allie's taste in men, I'll take the risk.

"Who is he?" I ask.

Allie squeals. "I knew I'd convince you! He's straight. I swear! I checked like *three* times. We'll talk more when I'm there. Take a shower!"

Twenty minutes later, I emerge from the ensuite bathroom with a towel on my head.

Allie's already there, unpacking the trunks, littering my room with make-up and twenty different dresses. She enrolled for a part-time course to become a professional stylist a few months ago. Whenever she's got an assignment, she uses me as her guinea pig.

"Sit down and shut up." She shoves me toward the chair standing by my dressing table. "Tonight, I choose what you wear on your face, head, and ass."

She's talented, and often, I resemble a piece of art by the time she's done, but her frivolous taste leaves a lot to be desired. Instead of protesting against the dark eyeshadow or the blood-red lipstick, I bite my tongue. Maybe a diametrical change in appearance will suffocate the growing part of me that obsesses over a particular enemy?

"Will you tell me something about the guy you've set me up with? His name, for example."

"Aaron Jones." She grips the backrest, dipping her head to meet my eyes in the mirror. "He's tall, muscular perfection. You'll *die* when you see him! Like, honestly, he's absolutely gorgeous! If I wasn't in love with Adam, I'd so go for Aaron." She flips the hairdryer on, cutting the chat short for a moment.

Then, she goes on, telling me the scarce information she has about Aaron while working with my hair. An hour later, she's done curling my locks into tight, spiral curls and sprays my face with a heavenly-smelling mist, sealing my fashion-model-worthy make-up.

I don't feel myself with a dark smoky eye, but I do my best to share Allie's enthusiasm.

"You're going somewhere?" Frank cocks an eyebrow when I enter the kitchen, all dolled up, wearing a black fitted dress that covers a whole inch more than just my ass.

Allie said she'd never speak to me again if I chose to wear anything other than the hooker-styled dress. Expensive and glamorous but still hooker-styled.

"We've got a date, Frank," she chirps, batting her eyelashes at my father, lips curved in an ear-to-ear grin. "It's right about time we find this beauty a man, don't you think? What a lovely coincidence that I just happened to meet the perfect guy don't you think?"

Frank bobs his head, utterly disinterested. He only cares about keeping me in line. "Is Adam going with you?"

"Yes." I straighten my spine, lifting my chin to artificially boost my confidence. "Can you give Burly a night off?"

It'd be awkward to have him there, breathing down my neck all evening. Dante hasn't been in touch with me since the dance studio two weeks ago, and I hope Daddy will start loosening the strict security regime. I almost hear his brain cells working before he bobs his head once.

"Have fun."

Have fun? Have I fallen through the looking glass?

"Thanks, Frank. We sure will." Allie grips my hand, dragging me outside, where Adam waits behind the wheel of his car. "We told Aaron we'll meet him at the restaurant," Allie explains when I cock an eyebrow, surprised that he's not there. She rubs her hands together, babbling about the guy for the duration of our journey.

Adam keeps turning up the volume on the radio, but Allie turns it down every time. And so, we listen to graphic descriptions of Aaron's sculpted biceps, triceps, and other ceps.

Twenty minutes later, we enter a restaurant not far from the invisible border that separates Dante and Frank's territories. Not far from Delta, which is only a few blocks away. Dante's probably there...

I dismiss the relentless thoughts, glancing around the space, navy walls, light-wood floor, and black tables surrounded by cream leather chairs. The place fits Allie's taste—luxurious. Large crystal chandeliers hang low over the plains, and floor-length curtains cover arched windows. Peonies decorate the windowsills, filling the air with their sweet scent.

Allie points at a table in the middle of the room, where a brawny, elegant man sits, nervously rolling up the sleeves of his shirt. An enormous, black and white mural of an owl painted on the wall behind his back steals my attention.

"Oh my God! I know, right?!" Allie elbows my ribs, mistaking my admiration of the art for the approval of Aaron, when she digs her long nails into my arm. "He's like *super* gorgeous!"

Not what I'd say, but she does have a point. Surprisingly, she didn't exaggerate when describing Aaron. He looks about twenty-four and wears a baby-blue shirt that struggles to contain the muscles Allie so graciously described earlier. An undercut top knot and a well-groomed beard make him appear rough, despite his delicate features. The evening looks up until we approach the table because I notice his eyes. They're *green*. In a flash, Dante regains control of my mind, wreaking havoc.

"I'm Aaron. You must be Layla." He kisses the back of my hand and, with similar old-fashion manners, pulls out a chair for me. "What can I get you to drink?"

"Moji—" I start but change my mind before the word fully rolls off my tongue. "No, white wine. Medium dry."

I love mojitos, but now it's something I share with one particular person... looks like this will be a long evening.

After checking Adam and Allie's orders, Aaron nods, leaving for the bar. I'd expect a waiter would take care of the drinks, but Aaron's already halfway across the room; his step eager, as if waiting on me will earn him a few extra brownie points.

"And? He's nice, right?" Allie whispers, leaning over the table. "He was *speechless* when I showed him your picture."

"How do you know each other?" I ask, ignoring the question. Many more will come throughout the meal.

"I met him at the gym. He's my personal trainer."

That explains his ideal physique. I stop thinking about the man with the most striking green eyes, but when Aaron returns, I can't focus on anything other than Dante again. Before the food arrives forty minutes later, Aaron tells a brief life story—he moved here from California with his girlfriend, who dumped him for someone else a month later.

"Why don't you go back to California?" I ask, interested, for the first time since I walked through the door.

Aaron smiles, clearly pleased that I took the initiative instead of merely answering his questions. "I sold everything I owned back in Los Angeles. My parents moved to Australia two years ago. I have no siblings, so nothing's waiting for me there. Besides, I like it here. You've got seasons. All we get is summer all year long."

"Sinner!" Allie squeals, pointing her finger at him. "You've no idea what I'd give to have the sun out all the time." She grabs Adam's hand. "Just think about it, babe! It's January, and we're sunbathing by the pool."

Adam's not thrilled by the idea, but he pulls her in for a sweet kiss. Jealousy gnaws at my mind like a woodworm. I never realized how good kissing is, but now that I know what it feels like, I crave Dante's lips more than his attention.

I'm halfway through my first glass of wine, but the guys are already done with their third drink. At this pace, I don't have to worry about the evening lasting too long.

"How about we hit a nightclub after dessert?" Adam suggests, pushing his empty plate aside.

My eyebrows hit my hairline. A similar sentence never left his mouth during the six years I've known him. Even Allie looks surprised, but Aaron's all game.

"Yeah, sure. I hear Delta's the best club in the city. We could go there."

Adrenaline rush courses through my bloodstream at the thought of seeing Dante.

And then I grit my teeth when frustration takes over. The bouncers won't let Adam into Delta, and Adam himself would never try and set a foot inside anyway.

"Everywhere but there," I say, pressing the cool rim of my glass to my lips.

"Why?" Aaron asks. "Something wrong with that place?"

"We won't get in," Allie says. "Well, no one but Layla."

Aaron waits for an explanation, eyes fixed on me. I glance at Adam for help, unsure how much I can divulge, and catch him nod once in a way that indicates no filters are necessary. Either he trusts Aaron, or Frank wants to find out how I feel about Dante now.

The latter, probably.

I rest my elbows on the table, crossing my legs. "Do you know who my father is?"

"Yeah. Everyone knows who your father is, Layla."

"Then you should also know who owns Delta."

Aaron draws his eyebrows together. "Dante Carrow..."

"Exactly. My father's men aren't allowed there because my father and Dante aren't too fond of each other."

"That doesn't explain why you'll get in."

There's no concealing the smile that curls my lips. "Let's just say Dante has a soft spot for me. Although I doubt the security would let me in tonight. Not after how I treated their boss a while back."

Adam twitches in his seat, the vein on his neck throbbing. "You've not heard from him since the dance studio?"

"No. I'm a smart girl who fulfills her Daddy's wishes, right? I told Dante to leave, and he did."

"Hey! What about Copacabana?" Allie changes the subject, uncomfortable with the tense atmosphere. "They've got like *the best* DJ playing on Fridays."

Adam excuses himself from the table, disappearing outside with a phone to his ear.

Snitch.

Dancing the night away with Aaron might positively affect my mood, so I agree with Allie and ignore the sinking feeling in my stomach. By the look of him, he's very much into me, and after another hour at the restaurant, his eyes no longer remind me of another green-eyed man.

Aaron twirls me around his hand on the dance floor in Copacabana as if I'm a rag doll.

Salsa, samba, rumba, cha-cha, and from the top again.

Thirty minutes later, we head back to the table on aching feet. A mist of sweat covers my neck, but a full-blown smile stretches my lips too. Aaron's an excellent dancer. I have no trouble reading into the subtle clues he sends, letting me know what's coming next. We formed a bond while dancing, and the mutual understanding is why I'll agree to a second date if he offers. There's also the bonus of not thinking about Dante when Aaron's around... using him to erase the boss of South Chicago from my system might be cruel, but as it's working well, I push my scruples aside.

Adam didn't bribe the bouncers to get us into a VIP box when we arrived, which is odd considering he prefers not to mingle with the crowd. He's been acting strange all evening, subtly digging for information about Dante as if I grab a drink, setting the glass down once it's empty. When my breathing stabilizes, I take Aaron back to the dance floor.

"I've not had this much fun in a long time," I say after twenty minutes when my legs are too weak to dance.

"My pleasure. Go back to Allie. I'll get you a drink."

Adam's alone at the table, drinking his Budweiser, eyes on the crowd of dancing bodies.

"Where's Allie?" I ask.

"Toilet. We need to get going."

"We just got here!"

"We've been here for an hour, Layla. Allie's not feeling well, so I'm taking her home." He looks around as if checking for eavesdroppers. "I want to trust you, Layla. If I let you stay here, will you promise you won't flee to Delta?"

He's thinking about leaving me here without a nanny?

What happened to his principles?

I nod before he thinks the idea through. "I promise."

The unwanted date turned into a pleasant night. It's still early, and I don't want to go home yet, hoping I can take Aaron dancing again once I regain feeling in my legs. He's kind, handsome, heterosexual, and his company soothes my cluttered mind. What more do I need?

The answer flashes before my eyes, but I lock Dante in a small, dark room in my subconscious, bolt the door and throw away the key. That should keep him from poisoning my thoughts.

Adam gets up, and thanks to his six-foot-eight height, he looks over hundreds of heads, searching for his girlfriend. "If anything happens, you call *me*. Only *me*, Layla."

"Nothing will happen. Dante hasn't contacted me in two weeks. I doubt he'll suddenly start looking for me all over the city. Relax."

He shoots me a skeptical look and, without another word, turns around, disappearing into the crowd.

CHAPTER
NINE
Layla

A large, colorful drawing of a human brain hangs in Aaron's living room. He brought me here after someone accidentally spilled red wine over his shirt at the club. He seemed harmless, so I agreed when he said he had a bottle of wine and asked if we could continue the evening at his house. We hailed a cab, and now I stand in his living room, looking at the framed brain, wondering *why*.

"Do you want to be a neurosurgeon, or have you lost a bet, and someone made you hang this here?"

He emerges from the kitchen with two glasses of wine, now in a plain white t-shirt that shows off his muscular arms Allie told me so much about.

"You don't see art in this?"

I chuckle, elbowing his ribs playfully when he smiles. "Why is it here?"

"That's all my ex left. She hung weird things all over the house. This one might be the weirdest, but I like it." He sits on the couch while I continue my journey of discovery.

You can learn a lot about a person by seeing what they surround themselves with.

Dante's house is full of quirky treasures that highlight his character. The Shelby parked in his living room, the shelf full of CDs, a well-stocked bar, and a dark color scheme. It fits his profession and personality.

Aaron is an athlete. The walls are decorated with medals and trophies, but other than that, the room is bland, almost empty. White walls, gray furniture. It looks as if he just moved in. I round the couch to sit, but Aaron grips my hand, dragging me onto his lap. Surprised by his forwardness, I cock an eyebrow, but he's not looking. Eyes closed, he inches closer to me, grasping the flesh of my hips so hard borders on painful. If he had tried that two weeks ago, I wouldn't object, but tonight my mind screams *no!*

Dante breaks the door of his mini prison, pacing all over my thoughts with an enraged look twisting his handsome face, reminding me how I felt when he kissed me for the first time... dizzy, almost drunk on endorphins; trembling like an uncoiled spring, my body and mind ruled by his presence. By the raw, irresistible hunger of his lips devouring mine.

There's none of that now. No excitement; no anticipation. I'm embarrassed, annoyed, and a little scared.

I dart away before Aaron's lips touch mine, my hand on his chest, keeping him at a distance. "I'm sorry, but no."

He looks at me, his face twisting in confusion when I stand quickly and step away, resting against the wall opposite the sofa.

"You don't like me?" he asks. "I thought we had fun."

We did. I can't fault him. He's well-behaved, well-mannered, and easy-going, but those qualities are no longer at the top of my list. Since two weeks ago, I've been attracted to confidence, bossiness, and a sprinkle of arrogance.

Aaron lacks all three.

"No, it's not like that. It's just..." I sigh, unsure how to proceed. "I don't know. We just met." In a flash, the pleasant evening turns uncomfortable. "I'll call a cab."

Aaron's up on his feet before I take the first step. He rests his hands on the wall on both sides of my head, locking me in a purposely built cage. Dante did that two weeks ago. I wasn't afraid then, but I am now.

"Stop messing around," I say, failing to strike a casual tone.

There's something in his posture; a threatening, determined vibe, that makes me quiver. For a second, I think he'll retreat, but he grips my throat hard enough to stop me from even thinking about escaping. His other hand travels up my thigh. Fear engulfs me so fast I struggle to keep up with my body's reactions. Aaron dips his head, forcing his tongue inside my mouth, and I pound on his chest, squealing because I can't scream.

"Shut up." He grips my wrists, tying them in one hand, the touch sharp enough to cut off circulation.

"Let me go!" I bite his lip, breaking the skin. "My father

will kill you when he finds out about this!"

A maniacal smile spreads across his face as he touches the bleeding lip. I don't dare look at the crimson trickle dripping down his chin.

My stomach sinks with the copper taste on my tongue as if I'm falling from a fifty-story building. My screams are cut short when he kisses me again. The taste of blood destroys my courage faster than a gun aimed at my head. Bile reaches my throat when he touches my panties. Repulsive thoughts infest my mind like small, biting insects.

I won't let him touch me that way.

Not in a million years.

Fear dies down, replaced by determination, and my instincts kick in, clearing my head of the panicked static. I swing my knee, ramming it into Aaron's groin. The punch isn't strong enough to knock him down but powerful enough that he lets go of my hands, gripping his jewels.

Before he has time to swear, I'm gone.

With my bag in hand, I sprint down the road, turning left, right, and left again. The short streets dotted with rows of similar houses blur together until I stop at a side street filled with small shops. I rest my back on the window of dry cleaners, my feet ache, my lungs burn, and I tremble like a kitten with a mixture of fear, shock, and adrenaline.

I steady my breathing, getting get my pulse under control before I start walking on weak legs. Buried in my thoughts, still shuddering, I wonder if I hadn't overreacted. Aaron's drunk. Maybe he didn't mean to hurt me...

I scoff, annoyed with my own naivety. The way he held me, the force he used to keep my now swollen, bruised wrists away from his face warranted panic.

My house is eight miles away. There's no way I'll walk the

distance wearing high heels after I just ran however many blocks. The neighborhood I found myself in isn't the best or the safest. I've had enough adventures for one night, so I take my phone out to call Adam.

Once, twice… no answer. I search the contact list for Burly's number to no avail. I try Adam again.

"Wait up, doll!" Someone shouts behind me. "Wait up!"

My heart rate soars faster than my pace. Not daring to turn around, I rush toward the main street looming in the distance. The man is closing in on me, and judging by the heavy footsteps, he's not alone. Fear reappears, gripping my throat like cold, wet hands. I can't outrun them. The street's empty; not a soul in sight. Adam's still not answering. I ignore what he said at the club and call Frank.

"The number you're calling is not available. Try again later."

A thin, bald guy cuts me off, blocking my way, a bottle of vodka in his hand. "Are you lost, doll?" Dilated pupils size me up. A faded swastika tattooed across his neck looks like a child had tattooed it. Multiple, neglected cold sores surround his cracked lips as he tugs from the half-empty bottle. He jumps forward, shoving me against a shop window.

"Don't ruin her, Loki," the other man says when Loki pulls out a long, rusty knife.

"Do you need help?" I ask, doing my best to stay calm.

"How about we help you? You're not from around here."

I inch away from the knife. "Don't touch me."

They laugh like two maniacs: like villains in superhero movies. "What will you do? You're alone, dolly." He inhales deeply, taking a drag of my perfume, eyes closed, lips parted in a repulsive manifestation of arousal.

I think I'll be sick; my heartbeats like crickets that try to scratch their way out of a plastic container. They cornered me on what must be the most deserted street in the city. I've only seen two cars in the last ten minutes. The third one just drove by, but it wasn't a cop car. Situations like this are standard on the poorer streets of Chicago, especially in this neighborhood. Riverdale's known for robberies, drug addicts, and rapes.

Loki presses the sharp edge of his knife to my cheek, sliding it lower ever so gently, but his hand shakes, and the blade digs into my skin. I might need a tetanus shot after this…. the blade looks and smells filthy. I hiss with fresh tears prickling my eyes. It's not the pain. That's irrelevant. I don't feel pain while panic tries to choke me at the thought of blood seeping from the wound.

"Do you know who my father is?" I ask, redirecting the train of paralyzing thoughts. "Frank Harston. Rings a bell?"

Every junkie in Chicago knows his name. The dark side of the city knows both my father and Dante.

Loki cackles, looking over his shoulder at the other man. "You heard her, Cannon?"

"Daddy's little girl." Cannon sneers.

The blade of Loki's knife breaks my skin again, lower this time. "You're down South. Your father means nothing here."

My knees buckle. Panic hovers nearby, ready to leap out at the least convenient moment and knock the breath out of my chest. Scaring them off won't work, and my composure starts to burst like a bubble, but with the undeniable defeat comes a sudden rush of bravery.

I shove at Loki's frail, drug-addled body and run, aiming for the main street. Cars loom in the distance, filling me with hope, but I'm too far away for anyone to see or hear me. Desperate to feel safe again, I call the last person who can help.

I swipe my thumb across the screen but never press the

phone to my ear. I trip on uneven pavement, falling face down. Tears trickle down my cheeks. My heart thuds against my ribs like a Conga drum. The sight of blood oozing from my scraped knee erases any remaining courage.

Cannon catches me first, bending down to grab my waist. He reeks of sweat, smoke, and piss as he heaves with the effort, rolling me over until I'm looking at his ugly face covered in a nasty rash, hovering above me.

"Leave me alone!" I keep my voice down because screaming might alert more psychopaths hiding in the dark.

The navy Dodge RAM that passed us a minute ago does a sharp U-turn in the middle of the road. Neither Cannon nor Loki pays the car any attention until it stops by the curb.

A tall, well-dressed guy jumps out of the driver's seat. "Let her go," he seethes, his voice low, dripping with fury.

Relief floods my system, but my tears come on stronger. "Please don't leave me here."

Cannon looks over his shoulder, holding me in a vice grip. "This is none of your business! Dolly got lost."

The newcomer turns to the sky as if he has no time for this nonsense, then grabs Cannon by the arm, twisting it back with an impassive expression. "Do you know who the fuck she is you fucking dimwit? Let. Her. *Go*."

Cannon jerks away, readjusting his position to ease the pain of his arm being twisted back at an unnatural angle. "Yeah, I do. Do you?!" A mist of spit flies out of his mouth. "She's Frankie's daughter! Dante's not gonna be happy you're helping the bitch!"

"Dante will fucking disembowel you when he finds out you touched her." Amusement tugs at his lips. "Start digging your fucking grave."

"But..." With fearful eyes, he looks from me to Loki as if he can shed some light on what's happening. "What the fuck are you talking about?!"

"You heard me," the man shoves Cannon to the ground. "Get the fuck out of here and make sure I don't see you again." He looks at me, his face impassive when he points at his car. "Get in."

I grab my bag and phone off the sidewalk and get in the passenger seat, no questions asked. Whoever he is, he knows Dante. He saved me from rape or worse: death. I don't care about his name if he gets me out of here.

Despite the fall, my phone still works. Sixteen missed calls wait on the screen.

All from Dante.

I hide my face in my hands. Tears no longer trail down my face, but I shake, whimpering despite trying my hardest not to make a sound.

The driver takes his seat, touching my back and making me jump. "Calm down, Layla." He moves away, jaw ticking. "You good? Did they hurt you? What the fuck happened to your security detail?!"

I rest my back against the door, covering the bleeding knee with my bag. "How do you know who I am?"

"Who the fuck doesn't?" he clips. "I didn't have time for pleasantries. I'm Luca, Dante's main fighter."

CHAPTER
TEN
Dante

I sit in the office at the club, a bottle of whiskey keeping me company. Twenty monitors covering the wall usually display the feed from cameras all around Delta but now stream a clip of Layla and me at the bar two weeks ago.

How did I get so fucking hooked on this girl after spending two evenings with her? How's that possible?

Well, I'm a living example that it's very much possible.

Dante

My laptop's speakers repeatedly blast one song—"One Way Or Another." Layla's favorite. I've listened to it non-stop for two weeks; ninety percent of my time is spent thinking about her smiles, kisses, and how crazy she makes me. Thinking of ways to convince her to give us a try. Ten percent is spent convincing myself I should let her be.

Spades enters the office with Nate around midnight.

"We've got a problem." Nate plops down on the sofa.

As if I don't have enough fucking problems.

"What is it this time?"

"FBI busted three of our guys in a raid." He rubs his face, exchanging a knowing look with Spades. "They hit our warehouse and confiscated two containers."

Spades rests his elbows on his knees. "They knew the container numbers, Dante. They knew where to go, and they knew what the fuck to look for."

"If they knew, someone must've tipped them off." I light a cigarette, turning around to dim the monitors. "Any suspicions?" They shake their heads. "Who did the FBI take?"

"Gareth, Newton, and Phil. They're in temporary arrest for now, but Jackson called our lawyer, so—"

"Get rid of them."

"All three? Dante, Gareth knew the risks. He won't talk. You're paying him too fucking much."

"*Call* Howard," I emphasize. "You can spare Gareth at your own risk, but an obituary is all that's to be left after Monday for Newton and Phil."

Howard is one of our many acquaintances. His men are scattered around major prisons throughout America, ready to kill anyone for the right money. I've used his services more than once in the past. He's not cheap, but neither is freedom. My freedom is priceless, just like the freedom of

Spades, Nate, and all my most trusted men.

Nate glances at Spades, probably looking for support, but Spades knows there's no arguing with me. He motions his chin, urging Nate to make the call.

"Aren't you overreacting?" he asks once Nate leaves the room. My distracted mind is the only reason he dares to question my choices.

"They'll get a minimum of ten years. At some point, they'll start talking. You're going down first when they do, and then it's Nate."

I won't risk it. Nate and Spades are like my brothers. We started this together, and we'll retire together.

My phone's ringtone stops our conversation. I smile when *Star* flashes on the screen. "You missed me?"

The hastened clicking of heels and Layla's uneven breaths are the only answer. I think her phone pocket-dialed my number, but uncharacteristic worry blooms in my mind, and my muscles tense like a guitar string. I call her back only to reach the answering machine. I jump to my feet, dialing over again, my mind like a nest of pissed-off rattlesnakes. I don't have the slightest idea where she might be, but I've got a plan at the ready regardless.

I don't know *what* is wrong, but something *is* definitely fucking wrong. I can feel it in my bones.

"Hey," Layla answers, halting me halfway to the door. She sounds upset, frightened, fucking *tearful*, and that distressed quality to her voice flips my stomach.

"What's wrong?"

"Nothing now," she whimpers, sucking in a sharp breath. "I'm sorry I called, but Adam wasn't answering, and neither was Frank, and I don't have Burly's number, and..." She exhales again as if trying not to cry. "I ran into two junkies on Riverdale."

I squeeze my neck with a trembling hand.

Anxiety rages inside my overworked, tired mind filling up with an array of dark scenarios. "Tell me you're okay, baby."

"I'm okay," she utters unconvinced, close to tears again. "Luca was in the right place at the right time."

I let out a shaky breath, a touch calmer that one of my men is looking over her. "Let me talk to him."

"She's fine," Luca says, infuriatingly casual. "Shaken up, a touch battered, but—"

"What the fuck does *a touch battered* mean?"

"Nothing serious. A few cuts on her face and a few bruises at most. They just scared her senseless."

Just? His *just* is more than I can handle. "Get her over to Delta. Meet me at the underground parking lot."

"Yeah, whatever," he heaves, annoyed with my curt, commanding tone. "We'll be there in ten."

I can hardly keep myself from hurling my phone at the wall when he cuts the call. Instead of a dramatic response, I down the last of my whiskey and light another cigarette. The last time I felt so out of place was six years ago when I restrained Dino minutes before Frank, Morte, and I threw him into Lake Michigan.

"Is everything alright?" Spades asks, every word worth its weight in gold with how slowly he speaks, aware of my short-temper and a shitty attitude. "You look like you're about to fuck someone up."

"Layla got cornered by two junkies on Riverdale."

"Someone's definitely getting fucked..." he murmurs under his breath. "Should I call Cai, Luca, and Jackson?"

"Luca's with her." Thank fuck for that, or I'd be climbing the walls right about now. It's crazy how protective I am toward her. "And I'll take care of the fuckers myself."

I grip my leather jacket, then take the lift to the underground parking lot, lighting one cigarette after another, waiting for Luca to arrive.

His Dodge RAM pulls up beside my Charger ten long, torturous minutes later. I yank the passenger side door open to check on my Star. Something fucking snaps inside me at the sight of mascara smudged under her red, puffy eyes. Blood is smeared across two cuts on her cheek, and a green bruise starts showing on the side of her neck. Her knee is scraped, and more blood is smeared down her leg.

My jaw locks painfully.

"Don't look at me like that. I'm okay." She sounds better than over the phone, but a glimmer of fear flashes in her eyes, pushing me that much closer to madness.

"Always call me first, Layla. Always." I help her out to drape my jacket over her shoulders, acting against instinct when I don't lock her frail frame in my arms.

She didn't call to see me. She called because no one else bothered to answer their fucking phone. Maybe she does trust me a little bit.

"Get in." I open the back door, then take her place at the front. Luca starts the engine, reversing out of the parking space. I stay quiet for a few minutes, trying to calm down, but every time I blink, the bruise on her neck flashes before my eyes, demolishing my composure. "What the hell were you thinking?!" I boom, my hands shaking. "A walk across Riverdale in the middle of the night? How the fuck did you end up there?!"

Layla curls into a ball, hiding her face behind a veil of dark, curly hair. She looks like a hooker in a tiny black number that accentuates her boobs and barely covers her ass.

"I had a date," she utters, picking her nails.

"Say what? A *date*?" Jealousy makes an appearance, kicking worry to the background for a brief moment. "And Romeo didn't fucking think to order you a cab home?"

I couldn't cope for two weeks because of her, and she went out with some fucker? Just like that? What kind of an asshole lets a girl like Layla walk home alone at night? When I see him, and I sure will now that he failed to keep Layla safe, I'll teach him some fucking manners.

Layla stares at her hands, chin trembling, lips sealed. I wish I could give her a few moments to calm down, but I'll burst into flames if she doesn't tell me what exactly happened.

I reach behind me, resting my hand on her thigh. "Baby... where's your security? Why were you alone tonight?" I fucking hate myself as I stroke her skin with my thumb. I'm manipulating her, knowing damn well how much she craves my touch and that it'll untie her tongue.

Her big, beautiful eyes pool with fresh tears as she shakes her head, swallowing hard. I'm this close to losing my shit. I swear, nothing has ever caused me more physical pain than seeing Layla in tears. I gesture for Luca to stop the car, resting my head on the headrest, and light up the sixth Marlboro in the last fifteen minutes.

"Start talking, Layla." I adjust the rear-view mirror to watch as she swats her tears away.

Fuck, I want to wrap her in my arms and hold her until she calms down.

"Take me home. Please, I—"

"We're going nowhere until you explain where Burly is, why Romeo didn't take you home, and how you found yourself on Riverdale."

The fear in her eyes fizzles out, morphing into a raging fire when she assumes an aggressive pose, crossing her arms, head up high.

"Frank gave Burly a night off. Allie set me up with her personal trainer for a double date. We had dinner and then moved to Copacabana." She hurls the words at me at the speed of light. If she had something heavy to hand, it'd bounce off my head. "I had fun, but Allie didn't feel well, so Adam took her home. *That's* where my security went. Aaron took me back to his place..." She stops, avoiding my eyes, staring at her hands and swollen wrists. "He scared me a little. I ran, which is why I ended up in Riverdale. I was walking back home."

I turn back around. "What did he do?" Unconsciously, she's massaging her sore, swollen wrists and I can't fucking take any more. Wrath sweeps over me like some biblical hurricane. "He *forced* himself on you?!"

"I don't know the first thing about it... maybe I misunderstood him, maybe—"

I jump outside, slamming the door hard enough that the widows shake before she has a chance to finish the sentence. I've never felt so unhinged. I don't know whether to walk, sit or stand. Twice in one night someone tried to hurt her. *Twice.*

I swear under my breath, yanking the back door open. "Name and address. Right *now*," I seethe, and the tone of my voice must tell her not to fucking argue.

"Aaron Jones. He lives on South Evans Avenue."

Luca knows where to go when I take the passenger seat again. I make a mental list of things I'll do to the motherfucker who touched Layla before shoving him in the trunk. Romeo's heading for a sad, imminent end.

Fifteen minutes later, we arrive at the dumpy street. Houses with lawns the size of my ensuite bathroom stand close together. Shitty old cars are parked in the driveways, and most street lamps don't work.

"Which house?" I ask. After a moment of silence, I find Layla curled in her seat once more, holding herself in a tight hug. Those should be my arms around her. "*Which* house?"

She bites her cheek, stalling. "It's nice that you care, but I'm not sure if he wanted to..." Her cheeks burn scarlet. "I panicked. Maybe a blatant *no* would've stopped him."

"Are you this naïve, or are you lying because you're scared I'll break his legs?" and *hands, and jaw. And turn his spine into a fucking jigsaw.* "Neither your wrists nor your neck would look like this if he wasn't trying to hurt you. Tell me which house, or I'll wake the whole goddamn street."

Layla sits up, flips the light, and looks into the rear-view mirror, the tips of her fingers ghosting the bruise across her neck. She tilts her head, examining two cuts on her cheek, the white of her skin a dramatic contrast to the dried blood.

She falls back, eyes wide. I think she's ready to throw up. "It's that one there." She points at the third house down the short road.

"Stay," I tell Luca when he unbuckles his seatbelt, ready to serve the fucker some justice. "He's mine. Make sure she stays inside. Don't let her out of the car."

The lock clicks when I close the door behind me, strolling up the short driveway. My muscles tense with every step. The ability to retaliate for Layla keeps me in a relatively rational mindset. Otherwise, I would've emptied the clip of my gun into the night sky by now.

I kick the door down fireman style. A narrow staircase opposite the entrance takes me upstairs, where I break down another door. Torn out of sleep, Romeo switches the night lamp on, illuminating the tiny bedroom.

"Good evening." I fist his t-shirt and hurl him at the wall as if he weighs no more than a bag of sugar.

He might be brawny, but he doesn't stand a chance with the pure fury coursing through my veins.

"What the hell?" He scrambles back to his feet, lips parted, eyes narrowed. "Who the hell are you? What's going on?!"

"Dante Carrow." I send my right hook sailing through the air to land on his jaw. "You touched *my* girl."

Romeo covers his nose to stop the bleeding. "I haven't touched anyone! I swear, I—"

Another blast, and the first bone cracks under my knuckles. Many more will break before I'm done. His neck will be last. I grip him by the collar of his t-shirt and send him tumbling down the stairs. His ribs crack, the sound bringing a sick smile to my lips.

"So, you're saying Layla bruised herself? You're saying you didn't try to fuck her?"

Romeo lands face first on the cream carpet downstairs, whimpering. He holds onto the wall for support, shaking like a leaf as he tries to haul himself back up. "I didn't know she's yours!" he cries, bloodshot eyes looking everywhere except my face. "Please, just—"

Another blast cuts him off mid-sentence. What the fuck does it matter whose she is? Even if she were single, drunk, or clingy, it wouldn't justify rape. Nothing does.

"Please." He clutches his ribs. "I didn't... she ran!"

I grip Romeo's neck when he takes a chance at fleeing. I cut his legs out from under him, so he lands back on the ground. His head bounces off the concrete one step outside the door, and he briefly loses consciousness.

I crouch beside him, yanking him by his short hair. "You should thank God Layla's in the car, or you'd be pumped full of lead by now. But she's watching, and seeing her scared drives me fucking insane, so call it your lucky day. You get to pray in the trunk for a little while longer."

The Beretta 92 in my holster is fully loaded and ready to go. Fifteen rounds of ammunition, all destined for Romeo's head.

I drag him to the car, deaf to his pleas. Luca steps outside, opens the trunk, and helps me haul Romeo in.

Layla chooses that moment to jump out of the car. "Leave him alone!" Her tiny fists connect with my shoulder. "He's had enough! Let him go!"

"Don't get in the middle," I hiss, keeping Romeo in place while he's tossing and swearing, punching the air. I land one more blast on his head to knock him out. It works a treat. I shut the trunk, all the while doused with a series of Layla's half-ass punches.

"He learned his lesson!" she cries, hitting harder.

Careful not to squeeze too hard or cause more damage, I grab her by the shoulders, forcing her back inside the car. "Stop fidgeting, Star."

"Next time, I won't tell you anything!" She turns her head the other way in a theatrical manner.

It'd be amusing if not for the words. "*Next time*? You want to see him again?!"

"No, I-I... just, leave him be. Please, he didn't do anything. I ran before he had the chance to—"

"If he had raped you, he wouldn't be fucking breathing right now." I would've killed him with bare hands. I'd batter him until he bled out on the front lawn outside his shitty house. "Put your seatbelt on."

Romeo starts screaming in the trunk half a minute after we pull away from the curb. Luca slams the brakes a few times, silencing Romeo for the time being. He'll scream again when I'll hold a gun to his head.

"Hey, Dad," Layla says out of the blue.

I jerk around, tearing the phone out of her hand. "What the fuck are you playing at? Why is Layla alone? Where's her fucking security?!"

"Why are you with her again?" he sighs, sounding bored. "She told you to stay away."

I tap Luca on his shoulder and point left, so he'll turn there. "One of my men found her on Riverdale cornered by two junkies. Would you rather he left her there?"

"No, of course not," he snaps. The concern in his voice sounds forced, unnatural. "But I'd rather—"

"Then be thankful Luca was driving by. You'd be looking for her in the gutter tomorrow if not for him." Chills slide down my spine just thinking about what could've happened.

"Thank you," he seethes, the words strained as if too tricky to pronounce. "And now, can you bring her back home and leave her the fuck alone? Stay away from her, Dante. You'll do more damage than all the junkies in this city."

A laugh escapes me. His daughter could've been raped tonight, or worse—drugged, raped, and beaten to death, but all he cares about is business. I hope he'll lose it all soon. There's a particular part of hell reserved for the likes of him.

"All I can damage is your fucking ego. I'll bring Layla home, and I have a gift, too."

I want to trial Romeo myself, but handing him over to Frankie might force the son of a bitch to look at my relationship with Layla from a different angle. He's fond of

Italian mafia culture and appreciates such gestures.

Layla meets my eyes when I return her phone, her pretty face clouded with uncertainty, but she grabs my hand, lacing our fingers together. "Thank you, and... I'm sorry."

It's not an average *sorry*. She doesn't mean tonight alone, but also the rejection from two weeks ago. Without putting herself out in the open, she's checking if I still want her.

"Stop the car," I tell Luca.

I hesitated once. *Never* again. I won't play games if she's ready to give us a go.

I want her.

I need her to be mine.

The RAM's tall enough, so when I open the back door, I take one step and being eye-level with Layla, I cup her face, covering her lips with mine.

Sweet.

So addictively sweet.

Her shoulders sag as her frail body relaxes under my touch. I hated every damn second I spent away from her the past two weeks. She presses her nose to my cheek, deepening the kiss with the same aroused urgency she kissed me last time, and her small, delicate fingers press into my jaw.

Having her close calms me right down. If she's with me, she's safe. "I'm taking you to Delta tomorrow. With or without your father's blessing, with or without Burly, you're coming with me. Understood?" A long journey to earn her trust awaits, but I'll gladly work on her doubts.

Tucking her long hair back, she presses her forehead against my torso. "I told you I'd get addicted. A gentle reminder..." She pulls away to meet my gaze. "Too many people use me, hurt me, and toss me aside like a broken toy." She rests her hand on my chest, keeping me away when I move to kiss her. "Don't try and shush me. I'll be waiting for you tomorrow but don't show up if you intend to put me back on the shelf once you get bored."

"I'll pick you up at eight."

CHAPTER ELEVEN

Layla

Frank waits outside the house with a glass of whiskey and a cigar. He stands at the top of the concrete steps, his face impassive as he watches the Dodge park by the three-space garage. Beside him, like an oversized statue, stands Adam.

Luca keeps the engine running when Dante leaves to let Aaron out of the trunk.

"Thank you." I say, meeting his gaze in the mirror.

He flips the lights on, illuminating the confined space, then turns around, gracing me with a tight-lipped nod.

"Let me go!" Aaron screams outside.

I open the door when Dante shoves him to the ground, and makes him kneel on the gravel, aiming a gun at the back of his head.

"I wouldn't move if I were you," he clips.

Aaron falls silent once he notices my father descending the steps, gracing him with his signature you're-worth-less-than-shit-on-my-shoe look before he raises his gaze to the man standing behind him. Instead of disdain or irritation, Frankie looks at Dante with respect.

"It was supposed to be a gift," he says, eyeing Aaron with a menacing scowl. "It's not wrapped, and you fucking broke it," he chuckles, clasping his hand with Dante, a rare, genuine smile on his lips.

My eyebrows shoot up. *What is going on?* Frank is *funny*. He never jokes around. It's been months since he smiled. After everything he told me about Dante, I expected a much colder, hateful greeting, but they shook hands like the dearest of friends. No snarky remarks or threats... it almost looks as if my father is happy to see Dante as if he missed him.

Mafia men and their stupid code of honor.

Frank flicks his wrist—a silent order for Adam. Ten seconds later, Aaron's locked in the trunk again, but he's not fighting or screaming this time. I don't dare defend him in front of Frank. Harsh consequences would follow for such deliberate insubordination.

Frankie moves his gaze from Dante to me, eyes roving my face with mild interest. "You good?" He never cares about my well-being, so his concern, however fake, is surprising.

"I'm okay."

"Then goodnight," he says, insinuating that the rest of their conversation isn't meant for my ears.

I spin around, looking at Dante. "Thank you."

"Goodnight, Star."

I spend the better part of Saturday waiting for Frank to come home so I can tell him about my plans for the evening. Dante earned an ounce of my trust last night, muting Frank's arguments. I'm sure he'll try to talk me out of seeing Dante, but I'm not changing my mind. I know what I'm doing; either he trusts me, or I prove him wrong without his blessing.

I open my closet, skimming the contents, looking for something I could wear tonight, but nothing stands out. I take my phone, dialing Allie's number. "How busy are you?"

"Not very. Why?" she asks.

"You need to help me get ready for tonight. Can you please come over?"

"Another date with Aaron?!" she screams in my ear. "How was it last night? Tell me everything! No! Don't tell me anything. I'll be there in twenty! Make me some coffee."

I collapse on the bed, sinking between a dozen fluffy pillows. Convincing Allie that Dante and I are a good idea might be more challenging than convincing Frank to let me out tonight. Her opinion's irrelevant, but I'd rather not lose her friendship if it can even be considered that. Genuine or fake, she's the only friend I've got.

She arrives, as promised, with two minutes to spare and a few trunks full of make-up and hair supplies. "So? Did Aaron pass the test?" She snatches a steaming cup of coffee from the table. "Go on! Tell me *everything*! Did you guys hook up?"

"It's not Aaron I want to look nice for tonight. Dante's picking me up at eight."

"Dante?" She pulls her eyebrows together. "Dante *Carrow*? Like... how stupid are you, babe?! Layla, he's your dad's enemy. He'll use you, and—"

"You don't know the first thing about him. Stop trying to educate me. Just be happy that I'm happy. that I care about someone who cares about me too."

"All he cares about is business. Stick with Aaron. I'm telling you, he's handsome, polite, and not a threat to your dad!"

I roll up my sleeves, uncovering bruised wrists. "He tried to rape me last night, and later on, if it weren't for one of Dante's men, two junkies would've probably killed me." I wipe the thick layer of concealer off my cheek, showing her the cuts. I almost threw up this morning when I saw my reflection and the dried blood that must've seeped from the wounds during the night because I cleaned up before falling asleep. "You should've seen Dante," I say with a small smile. "He was so worried... so *furious* when he found out what Aaron tried to do."

Allie rolls her eyes, but her face brightens with a tight-lipped smile. She jumps on the bed, patting the space beside her, and widens. "Do tell!" She listens while I gush about my relationship with Dante so far, her cheeks pink, eyes wide. "Okay. Let's say I won't give you a hard time for choosing the biggest criminal in like the *whole* of Chicago, apart from your dad, as your new boyfriend. I won't mention all the reasons he has to kill you, either. What's in it for me?"

"My eternal gratitude and the canvas that is my face at your disposal whenever you feel like practicing."

She clicks her tongue, unappeased. "Nice, but I was actually thinking about something like free entry to Delta. I can't get past security even if Adam's not around."

Dante won't change his mind about that, but there's no harm in asking. Especially if it means getting Allie off my back. "I'll see what I can do. Now, can you please tell me what I should wear? Nothing too out there. And it has to cover my bruised wrists and my scraped knee. Oh, and can you do something about this?" I point to my neck, where Aaron's fingers marked my skin with ghastly, green bruises.

Allie narrows her eyes. "You got a snowsuit?"

I hurl a pillow at her when she hops off the bed and starts rummaging through my closet. Twenty minutes of back and forth later, we settle on a fitted green dress and cover the scraped knee with concealer.

She gives me a pair of black heeled boots, then points at the chair in front of the mirror. "I'd love to cut it all off," she mutters, toying with my locks. "Short, asymmetrical bobs are like *the* thing now."

"I like my hair. I've been growing it out for four years."

Half an hour later, a stylish bun appears at the back of my head, held in place by a single, long pin. After a long, unnecessary discussion, my make-up is kept to a minimum— concealer and mascara. I don't like flashy make-up. Jess is the queen of the porn-star look. I'd rather not resemble her in any way.

"Hey, does Frankie know you're off with Dante?"

"Not yet." He left before I woke up and hasn't returned since, as if he's purposely avoiding me. "I've been waiting for him all day."

"He's downstairs. He was here when I came in."

My palms sweat as I leave my bedroom, almost flying down the stairs. Frank sits at the antique desk in his office, surrounded by thick clouds of cigar smoke. He's wearing a charcoal suit today, looking unapproachable. Women eye him up at every party hosted at our house, but Frank doesn't care about them. He doesn't even care about Jess.

Black curtains behind his back hide a large window, the only source of light in the room coming from a small desk lamp. Tall bookcases cover the left wall; old books, folders, and pictures of Frank with influential people fill the shelves.

I stop by the large, mahogany desk, hands behind my back so he can't see I'm picking my nails. "Dante's taking me out tonight. You can send Burly with me, but I am going."

"I know." He puffs out smoke through his nose like an enraged bull, eyeing me from head to toe to check if I look presentable. "He told me about it last night." He glances over my shoulder, his jaw working.

I don't need to check who lingers outside the door, listening to our every word. There's only one person around, courageous enough to openly spy on us. In character I get, dropping a few questions I want answering, for now.

"I won't lock you up," Frank continues. "If you want to keep seeing Carrow, then do so, but keep your mouth shut, Layla. My business is just that. It's *mine*."

"I thought you'd be mad..." I say, aiming for disbelief. I think I nailed it. My acting skills are nonexistent so thank God Jess is the only one who has to witness the show.

"Do I look happy? What more can I do? You're young, naïve, and you think you're in love. And Dante's... as you mentioned... *persistent*. He made it clear last night that he won't back down."

In love? He got ahead of himself there but convincing him otherwise is impossible. Frank always knows best.

"He's very possessive of you," he says, his expression puzzled like he can't understand why anyone would want me. "I don't trust him, Layla. You shouldn't either. Now, listen, and listen well because I'll only say this once." He swallows hard, his eyes softening while his tone remains clipped. "If you leave with him tonight, you're on your own. I mean it, Layla. If things go south, don't count on me. I won't help you. Is that clear?"

One sentence plants a seed of doubt in my head. Does he mean it? Is this a warning? A test? No, he can't mean it... surely, it's all just for show.

I trust Dante, or at least I want to trust him but knowing no one will come to my rescue makes following my instinct that much harder. Then again, it wasn't Frank helping me last night.

"I'll remember that." I bow low, mocking Adam.

Jess hooks her arm with mine when I step outside the office. "Don't worry. He's all talk, Layla. Besides..." she lowers her voice, "Dante's so hot even I'd have a hard time resisting the man."

I cringe at the mere thought of Jess and Dante together. I wriggle out of her embrace, walking back to the kitchen where Allie waits, holding my phone out for me.

"You've got a text from Prince Charming."

"And you read it."

Dante: Rookie will pick you up at eight, Star. He'll take you to my place, and I'll meet you there soon. Make yourself at home.

Growing up with a mafia boss for a father, I learned that evening meetings are the norm in their line of work. They don't do business lunches like the working class. Allie heads home when Rookie enters the driveway at eight o'clock sharp.

"Dante went to get even with Cannon and Loki. Spades

was hunting them all day but only found them half an hour ago," he explains when I take the passenger seat.

Frank keeps his business private, so I expected nothing less from Dante. Honesty is refreshing.

"Is Spades his right-hand man?"

Rookie starts the engine, casually resting his elbow on the armrest and leaning toward the car's center. "Spades and Nate." He smiles a boyish smile, the ivory skin contrasting sharply with almost black eyes and long eyelashes. "As you probably noticed by now, I'm his favorite driver. You met Luca last night, and there's also Cai and Jackson. We're the main entourage. You'll meet everyone tonight. We gather in Delta with our girls on Saturdays for a few drinks."

My outfit leaves a lot to be desired if I'm to meet their girls. My mother and Allie are excellent examples of what a mafia woman should look like—flawless hair, make-up, and revealing dresses. My long sleeve knitted dress is best suited for a nerdy schoolgirl. I should've let Allie try out the flashier make-up options.

"How did you convince your father to let you go without Burly?" Rookie asks, toying with his lip piercing.

We speed through the city more than a hundred miles an hour and whizz past a cop car, but they don't follow. Dante must own the cops down South just like Frank owns those up North.

"It didn't take much. I've been erased from the list of things Frankie cares about. If you lock me up, Daddy won't come to my rescue."

Rookie smirks, shaking his head as if dealing with a misbehaving child. "I wonder when you'll realize that Dante wouldn't have freaked out last night if he wanted to use you."

"I see news travels fast."

"You'd be surprised... you clean up well, though. Luca says they roughed you up pretty badly."

Those weren't the words he used yesterday while on the phone with Dante. He played it down as if he didn't want his boss to see me.

"Why, thank you. I guess Dante's reaction last night was out of the ordinary?"

"Hold on to something," he orders.

I grab the seat when the lights change at the junction ahead. Instead of braking, Rookie slams the gas, turning the wheel left to send the car flying sideways.

My heart pumps blood faster when a healthy adrenaline rush shoots through my nervous system. I'm buzzing, eyes wide, lips parted. Rookie looks unaffected, as if we hadn't just drifted through a busy junction in the heart of Chicago.

"Again!" I cry out, digging my fingers into the seat.

Rookie chuckles, fulfilling my wish at the next traffic light. "You make for a fun passenger, but don't mention it to Dante. He'd have my balls if he knew I'm endangering you."

"Don't worry. I'm not the type to kiss and tell."

Ten minutes later, he parks the car outside of Dante's two-storey, modern, all-glass house. "Going back to your questions, Dante acted very unlike himself last night and still acts odd today. Cai, Jackson, and Luca take care of the dirty work."

"He doesn't like getting his hands dirty?"

"Definitely not." Rookie taps a code on the control panel outside the main door, disarming the alarm. "I'll see you at ten." He turns around, leaving me alone in the empty house.

I switch the lights on, crossing the short entryway that opens onto the spacious living room. Dante's leather jacket hangs over the back of the couch, representing the only misplaced thing in the otherwise tidy space. His cologne mixes with cigarette smoke in the air, making me feel at home as I take a moment to search through the CDs before deciding on Kaleo. "No Good" plays from the speakers as I dance toward the bar to make myself a drink.

CHAPTER TWELVE

Dante

"I've got him," Spades says when the hands-free system activates. "He's in Amber. Can I fuck him up? Pretty please."

He's been chasing junkies all day long, searching for Cannon and his friend, whatever his fucking stupid nickname is. A few years back, Cannon owned the best brothel in the city. He was engaged to a supermodel and surrounded himself with rich, famous friends. Back then, we did business daily.

Until he slipped.

He fell for the *it's-just-this-once* nonsense. It's never just this once. Once you cave, you're doomed.

Cannon started with LSD but soon became addicted to everything he could get his hands on. His girl left, friends turned their backs on him, the brothel went bust, and Cannon fell through the cracks.

I glance at the clock, gripping the steering wheel harder. I promised Layla I'd pick her up at eight, twenty minutes from now, but getting my hands on Cannon takes priority this time.

"Don't touch him. He's mine." I make a sharp U-turn. Incoming drivers flash their lights, veering to the side, barely avoiding a collision.

"I'm coming to watch. I'll be there in fifteen." Spades cuts the call before I get a word in.

I step on the gas, dialing Rookie's number. "Spades found Cannon." I maneuver around the slow traffic. "Pick Layla up at eight and take her to my house."

"Sure, I'll leave now."

I stopped throwing my fists around four years ago once it got too tiring. I never enjoyed sporting bruised knuckles, so I appointed three guys to do the deeds: Cai, Luca, and Jackson. They're my main boxers, but I won't sit back while they beat the ever-living shit out of the fuckers who touched my girl.

I turn left, burning down the street where Amber is, the go-to place of all the junkies and degenerates—one of the leading outlets for my product down south.

Grinning like a Cheshire cat, Spades smokes, leaning against his car. "I haven't seen you land a punch in forever."

"Take a good look tonight. It might be a while before you see me land another one."

Cracking my knuckles, I get ready to unleash the fury, following Spades as he pushes the double doors with both hands, slamming them against the walls with a bang. The place reeks of stale beer, puke, and sweat. I'd never willingly walk in here if not for the prize lurking somewhere in the corner.

A cloud of smoke that looks almost blue—a mixture of crack, pot, and cigarettes—hangs in the air, illuminated by the bright fluorescent light. It has to be bright so the clientele can see their veins clearly. The bartender resembles a butcher from a low-budget horror movie. He lifts his head, but his eyes look in different directions. I'm unsure if he sees us until a scowl twists his tired, sweaty face. My presence doesn't bode well for anyone. He rakes his hand through the long, greasy hair, returning his attention to the task at hand—polishing a beer glass with a filthy cloth.

Most guests sit at small tables, daydreaming or dozing off, oblivious to their surroundings. A few guys talk quietly while someone else is tripping on the dirty used-to-be-white floor. He might be dying, but no one gives a flying fuck.

A skin-on-bones woman with protruding cheekbones and cracked lips sits nearby in a dirty wifebeater, tightening a fast-release tourniquet belt around her arm, a syringe between crooked teeth.

I step around the bar with Spades close behind and step over the guy thrashing on the floor, frothing at the mouth like a dog with rabies. Cannon sits at a large concrete table with four friends. They look alike—thin, sunken eyes and cheap, meaningless tattoos. Instead of salivating or daftly staring into the distance like everyone else, they're ranting in raised voices.

"You want help, or will you be an egotistical bastard and fuck them up all by yourself?" Spades asks, still excited.

"Do you know which one was with Cannon last night?"

"Loki." He points to a guy in a tattered black t-shirt.

"Make sure he stays where he is." I walk over to the table, taking a seat beside Cannon. "Good evening."

I've always been a little theatrical. I make a show, basking in my superiority, in the fear glimmering in the eyes of those who crossed me; their pleas like music to my ears when they beg for mercy.

Mercy that's never granted.

Cannon jitters in his seat, pupils dilated, unfocused eyes jumping all over my face. Looks like he's already had a few snorts of speed this evening. The evidence is there: a rolled-up one-dollar note and a few white lines on the table. "Dante, shit, Boss, what are you doing here?"

His companions follow his lead and sit up, trying to appear intimidating... it doesn't fucking work.

"I've been told you tried to score with Frankie's daughter last night." My tone borders on casual, shoulders relaxed, giving the fucker a false sense of security before I release a bomb and watch him shit his pants.

Cannon sneers, showing off a row of crooked, yellow teeth, two missing at the top, two more turning black. "I knew you wouldn't be pissed off! I told Luca that he should stay the fuck out of it, but he wouldn't listen. You should have a word with him, boss. He ruined our night! Frankie would've had a hard time recognizing the bitch if Luca let us finish. I guarantee it." He moves closer, the stench of his breath, like something old and rotten, fanning my face. "I'll finish it off for you. Just say the word. I know where Frankie lives." He looks at his friends, bouncing in the seat. "We'll grab her and have some fun, right?"

Everyone nods, eager to please me because they know

I'm the one who supplies their dealers with the product. One word from me, and no one will sell them shit.

"Yeah, just say the word, Boss," Loki says. "I'll fucking gut her like a fish for you."

"You're right," I say, my tone calm as I eye Cannon. "I'm not pissed off. That'd be an understatement."

Two creases dent his forehead, speckled with an angry, dry rash. "What do you mean? She's Frank's daughter, Dante! I was doing you a fucking favor, you ungrateful—"

"A favor? You touched my girl, bruised her, cut her, *scared* her, and you call that a fucking favor?!"

He retreats, his ashen skin turning paler, almost green. The realization of what will happen next petrifies him to the core. Rightly so. He jerks back, scooting away with the chair, but doesn't get further away than a few inches. "Don't do anything stupid! It was a misunderstanding, c'mon, I didn't know! She's all good, right? No harm done!"

Satisfied with his begging, I grip his neck, knocking his head against the concrete table in one swift motion.

Teeth fall out.

Blood splatters halfway across the table.

His jaw pops out of place.

Fuck, that must hurt. He screams, writhing and thrashing like a loose garden hose, but I hold him in place, pinned to the tabletop, so he won't splatter my clothes with, most likely HIV-infected blood. Two others jump to their feet, starting toward me, hands balled into fists smaller than Layla's. Cannon slides to the floor, covering his face when I let him go.

A foldable chair by the wall looks out of place, so I find it a new home, folding it across the face of the first guy approaching. His friend stops mid-step. Good for him.

It doesn't pay to play the fucking hero.

"Dante, I didn't touch her!" Loki raises his hands. "I didn't do anything! He wanted to fuck her, but I didn't touch her!"

Cannon lays on the floor, frantically trying to stop the nosebleed. His demented, howling whimpers worthy of a mental patient give me a headache, so I grip his neck and hit his head against the table again. He falls silent.

All the while, Loki is begging. I fucking love it when they cry, beg, and swear they won't *ever* do anything to cross me again. I step forward, but he jumps on the chair and then onto the table like a circus monkey.

He thinks he'll get away?

Good luck.

I don't have time for this shitshow. I'm fucking late for my first date with Layla.

I grip Loki's ankle, jerking him to the side. He dives, hitting the dirty floor head first. For a second, I think I broke his neck, but no. Not so lucky.

He rolls onto his back, arms folded across his face. "Please, stop. I swear I didn't touch her!"

"You wanted to." I yank him up by the collar of his t-shirt and smash his arm on the table, breaking both bones at once. "If I find out you so much as uttered her name, I'll find you and kill you. Slowly. Painfully. Got it?"

"Never," he squeals, tears streaming down his cheeks. "I swear, Dante! Never!"

"Good. Pass the message to Cannon when he wakes up."

I turn around and march out of the building with Spades and his wide grin right by my side.

"That was fun." He hands me a small towel and a bottle of water so I can clean the blood off my hands. "Better?"

"No." I toss the towel back in the trunk, then light a cigarette. "Even if I killed them there, it wouldn't turn back time." I squeeze the bridge of my nose. "All day, I couldn't stop thinking about what would've happened if Luca wasn't there."

"But he was. Stop overthinking, Dante. Get back home. Layla's waiting for you." He pats me on the shoulder, his grin more prominent now. "I'll see you two at ten tonight. I want to meet the girl. She's doing you good."

That she is. So fucking good... my little pissy, feisty Star.

Twenty minutes later, I watch *my* girl from the living room doorway. She hadn't noticed me arrive, busy cleaning the mess she made behind the bar. Either a small bomb blew up, or Layla has two left hands. Ice cubes litter the counter among mint leaves, sugar, and spilled rum. She glances around with a deep frown. Failing to locate what she's looking for, she picks the shards of used-to-be-a-glass with bare hands.

"Leave it," I say, crossing the room. "You'll cut yourself."

"I'm sorry, I made myself at home a bit too much."

A green dress hugs her petite body, highlighting her slim waist and the soft roundness of her hips. I grip her underarms and sit her on the countertop, away from the mess she made. I take a step closer, standing between her legs, dizzy when I have her this close.

Fear no longer taints her steel-gray eyes. She's calm, and that's how she should be all the fucking time.

"I missed you," she whispers, tracing the contour of my jaw with delicate fingers.

I breathe out, relaxing under her touch, and move my hands to her thighs, caressing her soft, smooth skin. We have an equally overwhelming effect on each other. The electricity jumping between us, the longing, the pure lust is more than I ever expected to feel. I grip her jaw, closing her parted lips with mine, pouring my emotions into one forceful, greedy kiss. I dip my head to graze my lips along her neck and kiss away the goosebumps dotting her skin.

No other woman ever reacted to my touch the way Layla does. Like I'm all she craves, all she needs. Theory confirmed when she tilts her head, giving me better access to her neck. The sweet scent of her perfume envelopes my confused mind, soothing the anger that's usually bubbling non-stop.

"Good girl." I slide her dress off one shoulder, kissing along her collarbone. I've imagined this moment every day for two fucking weeks. "*My* girl." I move my hands higher, climbing her thighs until my fingers disappear under the hem of the green dress.

Layla tenses, spine straight like a guitar string, but she doesn't move away like I expect. She clings to me harder, clawing at my shoulders to hold me closer. This is not the first time she's craved my touch, but it is the first time that I don't mind.

My fingers sink firmly into her thighs and keep climbing, exploring every inch she'll let me explore. I'm in for the wait of a lifetime before she'll want sex, but I'm curious how much she'll let me do.

Not much.

She turns rigid again when I touch the lace of her panties, my mind in turmoil once my fingers find a wet patch. She's soaked... aroused... so warm. Her eyes fly when I stroke her pussy through the lace fabric, barely putting any pressure. An ugly grimace distorts her calm, gorgeous face before two small hands shove me away with more strength than I'd expect in her frail body.

I take an involuntary step back. Fear clouds her face rendering me temporarily insane. My throat constricts as if someone's tying a rope around my neck, pulling harder and harder. Anger spreads like a malignancy when one thought hits me with the force of an avalanche...

I should've fucking *killed* Romeo.

By the look of her, reality blurs inside her head with the memories from last night. Her cheeks burn scarlet when she jumps off the bar, pressing the back of her trembling hand against her forehead. My hands shake, too, when I turn to pour myself a large, neat drink.

Layla walks away, curling into an almost fetal position on the couch, eyes focused on mint leaves drowning in her drink. She tries fishing them out with a straw as if her life depends on it.

I gulp half of my whiskey before I sit beside her, watching her face, so I won't miss her reaction. "Baby... are you scared because you think I'll hurt you or because you think I want to sleep with you tonight?"

"You don't want to?"

"Of course, I do." More than she'll ever know. I'm holding myself back on the shortest leash, trying my best not to rush her, but I am a red-blooded man craving what's mine. The image of her naked body writhing beneath me on my California King bed upstairs plagues me in my dreams. "I want to know if Romeo last night scared you so much that all you think about when I touch you is that I'll hurt you."

Her cheeks burn bright red, the color almost matching the Shelby in the corner, but she shakes her head. "He didn't scare me that much. I know you won't force me to do anything I don't want."

"That's right." I curl my fingers under her chin. "I will be your first, Layla. I'll show you exactly how good sex can be. I'll teach you every trick. You'll learn how to meet my needs and demand I meet yours, but it won't be today, tomorrow, or any time soon." Giving up on her body until further notice is the last thing I want, but I can't claim her virginity tonight. She has to trust me first.

"I don't understand. You want to sleep with me, but you won't? Why?"

I smirk, tugging her hand until she takes the hint and straddles me. "You're the one who needs to *want*, baby. to want, you need to trust me."

"I trust you."

"No. No, you don't. Not yet. You want to trust me. You want to believe not everyone is trying to use you. I've got time, Star, but don't push me away again. We won't have sex until I know you're ready, but I will be touching you. *Everywhere.* And I'll be very possessive when I do so."

Her red cheeks fade to light pink. "I'll let you know when I'm ready."

"No need. I can read you. You tensed when I touched your hips. I wanted to know how much you'll let me do before you say *no*. I just didn't expect that you'll panic."

"I'm sorry. I wasn't thinking straight—"

"Don't apologize for listening to your instincts." I rest my hands on her hips. "And, get used to this because my hands will be here a lot. Just as much as here," I squeeze her butt, "Also here." I cup her face, closing her lips with mine. "And now..." I pat her butt. "I should grab a shower, Star. We need to be at the club in an hour."

She moves away, and the pure joy dancing in her gray irises reminds me of her younger self. Back then, she looked at me just like this. As if I were her favorite person.

"Try not to demolish the house."

"I'll try." She sips from her glass, then spits a mouthful back with a wince. "This is awful. Wine might be a better idea."

Climbing the stairs, I yank my shirt off and stop when I hear Layla chasing after me. She catches up to me, one hand around my arm while the fingertips of the other brush the contours of my tattoos.

A few years ago, I spent countless hours at the studio. My back and arms are covered with Gustavo Dore's illustrations for *The Divine Comedy.* My mother is a huge fan. She even gave me the author's name. I read the book when I was old enough to understand it. When the time came for ink, there wasn't anything else I could've chosen.

Layla draws a line down my spine, her touch featherlight but sensual enough to rekindle my desire. I spin around, grip her wrists, and pin her body against the wall, closing her mouth with mine. Her eyes sparkle when I pull back, careful not to get carried away. We'll spend a lot of time making out if it's making her *this* happy.

"Are you done?"

"No," she says with a pout

"You might want to finish this another time."

I leave her with a frown marking her forehead, and three minutes later, I lock myself in the bathroom upstairs, jumping under an ice-cold shower. I will probably need many more before I find release in Layla's sweet pussy.

Fifteen minutes later, I load my Beretta 92 in the holster, draping a white shirt over my back, and get back downstairs, too fucking eager. Layla stands in front of a long mirror hanging out in the entryway, fixing her hair when I return downstairs.

"It won't get better," she mutters, smoothing out non-existent creases on her dress.

"It can't get any better."

She spins around, rolling her eyes. "If you had told me

we were meeting your people's girlfriends, I would've put on something nicer. A heads-up next time, please."

"You look stunning, Star."

"You'll change your mind when I'm standing with the supermodels your men probably date."

She's not whining or fishing for compliments. She's genuinely irritated that she won't blend in. She's right there. Too much fabric covers her body, and not enough jewelry adorns her neck for her to blend in with the other girls.

"If I wanted to date an overdressed Barbie from the cover of Vogue, I wouldn't be dating you. This," I run my finger down her arm, touching the green dress she wears, "Is exactly how you should look for me—modest but sexy. I didn't like you yesterday in that slutty dress."

"I didn't like myself either." She smooths the creases out of my shirt. "Allie chose that dress. Her taste is problematic."

Allie, welcome to the black book of people I don't fucking like.

Layla would've been safe at home last night if not for her. On the other hand, she wouldn't have a reason to call me, and we wouldn't be standing in my living room now. I'd choose not to have her over what she's been through any day.

"While I remember. Allie was wondering if she could come to Delta sometime. Security doesn't let her in."

"You should've asked before you said who chose your dress last night. I'm sorry, Star, but she won't get in. No one from Frank's entourage ever will." I glance at her parted lips and kiss her because... well, because I fucking can. "There's one more thing that doesn't suit you." I pull a long pin out of her hair, letting the locks fall down her back, surrounding her round, doll-like face. That's what she looked like when I first saw her, and that's how she's always supposed to be for me—sexy, sassy, innocent, *mine.*

CHAPTER THIRTEEN

Layla

The bouncers bow low, greeting their boss when we enter Delta. Smoke clouds hang above the thick crowd, filling the space with a fragrant aroma of oranges laced with just a hint of mango.

Almost naked waitresses with trays full of colorful drinks walk among the crowd, wearing nothing but snow-white bras and skirts so short their thongs are showing. Under ultraviolet lights, they shine bright like fireflies. Apart from alcohol, they sell small plastic bags filled with white powder or small pills. I hadn't noticed it last time.

Enormous mirrors cover the walls, reflecting the strobe lights that fly around the room in uncoordinated directions. A machine above the DJ station releases soap bubbles, and girls giggle, jumping around, trying to pop them. The floor shakes beneath my feet as Dante leads me through the POP music room, my hand in his.

Despite the early hour, the place is packed beyond capacity, thanks to a famous DJ who's starting his set at midnight. The crowd parts before us like the Red Sea before Moses. The crushing confidence surrounding Dante makes heads turn our way as people scramble to take another look at him. He's any woman's dream come true. Under the layer of ruthless arrogance hides an affectionate, passionate man.

My man.

What is it that he sees in me? A corny, inexperienced, pathetic nineteen-year-old craving constant attention. I'm not ugly, but I can point out a dozen prettier girls. He wouldn't have to abstain from sex if he chose any one of them. It can't be easy, and I can't think of one rational reason why he's so willingly enduring the torture, but I'm thankful. His kisses are addictive enough. I won't be able to keep him from invading my heart if he claims me whole, and loving him is out of the question.

I squeeze his hand, having a hard time believing he's not only real but mine too. Frankie was right six months ago when he said he knows what type of woman Dante's looking for. One like me...

Dante stops, inching closer so he won't have to shout over Britney blasting from the speakers. "Everything good?"

"Yes, all good." I rise on my toes, curious whether such a blatant manifestation of feelings will bother him while everyone who can see us watches us with wide eyes.

He doesn't skip a beat when I close his lips with mine, smiling and satisfied that he won't hide me like a dirty secret. We take the metal staircase and stop by the bar upstairs. Dante stands behind me, hands gripping the countertop, arms boxing me in, his protectiveness in the highest gear.

No one complains when the bartender walks past ten guys, reaching for a tall glass as he turns to face us. "Mojito?" he asks, even though he's not the same bartender that was here two weeks ago.

"And the usual for everyone," Dante says.

"I'll send a waitress over in five."

I'm overcome with stage fright once we move toward the largest booth in the club. Two half-moon white leather sofas that easily fit twenty people face each other, and a round metal table stands in the middle. A tall sheet of glass separates the booth, either protecting whoever is there or dulling down the music.

I tug my hand free from Dante's grip, and brush my hair out of my face for the hundredth time when I spot two blonde Goddesses worthy of a Miss America title. Then, auburn locks catch my eye, the owner a stunning girl who laughs with her arms wrapped around Luca's neck.

"They should envy your sense of style." Dante halts me mid-step. "Miniskirts and boobs showing are trademarks of undervalued teens. You look like a real woman."

"I'd say I look like a well-behaved schoolgirl."

The corners of his mouth twitch, eyes roving down my body. "Every man's fantasy."

"Girls at school hated me because of Frank. It'd be nice if

these beauties at least refrain from talking behind my back."

"You won't escape that. They'll talk because you're here with me." He tucks a loose strand of hair behind my ear. "You're the first girl I've brought here, Star."

Way to make me even more nervous.

"Clockwise," he says, starting with Rookie. "You know this one, his girl Jane, Spades, Nate and Bianca, Cai and Luna, Sandra and Luca. The smartass at the end is Jackson."

Compared to the four girls, I look like I fled a seminary for nuns. They're wearing flashy, revealing dresses, their necks adorned with more jewelry than any jewelry store I've ever been to. Despite the visual difference between us, I feel welcome. Furthermore, Sandra, the owner of auburn hair and a pretty, freckled face, smiles at me over the table as if we're best friends.

"I think I know you from somewhere," I say, looking at Jane. "Don't we have sociology lectures together?"

"Yes! Where's your bodyguard? God! Newson was fuming when she brought him to class!" she tells Rookie, squeezing his arm.

"Burly's off the hook now. Frankie no longer cares about my safety."

Dante leans closer, whispering in my ear. "That's *my* job now." He pecks my temple.

A waitress brings a tray with drinks a moment later, handing out twelve glasses to their respective owners. The mojito tastes much better than the ones I made at Dante's house.

I listen to the conversations for half an hour, joining in whenever I can so they won't think I'm rude. I am, but I'm making an effort not to be tonight. The girls seem friendly, but I'm immediately drawn to Bianca. She reminds me of Allie with one difference: a sense of humor. Allie has none, while Bianca's a full-on joker. She's goofing around, making everyone chuckle when she swears like a sailor, lighting one cigarette after another.

The waitress brings over fresh drinks five minutes later, and the men rise from their seats.

"A few things that need taking care of," Dante says, kissing me softly. "Back in half an hour."

"It's like this every week," Bianca explains, noticing my confusion. "They have a drink with us, then go away. They're usually back within the hour. You'll get used to it."

That depends on how long I'll be by Dante's side.

Sandra leans over the table, all smiles, and wide eyes. "Go on! Walk us through it! How did you two get together? Luca says you came here two weeks ago."

"It's the only place in Chicago where my father's people aren't welcome. I needed a breather without his men watching my every move."

Jane beams, joining in. "How did you get Dante himself to fall at your feet? He's not easily impressed. I've been dating Rookie for a year, but I haven't seen Dante leave the club with a woman. Not even once. What did you do to him?!"

"Um... nothing. I asked him to leave me alone when he offered to buy me a drink."

Sandra exchanges a knowing look with Bianca and Jane. "So, you played hard to get?"

"No. I simply didn't want him around. It shouldn't surprise you with all the hatred between Dante and my father."

"So, how come you're here?" Luna asks, arms crossed.

I'm growing annoyed with the nosy inquisition. I can't explain how my status changed from mafia boss's daughter to mafia boss's girlfriend because I still don't know how that happened. "Dante's doesn't exactly quit without a fight," I say, looking at Bianca bouncing in her seat. "Should we go?" I point to the dancing crowd.

"We can't go there," Luna says, turning her head the other way, lips pursed. "Our men don't dance, Layla, so, *obviously,* we're not allowed to dance with other men."

"Who said anything about other men? We can have fun together." I stand, pulling my dress down, but neither of the girls follow my lead. "Don't tell me you're scared of them. What will they do?"

"Layla, you can't go down there." Sandra pleads. "Didn't Dante tell you?"

"Tell me what? that I can't dance?" I scoff, finishing off my drink. "No, he failed to mention that. C'mon, get up. You can tell them it was my idea."

Jane saves me from an embarrassing situation, rising onto her stiletto heels. Once she's up, the other three stand too. We find enough space so we can all dance in a small circle. Disclosure and a remix of "You and Me" blasts from the speakers. My new friends enjoy the music, losing themselves in the beat. Seeing their kind smiles, I stop worrying about whether I fit in. I'm the first one forced to push away a guy who wants to dance with me. Luna does the same when a tall, dark-haired man reaches for her hand, swaying as if he's had a few too many. I don't want to get them in trouble, but if no one's hitting on us, Dante and his men shouldn't have a reason to keep us upstairs.

Or so I hope.

"I can't remember the last time I danced!" Bianca shouts over the music. "I'm so glad you're here!"

Songs blur together. I count eleven tunes before I realize men have been steering clear of our little gathering for a while. I glance around, smiling at two bodyguards who stand fifteen feet away by two tall pillars that support the balcony. They shove aside anyone who comes near our tight circle. I look up, knowing the security didn't devise this brilliant idea alone. Six pairs of eyes watch us from the balcony. Only Dante's missing. Rookie holds a glass of whiskey, pointing behind me. A second later, a warm arm snakes around my middle, and I'm turned around, meeting Dante's lips.

His hands slide down my body as he deepens the kiss, his tongue skimming mine slowly. "How about a break? You're barely catching a breath."

"Okay, a break sounds good. But only a short one." I gesture for the girls to follow us upstairs, where fresh drinks wait on the table.

Rookie shakes his hand, readjusting his wristwatch, eyes on me. I'm not sure if he's annoyed or amused. "I guess it was your idea to take them dancing?"

"It wasn't easy to convince them."

"There's a rule Dante apparently hadn't mentioned," Luca growls. "You stay here because we have enough shit to deal with without worrying about you." He rolls up his sleeves, exposing the colorful tattoos snaking up his arms. "You attract trouble like a magnet, so do us all a favor and stop rebelling."

Dante tenses beside me, leaning forward, ready to interject. I squeeze his thigh under the table, silently asking him to zip it. If I want respect, I have to earn it.

"Change your attitude, Luca," I say, unaffected by his reluctance. "You don't know me well enough or long enough for your tone to sit well with me."

Frank's pawns treat me just like Luca doe; like a silly little girl they can walk all over. I've dealt with men like Luca more than I should. Compared to the son of New York's mafia boss, Luca's child's play. He may look impenetrable to an untrained eye, but I've dealt with his kind all my life, and Luca sure lacks confidence. He cocks an eyebrow at me, making another mistake. I don't think he knows how to handle my attitude. The other girls probably never talk back, so he must've thought I'll recant and shut up. Wrong address.

He casts a loaded look at Dante, his jaw flexing as he grinds his teeth.

"Don't look at him," I snap, setting my glass aside. "He won't help you. You started with me, so you'll deal with me."

Dante chuckles while everyone around the table remains silent, watching us as if watching tennis, heads turning from me to Luca and back.

"You don't use your brain for work, so worrying about your girl shouldn't be so exhausting. Don't even start talking about safety. We're not up North where everyone wants you dead. You think anyone will dare touch Sandra knowing she's with you?"

"Not many people know she's with me. We don't print it in the local newspaper," he says in an arrogant tone. "They always stay here. They *never* object, so be a doll and don't get in the fucking middle."

Not many people know... how can they be so careless?

"Who does Adam date?" I ask.

"Allie Carter."

"And?" I urge, but he doesn't grasp what I'm telling him. "Did you read about it in a newspaper?" I look at Dante. "Didn't it occur to you it might be good if all the scumbags know who they should steer clear of?" Up North, all the junkies know which girls are off-limits.

"Luca's right, Star," Dante says, glancing at the girls. "You never said you wanted to dance, and we don't read minds. If you want to have fun, I don't see a problem. I'll make sure we have two more bodyguards on Saturdays, so they keep an eye on you." He glances around his men. "All good?"

No one disagrees but Luca's sulking. "Is this what it'll be like now? You'll agree with everything Layla says?"

"If she's right, then yes."

They stare each other down like two lions, ready to tear the other's aorta, but Luca's in the losing position. He looks away, aware that forcing his opinion on Dante won't end well.

"Do you have a sister, Layla?" Jackson asks, relaxing the atmosphere. "I could do with a feisty girl like you."

"Sorry, Daddy only made one of me."

CHAPTER FOURTEEN

Dante

Luca makes a show of ignoring Layla's existence. She poked at his ego with a very sharp stick. Not only did she snap back, but he couldn't fucking deal with her temper.

Welcome to the club.

Every time she shifts into battle mode, hissing like an enraged pussycat, I want her naked body writhing beneath me, begging for release. Her biting tongue works like a magnet. I regretted being a decent guy with each sentence she spoke to Luca. If she'd let me, I'd lock her in the bedroom for hours.

Spades tells me about the all-new Charger while my thumb grazes Layla's thigh. I've never touched any woman like this before her. Never touched a girl just because. Never sought physical connection unless my cock was involved. Things are much different with Layla... she craves closeness, and I love rising to her expectations. Love the smooth texture of her skin under my fingertips. Her warmth and scent.

She bounces softly under my touch to the music like the other girls. Spades stops mid-sentence, pointing his chin at Layla, one eyebrow half raised, half drawn into a confused question mark.

Turns out she's patiently waiting until we're done talking. I wouldn't mind if she'd cut in, but I'm glad she didn't.

I pull her closer to me and kiss her temple, keeping my lips there as I speak. "Good girl. What do you need, Star?"

She covers my palm with hers, lacing our fingers. "We're all heading downstairs. Can you get me lemonade and another mojito?"

"I can. Can you come back before you dehydrate, or will I have to come and get you?"

She pecks my lips, sighing ever so softly. "You'll have to come and get me, baby."

Baby. I've never had a pet name before. I'm not sure if I like it, but I don't comment, busy keeping desire at bay before I need another cold shower. That sure is a test for my fucking patience when she sighs like that.

The girls leap out of their seats when Layla rises to her stilettoes. They look ready to jump off the balcony just to get downstairs faster. I stand, holding my finger up to signal security. They know their job even without me pointing at Layla. Last night, everyone who works for me was informed who my star is and that there'll be hell to pay if a single hair falls off her head.

With a drink in hand, I stop by the railing to watch Layla dance. There's something innocent yet incredibly arousing about her delicate movements. For thirty seconds, she sways in sync with Bianca and Luna before she wanders away toward the DJ's station. One of the bouncers follows suit, aware of what will happen if they leave her unattended for even half a minute. A moment later, I'm rushing downstairs too, when a tall guy blocks her path, pulling her into his arms. Possessiveness kicks riot in my head, pushing me to break his hands.

"Daddy knows, but I'm a big girl now. I won't be bossed around," Layla tells the guy. "I'm here—"

"You're here with me, Star." I yank her to my chest, wrapping a protective arm around her waist like a python. "Introduce us," I add, glaring at the guy.

Layla tilts her head with a smile, lacing her petite fingers with mine. "This is Michael, my ex-boyfriend."

Right about now, I'm ready to laugh at my own blindness. Skinny jeans, concealer on his face, and theatrical gesturing. Everything about him screams *I like men but* consumed with voracious jealousy, I didn't notice.

This girl, the pretty little bug in my arms... she makes me fucking crazy. "Invite your friend upstairs for a drink."

Michael shakes his head a bit too eagerly. "No, no, no, I wouldn't want to intrude. I'm looking for my boyfriend. He's here somewhere. It was good to see you, Lay." He inches forward to hug her, but one glance at me changes his mind. He leaves, disappearing into the crowd.

I spin Layla around, and at the same time, a guy imitating Michael Jackson's moonwalk a step away from us bounces off my shoulder. I shove him away, still focused on Layla, but from the corner of my eye, I see how his face hugs the floor.

"*Lay*?" I ask.

"Hey! You got a problem, dude?" Fake King of Pop taps my shoulder. "I'm talking to you, dickhead!"

As an amateur boxer, he steers a half-assed punch. Unlucky for him, he almost hits Layla. His fist flies between us, landing on thin air, but it's enough to get me from calm to all-out raging.

I grab his shirt, towering above him. "Don't try that again. If you hit her, you'll be introducing yourself to God."

Either the alcohol makes him courageous, or he's just plain fucking dumb because he makes a fist. I hit his face before he decides his next move or reassesses the situation. The bouncer picks him up, knocks him down again with a powerful blast to his ribs, then hauls his ass out of the club.

"Lay, Laylee," Layla says, ignoring the last minute as if it never happened. "He always called me that."

"*Lay* sounds like something you clean the shower with. Don't let people call you that." I lead her back to the girls, but she walks around them, following me upstairs.

"Am I imagining things, or were you jealous?" She asks, failing to conceal the excitement.

"You'll get used to it." I press my lips against her temple. "Go sit down. I'll get your lemonade."

The bartender appears when my elbows touch the countertop. "Another round?"

"Yeah, send the waitress over but give me a glass of lemonade now."

Layla's in the booth, her shoulders back, chin raised, eyes shooting daggers at Luca when I approach. "You're mistaking me for someone who cares what you think," she says. "But just so you know, the guy Dante knocked out bumped into him by accident. It wasn't my fault." She snatches the lemonade out of my hand.

A slow glow of anger works its way up from under Luca's collar. "All just a big coincidence, isn't it? The thing is, everything turns to shit when you're around. What's wrong with you?"

"Never ending story." She rolls her eyes. "You want a list?"

"I won't sugar coat it for you just because you're dating the boss. I *don't* trust you."

"I ordered a mojito, not your opinion, Luca."

That one sentence sends my desire through the roof. I'm absolutely wild with the feral need to claim her body. Layla tucks her hair behind her ears, casually sipping through the twirly straw, and I can't focus on anything other than being inside her.

"You think you're so crafty?" Luca snaps. "You're all talk."

"Of course, I'm all talk!" Layla slams her hands on the table. "You thought I'd fight you?"

Everyone at the table looks between Layla and Luca as if they're watching Roger Federer play against Rafael Nadal. Everyone's expressions make it clear I'm not the only one in awe of her or annoyed with him.

"Dating the boss doesn't mean you can disrespect his people," he growls, determined to get ahead.

Layla squeezes my hand again as if sensing my patience wearing thin. "It doesn't mean you can disrespect me, either."

"Respect has to be earned."

"Exactly. Next time when you're on your period, let me know. I'll get you pain relief. Are you done for the night, or do you have something creative you'd like to add? I'd like to go back downstairs."

"You better don't fucking move, or someone else will get their face smashed."

"If you don't shut up, it'll be you," I snap.

Layla clipping his wings is amusing to watch, but enough is enough. Luca glares at me for a moment as if debating whether to keep talking, but he decides against it and lights a cigarette, sparking a conversation with Jackson.

I pull Layla closer, lowering my voice. "Go, Star. Join the girls, or I'll take you home."

She grips her waist, pinning me down with a forceful stare. "*Excuse* me, but I won't let him use me as his punching bag. I can go home, no problem, but don't count on me keeping quiet if you want me to stay."

"The way you hurt his ego is far more painful than my right hook. You're beyond sexy when you're aggressive. If I keep listening to you hiss, I'll take you home, and I won't give a fuck if you're ready or not, so go join the girls."

A cheeky, slightly shy smile curves her lips. She pecks my cheek, letting her lips linger on my skin a little longer before she walks away without another word. I watch her hips sway until a random guy blocks the view.

"What's your problem with her?" I ask Luca, readjusting my position to disguise the apparent bulge in my pants.

"It took five minutes, and someone got knocked out because of her. Saturdays are our time to unwind, Dante. Her stupid ideas don't fucking help."

"Since when do you care if someone gets fucked up?"

"I don't, but..." He exhales, folding his arms over his chest. "Snap out of it! Shit, just look at the whole thing the way I do.

You've saved her ass three times in two days. You got yourself a little damsel in distress, and we'll be doing all the work."

Rookie tears himself from his seat. "What the fuck did you do? Dante took care of everything himself. You didn't lift a finger, but you complain like you haven't stopped fucking people up for days. Lay off her."

Luca opens and closes his mouth, a fish out of the water, surprised that no one took his side. If he argues any more, he'll end up looking like Cannon or Loki.

I hold my hand up before he says another word. "Get the fuck out. Take Sandra and go home before I make you bleed."

"I didn't mean anything bad, Boss, but none of this feels right. She came out of fucking nowhere! She's Frankie's daughter!"

Why does everyone insist on reminding me who Layla's father is? I don't have Alzheimer's. I know damn well who her father, mother, grandmother, and great grandfather are, but that doesn't mean shit. Layla's here for me. She's here because the chemistry between us is undeniable. Because she cares about me as much as I care about her. Frankie has shit all to do with any of it.

"I know her family tree, Luca. It doesn't alarm me, so it shouldn't alarm you. Do yourself a favor and don't argue with her. She keeps shooting you down, and it's really fucking sad to watch when you can't handle shit."

He falls silent, sulking for the rest of the night, not one more word to Layla or me until the club closes. Good choice. He knew that one more sentence in her direction would cost him his teeth.

CHAPTER FIFTEEN

Layla

Since I started dating his enemy, Frank regards *me* as an enemy too. He ignores me when I speak, gracing me with furious glares. I don't care, but I am confused when he does this even when no one's looking.

"Don't make plans for next Saturday," he says when I walk into the kitchen on Wednesday morning.

Too little too late. Dante reserved me for all the days this week, next week, and every week.

"I've already got plans."

He scowls, highlighting the wrinkles around his eyes. "Cancel. You'll be here to entertain my guests."

"Another party? What's the occasion?"

I hate that I need his attention. It's not as if we talk about my plans or aspirations, but any conversation is worth its weight in gold. I still remember the times when Frank hugged me, and Jess told me she loved me every year on my birthdays.

Six years have passed since the last manifestation of their affection, not counting the trip to Aspen Frank and I took. Although it shouldn't count. Frank only played nice because he wanted my help. Everything changed when Dante took over the South. Among other things, the humanity that burned in Frank went out forever.

"The boss from New York is flying in. I still have to figure out how to explain why my daughter's dating my enemy."

"Don't tell him. They don't need to know."

"They know. His goddaughter lives in Chicago."

"Hold on." I look up, remembering who the boss of New York is. "Is Julij coming along with Nikolaj?"

Adam appears at the door with Burly at his side. "Should we wait in the office?"

"No, Layla's leaving." Frank points at two empty chairs urging his men to sit. A mocking smile tugs on his lips. "Yes, Julij's coming, and you'll be here, taking care of him. Don't object. That's the least you can do for me now that I'm allowing you to date Carrow."

"You're *allowing* me?" God, why do we always have company when I need to retaliate? I bite my tongue, finding a different way to hit. "Try and stop me."

I had the dubious pleasure of meeting Julij Aristow two years ago while we were in Dubai. He's an embodiment of everything that's wrong with the male population. He was twenty-two back then but acted like a teenager, like those stupid, rich football players in high school: loud, obscene, irritating, king-of-the-world type.

We argued for two weeks straight. He considered my aversion toward him as a sign of attraction. When he drank too much, he was pushy and vulgar. He never touched me, but I felt sick whenever he called me *sugar* with a thick Russian accent.

And now I have to spend another evening with him.

A rumble of large engine filters inside the house through the open windows when Dante pulls up onto the driveway. He took on the role of my personal chauffeur, driving me to and from college every day. To my surprise, Frank didn't argue against Dante showing up here house every morning.

The relationship between them is bizarre. Mutual respect overshadows the enormous hatred... mostly.

"You do know I've got my own car, right?" My bag lands on the back seat. "It'd be nice if I could use it sometime."

Dante grips the steering wheel harder, his knuckles white with the effort. "Good morning to you too. I don't know why you're pissy, but don't take it out on me." The engine springs to life, murmuring wildly as we pull out onto the main road.

He's a skilled driver, veering around other cars so fast it feels like they're at a standstill, but he's no match for Rookie.

"I'm sorry." I cover his hand with mine when we park outside my college.

Last week Dante sat me on the bonnet and kissed me while at least a hundred students watched him mark his territory and show off that I'm his—untouchable. When I joined Jane in the auditorium later that day, the whole student body knew all there was to know about my new boyfriend. Within a few hours, my status changed from nobody to the main topic on everyone's lips, including the professors. I've never enjoyed being in the center of attention, but I can't escape the nosy looks while I'm at college.

Today, more students wait outside, staring at the black Charger. Among hundreds of nameless faces, I spot Jane. She stands by the door in a summery brown dress, tapping her wrist to let me know I should get moving.

It's the middle of November, so the temperature outside oscillates around fifty degrees, but Jane doesn't care about the flu outbreak spreading among the students like wildfire. I'm bundled in a thick cardigan, warm boots on my feet, not daring to put my looks above comfort.

"Keep going," Dante says. "Why are you so pissy?"

"We'll talk later. Newson will have a fit if I'm late."

Dante cuts the engine, exiting the car, my bag in his hand. "We'll talk now. I want a word with your professor anyway."

"You know each other?"

"He does a bit of after-hours work for me."

Newson is a sociologist specializing in public opinion. I can only guess what he does for Dante.

I thought people were moving out of my way since Dante staked his claim, but I was wrong. They're literally running away at the sight of him. I had never taken an elevator inside this building before, but it's free to use today because everyone takes the stairs as soon as we approach the metal door. Even Jane chose to climb instead of riding with us.

"I can't see you next Saturday," I say when the door slides shut. "Frankie's throwing another party. He invited one of the bosses, and I'm supposed to babysit their son."

Dante rests his back against the wall with a soft smile. "You can't last one evening without me?"

We spend most of my free time together. He takes me to college every morning, picks me up after my last lecture, and takes me to his place. I don't get home until late, but Dante doesn't like driving me to Frank's. Spending one evening without him might prove a struggle.

"That's not the problem." I click my tongue. "I don't like the guy I'll be taking care of. He's a clown."

"You deal with Luca, so you'll have no problem dealing with whoever is coming."

"Luca's almost well behaved compared to Julij."

The small smile slips from his face. "Julij Aristow? Nikolaj's flying in?"

The elevator stops on the last floor. "I'll spend the evening faking smiles and dodging that idiot's obscene comments."

"Does Nikolaj know about us?"

"He's got a goddaughter in Chicago. News traveled faster than you predicted."

Dante thought it'd take a few weeks for the city to find out about us. One was enough. Gossip has an unbelievable kill radius. Like an atomic bomb, it went off outside the college building, and the shock wave traveled throughout Chicago, reaching as far as New York.

He pushes the door open, entering the auditorium as if it's his class. Jane waits at the top row, looking impatient and slightly disheveled. She must've ran to get here before Dante and me.

"Layla, how considerate of you to—" Newson pauses, his face pale when he spots Dante by my side.

"Bye," I whisper over my shoulder.

He pulls me back, grips my neck, and sinks into my lips, his tongue skimming the inseam of my mouth as if we're not watched by one hundred people. "I'll pick you up later, baby." He turns towards Newson. "A word. *Now*."

A fundamental change in his tone sends shivers down my spine. It sounds as if he's inviting Newson to hell.

"What does Dante want from him?" Jane squeals, bouncing in her seat when I sit beside her.

The room falls silent, and everyone's ears turn toward us. It's so quiet I can hear the dust settle over the wooden floor. I clear my throat, shaking my head so she'll stay quiet.

"Go on, spill it!" Her hand flies to her mouth, trying to keep the volume down. "Is he making sure you'll pass with all your credits?"

"No! Of course not!" I object too eagerly.

Silence breaks, morphing into an uproar of hushed conversations. I rest my elbows on the table, hiding my face in my hands, and ignore everyone's existence.

I last three hours of everyone's curious glances. I've got two more classes before I can get home, but the constant whispers turn my stomach. A few versions of the events that allegedly took place in the auditorium fly around the campus.

Rumor has it, Dante beat the hell out of Newson in front of the whole class. A different rumor is that he pulled out his gun to threaten Newson in the courtyard. There's also the one that has nothing to do with anything that happened. Apparently, Dante arrived at the university to *tell off* some guy who's in love with me. Since no jaw-breaking, gun-firing, or threatening is involved, it's safe to assume the author is a girl.

I ditch the rest of my classes a few minutes past noon and hide in a small café a few streets over. Cups clatter against each other while the barista rushes around, filling the room with a strong, bitter aroma of coffee. A rock ballad plays from the speakers, overshadowed by excited conversations. I sit out of the way, claiming a small table in the corner, and look out the window, covering the froth flower on my coffee with two sugars. Raindrops splatter against the glass forcing more people inside. In a few days, everyone should stop talking about me. A different topic will resurface, and I, or rather the identity of my boyfriend, won't matter. Or so I hope.

I grab a worn copy of *"Genius and Insanity"* by Lombroso Cesare and a few similar books from my bag, laying them out next to my laptop. With earphones in, I start my dissertation for Newson. It's due in five weeks, but all I have so far is a title. Locked up in the world of geniuses, I pay no attention to the world while Ellie Goulding mutes the surrounding noise.

It's Spades who stops me typing. He tears the headphones off my head, jaw working, nostrils flared. "What the hell, Layla?!" He pulls his phone out of his pocket.

It's dark outside. When did it get dark? I glance at the time, my eyes growing wider. It's half-past five.

"I've got her," Spades says to whoever's on the line. "We're in a café on forty-second street ... yeah, she's good."

A hot sweat washes over me as I search for my phone, buried under my books. Twelve missed calls wait on the screen...

Spades plops down in the chair opposite mine with a heavy sigh. He's by far the least handsome of Dante's men, tall, overweight, with a nose that looks like it has been broken half a dozen times and thin, almost invisible lips.

"Everyone's been looking for you for over two hours." He cracks his neck with a sigh. "Why are you hiding?"

"I'm not hiding. I ditched the last two classes and came

here to write my dissertation. I don't even know when it got dark. Dante's angry, isn't he?"

"Angry? He's fucking fuming." With another heavy sigh, he raises his hand, squeezing the bridge of his nose. "I like you, Layla, but Dante's got hay instead of brains because wherever you're concerned. If it ever affects business, I'll stop liking you. Fast."

I'm sure Dante has more than enough problems without me causing more trouble. Despite still thinking that every man's primary responsibility is worrying about his woman, it doesn't apply to situations like this.

My stupidity shouldn't be his problem.

"I'm sorry, I just—"

"You're *okay*, Layla. That's all that matters today. Just don't disappear without a word again."

A black Charger parks on the curb by the café window. I start shoving my books inside the bag, thinking of a decent apology, when Dante barges inside. I take a step back, standing behind a chair.

It's irrational, but his narrowed eyes, heaving chest, and the vein throbbing on his neck have me looking for cover.

The makeshift barrier makes no difference. Dante shoves the chair aside, making much unnecessary noise when it topples over. He grasps my neck, yanking me close enough to reach my lips, the kiss urgent, desperate. His tongue strokes mine and he draws me closer, one hand tangled in my hair, the other snaked around my back. Muscles on his don't relax under my fingertips.

They have no give in them, not even when he inches back slowly, and his stormy green eyes rove over my face, jaw working in tight circles.

"Cutting class?" he forces the words past his lips, each one sharper than a blade, but he's not yelling. "Where's your phone, Layla?"

"I'm sorry, I got distracted. I didn't hear the phone—"

"You got any fucking idea how many people are out looking for you right now?"

My instincts kick in, and remorse dissipates, replaced by a burning sensation in my throat. I won't act like someone I'm not. That's not how our relationship will ever work. My immediate reaction to aggression has always been aggression.

I shove him back. "Who asked you to look for me?" I grab my bag, marching outside because we're making a scene, and I've had enough attention for one day. Dante follows, grasping my arm two steps outside the door. I push him back again. "You're making a mountain out of a molehill. No one asked you to look for me! You're the only person who could gain anything from my disappearance." I shove my finger into his chest. "I said I'm sorry. I said I got distracted. I didn't hear the phone. I won't repeat myself all night, and I sure won't inform you about my every move, so stop freaking out or leave me alone."

"And how am I supposed to do that?" He takes a step closer. "You knew I was coming, Layla. I show up, and you're not there. What the fuck did you expect me to do? Go home?! You should've called!"

Spades joins us, glaring at his boss. "Stop scaring her."

They step aside, talking in hushed voices, or rather Spades talks while Dante pumps his fists and grinds his teeth, clearly unappeased with whatever Spades says. After a minute, he turns around, getting into the Charger without a backward glance my way.

"You think he scared me?" I fold my hands over my chest. "Do you know me, Spades? I'm not scared of Dante. It takes more than shouting to scare me."

"Yeah, figures. C'mon, I'll take you home." He points to the parking lot across the street. "And don't argue. The only reason he left without a fight is that I promised I'd get you home safe."

I don't feel safe in taxis, so objecting is out of the question. Especially since it's freezing outside.

"That's what I meant about the hay brain," he says when we speed across the city. "He needs to calm down."

"I don't need a controlling, breathing-down-my-neck man in my life. I've got enough of those. I won't be reporting back to Dante every five minutes. You can tell him I said that."

Spades chuckles under his breath. "He wasn't pissed off that he couldn't reach you, Layla. Not by a long shot. He was scared something happened to you."

Oh. My mouth parts, and warmth engulfs me like a soothing balm. I might be selfish, but I love how much he cares; how protective and worried he is.

Spades slows down as the lights change at the junction a few hundred yards away, but we never reach it. A Charger jumps out from a side street, and Dante stops in the middle of the road, forcing Spades to emergency brake. The seatbelt prevents me from breaking my nose on the dashboard. Dante jumps out of the car, jaw set, eyes focused as he marches straight at us.

Spades gets out, leaving the door open. "Are you fucking insane? You were supposed to go home!"

"Shut up." Dante pulls the passenger door open. "Are you scared of me?"

"No."

"Then get out."

"I don't take orders. Get a dog."

Tension leaves his face, and a small smile tugs at his lips. "Get out of the car." He takes my hand. "*Please.*"

I can't say *no* when he says *please.* I follow him back to the Charger, expecting an argument or a heated discussion at least, but he's silent all the way home.

Once in the living room, he drinks half a glass of whiskey in one go before he even looks at me. "Is there anything I can do so you'll stop thinking I want to use you?"

"Treat me like your girlfriend, not like your pawn."

He lights a cigarette, sitting beside me on the couch. "When have I ever treated you like one of my people?"

"Do you hear yourself when you talk to me sometimes? You can't boss me around, Dante. I'm yours, but I'm not your property. You don't pay me to follow your orders, and I won't let you dictate what I'm allowed to do."

"Layla, I'm not acting this way to annoy you. It's a habit."

"A habit? I care about you, you know?" I look at him to make sure he's listening. "It's been a month, but I can't imagine being without you." Which is something I feared from the beginning. Something I swore not to let happen. "You know how to manipulate me. You know what I need and how much I lack attention, but I won't let my man treat me the way my father and his people do. Either stop ordering me around, or if you can't tone it down, then—"

"I can."

Neither of us wants to hear the end of that sentence. He puts out the cigarette, pouring himself another neat whiskey. I don't expect him to say that he cares. It'll take time before he admits it aloud. Dante's careful with words.

"I won't control you. I don't have to know where you are at all times, but when you're supposed to meet me, and you don't show up, don't pick up the phone, and no one knows where you are, I will look for you." He moves closer, kissing my lips. "Always." He kisses again. "Until I find you."

I sit astride his lap and drape my arms over his shoulders, turning the innocent kiss into a battle of lustful passion.

He lays me down, covering my body with his broad, heavy frame. "Stay the night, Star."

I shake my head, despite wanting nothing more than to have his arms around me all night.

"Stay, baby," he whispers, kissing along my collarbone. "I want you to fall asleep next to me."

"I don't have clothes, a toothbrush, or shampoo."

"Shops don't close till ten."

I close my eyes with a sigh, unable to say *no* again. "Frankie's going to lose his mind."

CHAPTER SIXTEEN

Dante

Layla sits on the floor in my bedroom, surrounded by ten bags filled with clothes, shoes, and cosmetics.

"Still mad?" I hand her a cup of steaming hot chocolate.

"I'm not mad. Just not happy that you didn't let me pay."

We argued at the till for five minutes over who'll pay for her new clothes until she threatened to put everything back and go to Frank's for the night. That didn't sit well with me.

I snatched the bags, paid the cashier, then dragged Layla to five more boutiques until she hit the daily spending limit on my card. She stopped waving her card around but didn't stop huffing.

I open the walk-in closet to make some room. "Don't take out your wallet when you're with me. Forget you own a fucking wallet. Money is my area."

"And what's my area? Looking pretty? Agreeing with everything you say?"

"I'm still waiting for you to agree with me on something. Anything, really. All you do is argue."

She rolls her eyes, placing the sweaters on a shelf. I swear she was folding them just now, but it looks as if she just threw them in there.

My OCD gets the better of me. Everything in my closet is carefully planned; shirts hang by the jackets, all color-coded. Sweaters, t-shirts, and pants are neatly folded. Not one piece of clothing is out of place.

"I like teasing you," she says, smirking under her nose.

"Give me that." I grab the sweaters.

"Am I disrupting your Feng Shui?"

"Sit or go take a bath."

She hooks her thumbs in the belt buckles of my pants, rising on her toes to reach my lips. "I'm not allowed to pay; I can't fold clothes properly..." she whispers, biting my lip. "Is there anything I do well?"

"You're a great kisser; you smell delicious, and you're incredible at getting on my nerves." I slap her butt, pushing her gently toward the ensuite. She dives under my arm, snatching my white shirt off the hanger. "You bought two nightgowns, but you'll sleep in my thousand-dollar shirt?"

"I didn't buy those. You did. And..." She wrinkles her nose

at the see-through nightdresses waiting for her on the bed, "I'll be cold in that."

"I'll keep you warm. Give back the shirt."

A mischievous grin twists her lips, and her eyes sparkle as she holds my gaze, ripping off the top button. "Oops... I don't think you'll wear it again. It's no good," she fakes a sad face. "I'll sleep in it, baby. Okay?"

Little devil.

I grip her by the waist and throw her on the bed, hiding my face in her cleavage. Desire tingles every inch of my body when I graze my nose up the valley of her breasts, sliding my hand up her waist. "Incredible," I whisper, ripping her blouse down the middle, exposing her stomach. "At getting on my nerves." I kiss her ribs, inhaling her sweet scent, on the verge of bursting out of my boxers when she arches back, exhaling slowly. "You're so soft, Star... so warm." I kiss around the edge of her bra, grazing my nose between her boobs to reach her lips before I roll over to the side, handing Layla my no-longer-favorite shirt. "It's yours, but I'll strip you down when you fall asleep."

She smiles, seeing through my bullshit. I'm too fucking worried to jeopardize her growing trust in me to put a foot wrong. The water in the bathtub starts running a minute later once Layla leaves me to fold her clothes. She keeps tugging on the door handle, checking if she locked the door.

"If you check again, I'll knock the door down," I shout.

She giggles, tugging again. The closet is again immaculate when she comes back half an hour later, hair wet, skin rosy, no more than three buttons fastened on her breasts. Her pebbled nipples press against the fabric, standing proudly. That sight, the hint of perky breasts, coupled with my wild-running imagination, turns my brain to mush.

I lock myself in the bathroom and spend ten minutes under ice-cold water, reining my craving for her body. I'll enjoy sex more once Layla trusts me. I'll appreciate her more once she's ready. At least that's how I'm pep-talking myself ahead of holding her close all night.

She stares at the ceiling, her body hidden under the satin sheets, when I crawl beside her, resting on my elbow, my other hand tracing the flawless curve of her hip. My desire is safely capped, but there's no way I won't touch her while she's right here in my arms, almost naked. She pushes me onto my back, drawing a line of open-mouth kisses from my shoulder up my neck until she finds my lips.

She's tense, but the touch of her hands and how she sinks into my lips feels greedier tonight. Desperate, somehow.

The overwhelming need to feel her naked, warm skin on mine resurfaces. My hands disappear under the hem of the shirt. I glide them up until my fingers frame her breasts. Once again, she goes perfectly still in my arms. Her lips no longer work with mine, but she doesn't jerk away, which is half the success.

"Good girl," I whisper, working my way back to her lips, exploring the silk of her mouth with my tongue as I move my hands lower, caressing her ribs.

She's not ready for much, but she'll trust me more with each step we take. Her breathing quickens, matching the rhythm of her heart when I flip her onto her back, hovering over her frail, warm body. I can fucking feel how wet she is when I touch her lacy panties with my thigh. I want to dive between her legs, lick her bottom to top and finally check how she tastes. I want to feel her vibrating beneath me as she comes, losing her goddamn mind from the influx of ecstasy.

Her long nails draw lines along my shoulder blades when

she yanks me down, flush against her hot body. A fire roars in my head, the touch of my hands more urgent every second, but I tame the primal hunger. She might act courageous, ready, and willing on the outside, but inside, she's not ready. She tenses every time my fingers graze the alluring roundness of her breasts or the inside of her thighs.

And so she throws me way off when she pops the first button on the white shirt she wears. Her hands tremble, and she stops breathing, biting her lip nervously, staring at her fingers touching the second button.

The air around us thickens, growing hotter by the second. Desire runs through me, a flame intense enough to vaporize diamonds. My primal instincts fight to take over and bury myself deep inside. Claim her. Mark her as mine. I fight to see reason and do the right thing when she pops the second button, letting out a shaky breath. She quivers like a frightened baby deer but moves her hands lower again. The growing panic rooted in her expression works like a bucket of water over my head.

I catch her wrists before she dooms us both. "Don't," I snap, my voice rough but the authoritative note clear. "I'm not taking that first tonight." No fucking way. Not with hesitation and fear looming in her beautiful, big eyes. Not while she's shaking like a timid kitten.

"Let me go," she whispers, kissing my jaw, looking everywhere but my face. "You said you'll be my first. It's just a matter of time. Why not tonight?"

"Because you're not ready, and you don't trust me. Because you're scared and one button away from bolting out of here. Because you're only doing it for me. Should I keep going? I said I'll be your first, Layla, but I also said I'll wait."

I'm expecting a phone call from the Academy in the

morning because I just won the Nobel Peace Prize by a landslide. I'm twenty-eight. There's nothing unusual about sex, nothing that'd justify making such a fuss. Sex is normal. Natural. It's an inseparable companion to any relationship. There's nothing extraordinary about it.

For me.

Layla's innocent, untouched, and that makes sex a big deal. I won't fuck this up for her. Or let her fuck it up. Especially if first thing tomorrow morning, my status would change from *in a relationship* to *it's complicated* or worse, *single.*

"But—"

"You can't even look at me, Layla."

Her cheeks flush pink, but she meets my eyes, pecking my lips. "You care about me..." A mixture of embarrassment and glee flashes across her face.

I let her go, jerking to a sitting position. Lust deflates from my body with a hiss, leaving no trace to prove it was there five seconds ago. "Was that a test?"

"No! of course not." She wraps her hands around me, her cheek pressed against my back. "I just want to do something nice for you. Reciprocate somehow."

"Reciprocate?!" I jump out of bed, ready to punch the fucking wall. "What for? A few dresses?!"

"Dante—"

I slam the bedroom door behind me hard enough to rattle the frame. Pinching a cigarette between my teeth, I march outside in nothing but boxer shorts despite the cold evening. I tug on my hair, digging my fingers into the nape of my neck, feeling fucking powerless. She drives me up the wall, that girl. She's not supposed to think she owes me anything.

She's mine.

I take care of what's mine.

159

Always.

I hang my head low, inhaling and exhaling the smoke. Five deep drags clear my head enough that I start seeing past the rage. The freezing air helps too. Sex was my go-to thing whenever I needed to let off some steam, but that's not been an option since Layla stumbled into my life. My temper rears its head more often, the pent-up frustration kicking my crazy into overdrive.

I throw the cigarette over the balcony railing, heading back upstairs, expecting to see Layla packed and ready to leave.

Nothing further from the truth.

She's right where I left her, sitting on the bed, all buttoned up, legs under the sheets. She's *nineteen*. Nine years younger than me, but she's much more mature. It's true what they say about men. We only mature up to a certain age and then grow old. Women, on the other hand, mature throughout their lives.

"I'm sorry, it came out wrong. I just—"

"I'm not a horny teen, Star." I sit beside her, running my hands through my hair. "Sex can wait. There are plenty of appetizers before we move onto the mains, and we won't until I know you're ready. Until I know you *want* to take that step. Understood?" I kiss her head. "Don't ever tell me you want to reciprocate. I'll spoil you because you're mine, not because I expect something in return."

She bites her lip, playing with her fingers. "I probably believe you're here for me and that I'm Switzerland."

"*Probably?*" I smirk. "You have to know it. Believe me, baby, when you're ready, I won't let you out of bed for a very long time." I fall back, my head hitting the pillow, and I tie my hands under my head.

Layla lays down beside me, her lips swollen from my kisses.

"You're not making this easy, are you?" She nuzzles into my side. "I shouldn't want to love you."

Love?

She wants to *love* me?

One sentence and the arrogant fucker I am turns into a plush toy. "You're delirious, Star. You must be exhausted." I wrap my arms around her, kissing her head.

I hope she'll love me.

I hope she won't be able to live without me because I sure as hell can't imagine my life without her.

CHAPTER SEVENTEEN

Layla

Two weeks flew by and judgment day crept up on me unnoticed. The house is filled with people from the early hours of the morning. An army of staff employed to cater for the party took over downstairs, preparing food or redecorating the living room. Two Chesterfield sofas, a coffee table, and Jess's beloved Persian carpet were placed in storage. In their place, a pop-up bar appeared by the window.

A young man dressed in a white tuxedo polishes champagne flutes while the event coordinator, a strict-looking brunette in horn-rimmed glasses, yells at the staff to get moving. Food is piling up in the kitchen while an older gentleman wheels in a barrel of fine, British ale—Nikolaj's favorite. Flowers were delivered an hour ago. Large bouquets of pink-and-white lilies. Their aroma makes me feel light-headed. Soirees at Frank's are usually held in the back garden under a beautiful canopy of tiny, white lights, but at the end of November, the weather doesn't favor outdoor parties. Jess locked herself in her bedroom with a make-up artist and a hairdresser five minutes after I woke up.

Frank supervises the staff to avoid slip-ups growling at people for no reason. Why he hired the coordinator is beyond me. He argues against most of what she says.

Nikolaj's due at six p.m. with his wife, son, and pawns. It's not even ten a.m., but I'm already tired of this day. I'm working on my dissertation, which is almost impossible with the shouting and general madness happening around here. I can't hear my own thoughts.

Frank sits opposite me, two wrinkles across his forehead as he pretends to read the newspaper but keeps a watchful eye on everyone around.

"Where's this going?" The man with the barrel asks one of the waitresses.

Frank exhales an exasperated puff of air, tossing the newspaper aside for the eighth time in twenty minutes. "Living room." He points the clueless man in the right direction.

Ten seconds later, the coordinator walks in, her face red. "Beer was supposed to stay in the kitchen!"

"I've changed my mind," Frank clips, visibly pleased to annoy the poor woman.

Sadistic bastard.

I take my phone, scrolling through the contacts to find Dante's number. I need an out, or I'll end up in the looney bin before the party starts.

"Good morning," he grumbles.

I imagine him with his eyes closed, head on the pillow, and the phone resting on the side of his face. A small smile curves my lips. "Get me out of here."

"Don't tempt me. This bed is so fucking uncomfortable without you in it. Why do you want to get out of there? You're supposed to be babysitting Julij, remember?"

"He won't arrive until six. I want to work on my dissertation, but it's like an Indian market here. I'll stay out of your way. I promise." I await his decision while he breathes down the line. "Pretty please?"

The bed creaks under his weight. "Fine. I'll pick you up in half an hour under one condition."

"Whatever you want."

"Don't say that, baby. Don't put images in my head. It's bad enough you torture me in my sleep. Now, I'm not taking you back to Frank's until quarter to six. Pack your dress or whatever you're wearing tonight. You'll get ready here."

"Deal." I cut the call, peering up at Frank. "I'll be back before Nikolaj arrives."

"Why don't you fucking move in with him already?"

Ah, if only he knew that Dante wants nothing more. He didn't ask directly, but started referring to his house like ours, bought me a dressing table, and stocked the fridge with my favorite foods. He rarely takes me back to Frank's for the night. It's scary how much Dante cares about me. We haven't even had sex yet, but he acts like we've been together for months.

I'm the opposite.

Or at least I want to believe I'm doing everything in my power to fight the feelings, but the truth is I'm failing spectacularly. Frank's words from our trip to Aspen reverberate through my mind, reminding me that no matter how incredible Dante is, I shouldn't love him. It's like fighting the wind, though. He's endured weeks of celibacy, and that gesture alone is enough to believe that he cares about me more than he's ever cared about anyone else.

Too many curious ears listen in on my conversation with Frank, so I let his comment slide. There's always someone around. I expected Frank to stage a meeting somewhere private, so we could talk without watching our every word, but so far, he's not asking about the details. Either he's really starting to trust me a bit, or he's always got eyes on me.

I won't be surprised if he has a spy among Dante's people.

I retreat from the kitchen, not gracing Daddy with another look, and rush upstairs to pack. Once the bag with books is ready, I zip a navy evening dress I chose for tonight into a dust cover. It's floor-length chiffon with a side split starting at the thigh. With a hair tie in-between my lips, I rush downstairs when Dante arrives. Without a goodbye in anyone's direction, I leave the house to find my man out of the car, ready to help me with the bags. He locks them in the trunk and drapes his hands over my shoulders, pulling me in for a deep kiss.

"What?" he asks, seeing me chuckle as I get in the car.

"Trying to enrage Frank, are you? I'm sure you're aware how much he enjoys watching people when they've no idea they're being watched."

"Unless they do."

I roll my eyes, buckling up. "He knows we're dating. Seeing you kiss me won't do any damage. He doesn't care."

"Yes, he does. It wasn't a power play, Star. I just want him to know that even though the war is raging, he has already lost one battle. You're *mine*. No matter what Frank says or does, you now trust your gut instead of following his orders."

Shame hits me hard, but I mask it with what I hope to be a believable smile. "That I am. Let's go." I attempt to tie my hair into a messy bun, but Dante takes the tie out of my hand, pulling it onto his wrist.

"Why aren't you in bed? I took you home six hours ago."

"The catering company rolled in at nine and woke me up." I take another hair tie out of my bag. "I don't like working with my hair getting in the way," I say when Dante frowns.

"How about you go back to bed with me instead of writing that paper? That way, you can let your hair down, and I can get some quality sleep. It's inconvenient not to have you snaked around me at night."

I spent the last eight out of ten nights at his place, and I felt out of place when I climbed into my bed this morning.

"Are my ears ugly?" I ask when he tries to steal the second hair tie.

"Your ears are fine. I don't mind your hair up, but it does make it damn near impossible not to kiss your neck when it's on display like that."

His compliments are like no other. Never straight to the point, never forced, always thrown in there casually as if he's commenting on the weather.

"You can kiss it all you want." I lean over to peck his cheek. "I've got a month to hand the dissertation in. You've been monopolizing all my time lately, and I hadn't done much writing, so I won't crawl back in bed with you, but you go. At least you won't disturb me."

"You mean I won't distract you."

"Sure, keep telling yourself that."

He squeezes my hand briefly, letting go to change gears. "Will you escape the party to come over to Delta tonight?"

"I don't think so. Nikolaj can drink the ocean. Frank managed to sober up twice in Dubai before Nikolaj got drunk. If they're planning on drinking like that tonight, I won't leave the house until Monday."

Frank failed to inform me about the reason for Nikolaj's visit. He doesn't typically invite himself over out of the blue. Julij's attendance is also a novelty. I haven't seen him since Dubai despite seeing Nikolaj half a dozen times. He keeps his son out of the picture, away from his dealings, so his sudden involvement makes me wonder.

Twenty minutes later, I set my books on the dining table. Dante throws his keys on the countertop, kisses the crown of my head, and heads upstairs to catch up on sleep. My dissertation grows at a steady pace for a few hours.

"How are you doing?" Dante asks sometime around one o'clock in the afternoon, making me jump out of my skin. "Relax, Star." He dips his head to kiss my neck.

"Good. Great, actually. I have to study here more often. It's easier to focus." Dante kisses me again, his warm breath making me tremble. "But only when you're not around."

Despite our short relationship, I know him so well that I don't need to see him to know he's smiling.

"Break time?" he asks, setting one of the books aside.

I glance at the clock, weighing my options. "Lunch break, please. I'm starving."

"Takeout, or do you want to go to a restaurant?"

"Order in. I'd rather not waste time stuck in traffic."

Dante pulls me onto his lap when I get up to make another coffee. "You'll be writing all day and entertaining Julij all evening. When will you have time for me?"

"I'm not supposed to be here at all today."

"But you are. I won't see you tonight." He grips my hips, caressing me softly. "I need to make the most of our time now."

It's nearly impossible to object when he watches me as if nothing else matters. "Okay, let me write until the food gets here, and then... yeah, what then?"

"We're watching a movie."

"You want me to ditch my dissertation to watch a movie?"

"And, so I can kiss you."

I drape my hands over his neck. "Only if you hug me too."

He lets me get back to work while he reads *"Artistry of the mentally ill"* by Hans Prinzhorn. "What are you writing that dissertation about?" he asks half an hour later, setting a pizza box on the table.

"Enjoying the book, are you? I'm writing about the links between genius and mental illnesses or rather, I'm trying to prove a theory."

"You're trying to prove that geniuses suffer from mental illness more often than ordinary people?"

I shake my head, swallowing a bite of pizza. "I'm trying to prove that genius is a form of mental illness. I read a quote once: "We're all crazy, but people who can analyze the craziness are philosophers." Following the lead, I found another quote by the same author." I point to *"Genius and Insanity"* by Lombroso Cesare, "In which he states genius is one of many forms of mental illness. The idea got me hooked."

"Pretty and smart... you need to start messing up, Layla. You don't have nearly enough flaws."

"I snore," I admit, taking another bite. "I'm clumsy, lazy, and cruel, but you think that's positive, just like my sassiness, innocence, and emotional instability."

"I considered the last one a flaw at first, but now I like that you need attention because I like it when you need me."

"Give it time. You can't see my flaws yet, but once the blindfold's off, you'll see many things that'll drive you insane."

That's unavoidable. During the first phase of every relationship, our bodies are ruled by endorphins, hearts skip a few beats, and legs grow weak at the sight of our crush.

The other half is always perfect at first. It takes a few weeks to notice the small, annoying things once the excitement wears off, but feelings are more important than the fact the other half won't take their cup back to the sink or can't fold a sweater.

I have flaws like everyone, but Dante doesn't see them yet, just as I don't see his. He's my winning lottery ticket. My dream-come-true. The best thing to ever happen to me and the worst decision I ever made...

"Back to your dissertation. You're writing about genius being a mental illness. Have you done any research, or are you basing everything solely on literature?"

"Are you asking if I've had a chance to talk to a genius? Unfortunately, no. I'm roaming through hundreds of books, trying to piece together something new."

"Wouldn't it be better if you included a new example?"

"Of course, it would, but I don't know any geniuses."

"I do. Quite a few."

My lips form one line. "Define genius."

"It means a highly intelligent person or one with remarkable skill in a particular area of activity."

"And you know a few?"

He nods, washing down the pizza with coffee. "Have you ever heard of Isla Gale?"

Who hasn't? Isla is Mozart in a skirt. Frank played her concertos at home when I was a little girl. He spent hours sitting by the gramophone with his eyes closed, listening to the music. Later on, when he became a bitter buffoon who lost half of the city to Dante, music ceased to exist in his life.

"You know Isla Gale?"

Dante smiles a self-indulgent smile. "You're looking at her son, Star. Do you want to meet her?"

"Are you serious?! You're Isla's son?! Wow... I sure know nothing about you." My eyes widen when his question registers with me. "You want to introduce me to your mom?"

He pushes his plate aside. "Her, and her more or less brilliant friends. She's touring Europe now, but we can visit her on the second weekend of December. You'll then have a week to hand in your dissertation."

"I can do it. I wouldn't miss the chance even if I were to pull an all-nighter."

"Okay. We're flying to New York on the ninth."

I'm both excited and nervous about meeting his mother, even if it's an educational meeting rather than Dante introducing his girlfriend.

Although this time, one doesn't rule out the other.

We spend the next two hours in front of the TV. The movie's only background noise as neither of us pays any attention. We tease each other more than anything, but I'm disappointed once the end credits roll. I never would've thought a mafia boss could be so normal. In the movies, they're portrayed as ruthless and calculated.

Dante's nothing like that when we're alone. He enjoys small things.

I check the time on my phone. It's only four, but I wouldn't put it past Frankie to summon me ahead of time. "I'll take a shower and start getting ready."

"Yeah, okay. I'll get your dress from the car."

I climb the stairs, pulling the hair tie out of my hair, then hang the towel close to the shower doors, so I won't turn the floor into a small lake when I get out. It's not until I stand there in nothing but my panties that I turn the shower on to let the water warm up.

The only thing I fail to do is lock the door.

Dante walks in, freezing mid-step, his eyes hungry, swimming with desire. "I thought..." he starts but doesn't finish. He sets the bag on the floor, hangs my dress on the door, then turns around and leaves.

My cheeks burn hot, but a wave of desire hits me like a freight train. I take a tentative step to find Dante, but the door flies open again, and he bursts inside, determination showing in his eyes. He grips my waist, pushing me under the stream of warm water, his lips on mine before I can blink, the kiss urgent, almost brutal.

I still hold onto my breasts while water soaks my hair and Dante's clothes. He pins me to the wall, never breaking the kiss, his hands all over my body.

"Take it off." I tug on his soaked t-shirt.

He lifts me up, his hands under my butt for support, my legs around his waist. He pins me to the wall, yanking the t-shirt off over his head. The touch of his skin on mine sends a brand-new wave of desire deep inside me. The sight of his firm, tattooed arms, and broad chest drives me wild, but the second a soft moan escapes my lips, he stops.

"I need to leave, baby."

My hold on him tightens. "No, you don't."

He bites my ear, breathing quickly. "Layla—"

I grab his shoulders, pulling him in for a kiss to shush him. He holds me flush against the tiles, his lips moving down my neck. My stomach twists with anticipation when the pad of his thumb toys with my nipple.

I want him, but taking the lead is out of the question. Dante has to be in control, but first, he needs to realize where my mind is.

"Take me to bed," I say in his ear.

His fingertips dig into my waist, the kiss greedy and demanding before he breaks away to look straight into my eyes. "You sure?"

"Yes, just..." I trail off, unsure how to voice my mind. "Walk me through this, okay?"

He presses another kiss on my forehead. "Step by step. I've got you, Star, but don't think you can't back out."

"I'm yours... I'm not backing out."

He smiles a smile I might be head over heels in love with already. He kisses me, his lips demanding, restless, his hands frantic, possessive. My mind is consumed by a mixture of anticipation and dread while my body reacts to his impatient touch. Warm water trickles down our naked bodies. I'm thirsty for more, arching my spine to cling closer to him, desperate to reduce the distance between our bodies to nothing as pleasant chills make my head spin. I weave my fingers in his hair, move lower to touch his back, then up again to cup his face. I try to touch him everywhere, all at once. A soft moan leaves my lips when he bites on my earlobe.

Dante turns the water off, carrying me out of the bathroom to throw me on the bed. I expected something different than what comes next. He doesn't take my panties off that very moment. No, he works me up with his lips, getting me ready, all hot and bothered to the point where I'm sure he won't need to slip inside me to make me come. He pulls a foil packet out of the nightstand drawer. The sound of it being ripped by his teeth makes me tense just a touch. Enough for him to notice.

"Relax," he says in my ear. "I'm not going in until I have you breathless."

I'm already breathless, already aching, but Dante wants more. His hand slips lower, his fingers pressing against me, moving in small circles. My eyes fly open, and my cheeks reach the same temperature as the fire building up inside me.

"Don't go shy on me now. It doesn't suit you. You're beautiful, and you're *mine*. I'll make damn sure you enjoy this. Focus on how you feel."

I close my eyes again, my hands on the sheets, then on his back, the pleasure multiplying. I claw at his shoulders, looking for an outlet for the pent-up tension.

He bites on my earlobe, his fingers moving faster, and I let out a quiet moan, the sensation becoming too much to handle. He smiles against my lips at the sound, then moves his mouth to my breast. That's all it takes. I stop breathing, clutching his hair while another moan, much louder, escapes me as the orgasm hits me hard.

"Good girl, that's it... don't hold back."

I'm only partially aware that he's removed his pants and of what's happening until I feel him spread my legs with his knee.

"Easy, baby," he says, grazing his nose up my cheek, and I feel him press against my entrance. "Eyes on me." as soon as I meet his gaze, he thrusts his hips forward, taking my virginity in one swift movement.

I gasp, holding my breath and claw at his back. My eyes shut tight while I wait for the pain to subside.

"Layla, look at me." The concern in his voice is like a living entity. It takes a few very long seconds before I let all the air out of my lungs, opening my eyes. "Tell me you're okay."

"I'm okay, just—" I bite my lip, entwining my fingers together at the nape of his neck.

"No rushing," he assures, pulling out slowly, his lips on my forehead. "God, you feel so fucking good, baby."

So does he. I feel every inch of him, sliding in and out in a cautious, calm rhythm as he allows me time to adjust. I lift my head off the pillow to close his lips with a kiss, my hands on his face. He holds me by the waist, the other arm bent at the elbow for support.

The rhythm of his moves turns eager quickly. Pain disappears, morphing into pleasure. Dante fuels the fire, worshiping me with every kiss and thrust. Never, not in my wildest dreams, did I think sex could be so amazing. All the feelings I tried to keep buried are amplified now that I gave him my all.

I shouldn't... I'll cry in the end, but I can't help it. "I love you," I say into his mouth and feel him shudder.

He knows. He felt it long before I understood it, but I want him to hear it. His hot lips press against my cool forehead. It's a small gesture, but those simple things put my mind at ease. He loves me but saying it out loud isn't something I expect to hear soon. I don't mind. I can wait.

Dante pulls out for a second, driving back into me harder, turning my world upside down. I rediscover his lips as I scratch his back, pulling him closer, as close as possible, when the pleasure floods me again.

"Can you... can I—"

"Yes. You can come again. And you will."

It takes a bit of effort on his part. His pace quickens bit by bit, his body on fire against mine. My moans ricochet off

174

the walls, growing louder. Dante's just as breathless as I am and his hold on me tightens with a low growl that comes from deep within his chest. that sound is enough to send me hurtling toward another orgasm. He moves his hips faster before he stills for a few torturous seconds while my legs shake as the orgasm sifts through me like a prolonged roar of thunder.

"All that time..." Dante rises on his elbows. "You've no idea how many cold showers I've had since we met."

I'm too exhausted to laugh. "It was worth the wait."

"That it was. I'm not letting you out of here for a week, and it'll be a very demanding week."

"We have to eat."

"No, we don't." He climbs out of bed. "But we need to get you on the pill." He disappears into the bathroom and comes back out a minute later with a warm washcloth. "You're staying in until Monday." He presses the warm cloth between my legs. "You'll be sore, baby." He lays beside me, pulling me to his side, one hand still between my legs.

I glance at the clock on the nightstand. "I can stay in bed for ten more minutes, but then I need to get ready."

"Fuck, I forgot about the party."

I roll onto my stomach to kiss his neck. "Thank you."

"What for?"

"For being here, for caring for me. I'm not used to being treated as if I'm—"

"The most important thing in my life. You are. Nothing matters more than you."

CHAPTER EIGHTEEN

Layla

"Frankie, my old friend. It's good to see you." Nikolaj reaches out to embrace Frank.

As a pedigree Mafioso, he's in a snow-white suit with a brown coat draped over his shoulders, a cigar in his mouth, and burgundy shades on his nose. If he had a hat, he'd look like Al Capone. Almost.

"Nikolaj, it's good to see you too."

I stand to the side, nauseous, when Nikolaj hugs me as if I'm his daughter, although he wouldn't accidentally grab her ass. Mrs. Capone, Tamara, blows two kisses in my direction before admiring my long, backless dress. Her compliments fly over my head. I do my best to play my role, smile and praise her earrings. In my head, I'm throwing up a rainbow.

Julij joins half a minute later. He's also in a suit, but he's not trying to imitate The Godfather. He's grown into a man since Dubai. The mocking expression he wore back then is no longer in sight. He shakes my father's hand, greets my mother, and approaches me. "Layla. You're prettier now."

Julij, ugly as always.

"Hey, Julij. How was your flight?"

I don't want to be here. All the more because Dante was right. I'm sore. I want a hot water bottle between my legs and Dante's chest to cuddle for the rest of the night.

But I'm here, warily gawking at Julij, who offers me his arm. The hallway's bursting at its seams now that Nikolaj's people have arrived. Frank's pawns, including Adam, are having a blast in the living room, standing in strategic places, not moving a muscle.

The first hour of these soirees is reserved for business talks, so I'm not surprised to see Frank lead Nikolaj to his office. Jess, the gracious hostess, shows her guests around. I have no choice but to accept Julij's arm. We snatch two glasses of champagne from a passing waitress on our way out the back door.

"I owe you an apology, sugar."

My eyebrows form a line as I tilt my head, studying his face. We don't know each other well, and the only impression he made in the past was strictly negative. Until now, I had no idea he knew the meaning of *sorry*.

"What for?"

"For my behavior in Dubai. I'm not usually such an idiot."

He doesn't sound like he's teasing. Besides, it's been four minutes, but I haven't felt the need to smack him yet.

"Is it Dubai or the alcohol that turns you into an idiot?"

"You do. Or did." He shrugs, attempting to hide a smile. "I guess I tried to woo you."

Julij's face would've been soaked in champagne if I hadn't already swallowed. "Are you kidding? You call that wooing?"

"Rough advances?"

"Rough? They haven't invented a suitable word to describe the kind of ass you were!"

He laughs out loud. "You're still so polite. An ass is an understatement of the century. I was a fucking dickhead."

"Polite? "Do you know me? Were you really trying to hit on me? By throwing me in the pool and arguing every minute of the day?"

"I liked that you talked back." He smirks, his light blue eyes sparkling. "You didn't let anyone walk all over you."

Who would've thought guys like feisty girls? I thought *Cinderella* types were the ones snatched first, but it looks like not only gays are interested in me. "I still don't."

He elbows me playfully. "If what I heard is true, you no longer need to worry about idiots like me. Your boyfriend will snap their necks before they get anywhere near you."

I cross my arms over my chest. "Did Mr. Capone tell you to talk to me about Dante? I hope you're not here to chastise Frank for my choices."

"Mr. Capone?" Julij asks with a chuckle. "I guess you're right. Nikolaj does look a bit like Al."

Not unlike me, Julij doesn't refer to his father as *Dad*. He uses his name. That's how they wanted it to be. I only use

Dad if I want to annoy Frank.

"And don't worry. Nikolaj didn't come all the way here to talk about your boyfriend. I can't say he didn't find it interesting, but it doesn't matter. I won't try to change your mind." He finishes his champagne, takes my glass, and disappears to find the waitress.

He shakes hands with Adam, making me realize that not only has his behavior changed but his posture too. He's no longer a frail, skinny boy. He stands straight, taking advantage of his height, and keeps his shoulders back, showing off his muscular chest. The blond hair is no longer a medium-length mess, trimmed on the sides and styled back in line with current trends. Allie would approve. She'd most likely eye his high cheekbones with a dreamy face, but she's not here yet.

A moment later, Julij returns with alcohol and a plate of salmon canapés.

"I don't want to sound rude—"

"Yes, you do."

I elbow him a bit harder than he did me. "What do you have to say on the matter? Frank tries to make Dante look like an Egyptian plague, but his arguments hit a wall, and it's not like your father can do more than voice his opinion. You can't even do that while Mr. Capone is the boss, right?"

"Right." He takes a packet of Marlboro out. "Shit, this is..." he motions to the cigarette. "One day, it'll kill me, just like it's killing Nikolaj. Mr. Capone has cancer, Layla."

I rest my hand on his arm. "I had no idea."

"He doesn't have long left. That's why we're here. to inform Frankie that New York will soon be under my control."

I don't know what to say. My affiliation with Julij is, in ninety-nine percent, awful. I only got a glimpse of his real

179

personality tonight, and even though he seems okay, I don't know how to comfort him.

That's if he needs comforting.

He snaps me out of my thoughts when he steps closer, minimizing the distance to less than a foot. "Don't worry, sugar." He touches my cheek, his thumb grazing the skin softly. "We're all heading there."

The air around us thickens as the atmosphere changes to an intimate one. Before I understand what he's about to do, Julij wraps his hands around me, hiding his face in the crook of my neck. Relief washes over me like a cleansing waterfall. I half expected him to kiss me, and it'd be a shame to ruin my immaculate behavior tonight by shoving my elbow in his face. Frank wouldn't approve.

I move my hands to his back, not to discourage the closeness. In our world, parents aren't affectionate, but they are our parents. I can only guess how difficult it must be for Julij to wait for his father's death. If it turned out Frank had a few months left, I'd be devastated.

"I'm sorry," I say truthfully.

Our fathers are close, and even though they're business partners first, there's a mutual respect there. The real kind. Mr. Capone has been a guest at our house for years now. Besides his hands sliding too low down my back, he's a pleasant man. He's never hurt or offended me, but I refused to see it until now, hating all of Frank's acquaintances on principle.

Julij moves away with a heavy sigh, taking a drag of his cigarette. "Frank and Dante's conflict only brings trouble to the table. It'd be much more lucrative if they buried the hatchet. Maybe you're the key."

"Hell will freeze over before they make up."

"You're probably right. Neither of them is amicable but never say never. There are hundreds of examples in history where women saved the day." He grabs my hand, pulling me toward the door. "Come on. It's time to make a good impression."

"It's going to be a long night."

"Well, good thing you have me to keep you company. You'd die of boredom otherwise."

Explaining the connection that just formed between us in the short amount of time is impossible. A thread of understanding, like a spider's web, weaves between us. Deep in my heart, I know it'll stay there for years. When not acting like a jerk, Julij radiates positivity. He's real, and even though I shouldn't be this careless, I trust him.

Nikolaj whisks him away a moment later. I'm left with an army of pillars and three women too excited about the pink table setting... Allie finally joined the herd.

Admiring Tamara's nails, I down another glass of champagne. Before she tells me which shop on Fifth Avenue she bought the varnish from, Allie drags me to the side to ask a million questions about Julij. As I expected, the dreamy eyes make an appearance. There's no denying she loves Adam, but she likes to look.

At nine o'clock, the door to our house opens as the rest of the guests arrive. An abundance of well-dressed women and handsome men fill the space. There's the bank director, the chief of police, and even the mayor. Not to mention all the criminals. An explosive mixture, yet everyone gets along well. As always.

I mingle, deep in my role to ensure Frank won't have a reason to reprimand me later. Julij sneaks me out for a chat every thirty minutes, and for the first time, I enjoy a party hosted by my father.

"Call me if you ever need anything. Whatever it may be," Julij whispers in my ear when we're saying our goodbyes outside. "Promise you'll call."

I kiss his cheek. "I promise. It works both ways, Julij."

He curls his fingers under my chin. "I'll see you, sugar."

Seconds later, the door to a white limousine closes behind him. The party ended much earlier than I expected. With Nikolaj's condition, heavy drinking is out of the question. An evening I expected to be awful turned out pleasantly fruitful. I gained a friend.

CHAPTER NINETEEN

Dante

Star: Order me a mojito, please.

Layla's text arrived thirty minutes ago. I rise to my feet because she's due any minute. I really fucking hope she hasn't changed. The backless navy evening dress she chose for tonight is the sexiest yet most elegant thing I've ever seen on a woman.

"Is Layla coming?" Sandra asks, eyes big and round.

"She's on her way."

No one told them to stay in the booth, but without Layla, they lack the courage to make a move and remain seated, glancing longingly at the dance floor.

The bartender approaches before I reach the bar, wipes the countertop before I rest my elbows on it, and passes me an ashtray before I light a cigarette. He's new. He started last night. So far, I can't fault him.

"What can I get you, Boss?"

"Mojito." Before I finish smoking, a glass with two fancy straws appears in front of me.

"Jesus, what the hell happened there?" He asks, gawking over my shoulder.

I follow his line of sight to find at least thirty guys throwing punches left and right. Fights are common in Delta, but it's usually two or three men fighting, and the security handles them within seconds. This time, my fighters' help is needed. I turn to signal Cai, Luca, and Jackson, but they're already on their way. Spades and Rookie follow suit.

With a cigarette in his mouth, Luca rolls up his sleeves and then knocks out the first guy in his path. He punches two more before guy number one hits the floor. He's a pro, a merciless killer lacking inhibitions. Spades has fun dodging punches and kicking those that are already down. He prefers to fight with a weapon—a baseball bat or brass knuckles.

The crowd of onlookers thickens, but not before Jackson freezes at the top of the stairs, his body rigid, eyes trained on something out of my view. I follow his line of sight. It's not until someone trips that I notice Layla. I'm on the move before my brain processes the information, my body in a state of instant readiness, not allowing fear to stop me when a rush of ruthless protection floods my veins.

"Don't just fucking stand there!" I bellow at Jackson.

Four bouncers are at the bottom of the stairs. A few steps higher, Luca and Cai surround Layla, beating the living shit out of anyone who comes near her. My fists fly to the sides in reflex as I force my way through the chaos.

Even though I'm hitting blind, not daring to look away from Layla, I don't miss once. She tries to fuse with the wall, her eyes focused as she looks for a safe way out of the mayhem. I jump over an unconscious, bloody mess and catch her hand, pulling her into my arms, shielding her petite body with mine.

"You good, Star?" I ask, checking her over for injuries.

"Yeah, I'm okay." Instead of fear, her voice is full of irritation. "I couldn't move."

My erratic pulse slows for a second before it picks back up as my right hand, entangled in her hair, finds something wet. "Fuck! You got hit?!"

Her eyes lock on my hand, and she turns ashen, trembling as if it's an arctic winter.

"Layla!" I shake her harder than intended. She's holding her breath, mindless animal panic in her eyes. "Breathe, Layla. You need to breathe, baby... in and out..." She nods, sucking in a harsh breath, fearful eyes trained on mine. "Good, again." I inhale deeply, urging her to do the same.

Once her panic lessens, she opens her mouth to speak, but all she can manage is one word, "Blood."

I read her lips more than hear the word. Thirty guys fighting didn't scare her, but blood stripped her courage in a blink of an eye. I wipe my hand on the edge of my shirt and tuck it into my trousers.

"You're okay." I cup her face, looking into those steel-gray irises. "You're okay, baby. Come on, I'll get you out of here." I say, lifting her into my arms.

We climb the stairs, passing the few guys that still stand. Security, along with Cai and Jackson, ends the brawl while Luca takes out his frustration on a broad, unconscious gym-goer. He pummels his fists into the guy's face as if it's a speedball used in boxing.

I place Layla on the sofa in my office, still pale, eyes on my trousers where I tucked the crimson hem of my shirt. "Look at me." I take her cold, trembling hands in mine. "Are you feeling faint?"

She snaps out of the trance, inhaling deeply. "I'm sorry, I can't look at blood. I panic."

"Don't be sorry. It's okay."

She jumps, startled when Luca barges in. He stops in front of her while I brush her hair away to check the damage.

"You got hit?! Shit!" Luca bends down to get to her eye level, his fists resting on the coffee table. "Who hit you?"

"A better question is, what did he hit you with? This doesn't look good." The last time she got hurt, I had a hard time controlling my temper. This time it's different. I'm still worried, still furious, but watching over her puts my mind at ease.

"He aimed at someone else. It was an accident, Luca," she says, her voice close to normal. "And I'll be okay, Dante."

"I don't give a fuck if he wanted to hit you!" Luca bangs his fists on the table. "What did he look like?!"

It does nothing to scare Layla but a lot to piss me off.

I smack the back of his head. "You'll regret this when you're throwing up your teeth on the pavement."

"They all look the same," Layla says, ignoring the power-play. "Tall and ripped."

The door swings open again, and all my people walk in.

"You need stitches," I tell her while Luca sulks on the couch. "We're going to the hospital." I glance at Spades. He had things to take care of, so he didn't join us at the club until thirty minutes ago. "How much did you drink?"

"A few sips at most."

"Good. You're driving."

Layla stands, pale again. "We're not going anywhere. It's nothing. I'll be fine." She fists my jacket, resting her forehead on my chest.

If the cut wasn't as deep, I'd patch her up myself, but this can't heal on its own. "Not this time. You need stitches."

She hesitates for a moment. "But you're coming with me."

"I won't let you go or out of my sight."

Once in the ER, I walk on Layla's left, blocking her view of the patients. There's enough blood around to do a few transfusions, and I don't feel like witnessing another panic attack. A girl sitting on the floor by the vending machines can't be much older than Layla. Her face looks as if someone battered her with an iron. An older man hurls into the trash can while nurses rush around, patching up minor cuts.

We pass two police officers standing to the side with a group of bulky guys who must've arrived from Delta. I look at every one of them as if I can telepathically find the one who hit my girl. I'd tear him apart bit by bit.

A nurse frowns at us from behind a tall reception desk when we head straight for the door leading out to the ward. "Where do you think you're going?" She holds out a wad of papers. "You need to fill this out."

"Pretend you can't see us."

"Excuse me?" She jumps out from behind the desk, blocking the way. "Who do you think you are? There's a line. Fill this in, or I'll call security."

"My name is Dante Carrow. You can shove those papers, you-know-where. Security will kick *you* out of here well before me. This," I point to Layla, "is my girl. She needs a few stitches. Doctor Carrow will take care of her in two minutes. Stop me again, and you'll wave bye-bye to your job before you can say *what*." Giving the woman no time to react, I drag Layla behind me toward the elevators. Once again, my stunt goes unnoticed. "No comments?"

"Compared to Frank, you're almost polite."

"I know you've seen your share of similar situations, but I expected you to step in."

"I've been taught to keep my mouth shut." She shrugs, watching the numbers change on the screen above the door. "I only object when someone might get hurt because of me."

Dr. Carlton Carrow, dressed in a white coat with a stethoscope hanging over his neck, waits for us in the doorway of his office. At first glance, he's like any other doctor. He isn't, though. He's a surgeon and my cousin, which makes him pretty fucking unique. Whenever one of my guys is shot or battered, Carlton puts them back together.

"She needs stitches," I say, shaking his hand. "Some fucker split her head open at the club."

Layla mumbles her name like a timid school girl switching schools in the middle of the semester. She sits on the bed, hands in fists, eyes closed even before Carlton gets anywhere near her.

"She can't handle the sight of blood," I explain. "And while we're here, we need to get her on birth control."

"One thing at a time." He checks the wound and cleans the dried blood, grabbing a hemostat. "Three stitches should be enough. You'll feel a bit of pressure."

Layla stills, frozen like a statue. The fear etched into her expression cuts me so deep I feel like my lungs are filling up.

I wheel a chair from the desk to the bed and take her hands in mine. "How was the party?"

She starts breathing again but clutches my hands so hard she cuts off circulation. "Julij apologized for Dubai and has been on his best behavior. We had fun." A smile on her lips tells me she can easily imagine my surprise. "I know. I didn't expect it either. Turns out he tried to woo me back then."

"Uh-oh," Carlton smirks.

"No, it's not like that. He's over it, I think."

"Are you telling me you spent the evening babysitting a guy who's in love with you, and you had fun?"

She smiles again, relaxing a bit. Too bad my mental well-being gets the kicking.

"Jealous, are you?"

I ghost my lips over her knuckles. "Not at all."

Carlton fake-coughs, sets the hemostat aside, and moves on to clean the stitched area.

Julij's not one of my enemies. We only met six months ago when I visited my mother in New York. Nikolaj hunted me down and invited me for a drink. He wanted us to work together behind Frank's back, but while they remain business partners, I want nothing to do with the New York King.

Thanks to my partners from Detroit, or their chemist, to be precise, I supply the best coke on the market. More addictive than street shit and less lethal, which means more long-term customers. That's what Nikolaj would love to get his hands on. I've got a good thing going with the V brothers from Detroit, and easy access to the ports from Atlantic City, so Europe's within my reach. New York's closer, sure, but it means working side by side with Frank which won't ever happen, so I shot Nikolaj down.

Julij joined the meeting, acting as if he owned the goddamn state. He was hitting on the waitresses, snapping his fingers at Nikolaj's men, and looking down at me despite being a fucking newbie in this world. I wasn't thrilled that Layla had to deal with him tonight, but she has a knack for putting people in their place. I wasn't too worried before the party. Now, knowing she likes the brat who's apparently in love with her, I want to dislocate his jaw.

"All done," Carlton says. "I put dissolvable stitches in, so no need to come back. Keep it clean, and don't use a brush or sleep on that side. You wouldn't want to pull the stitches now, would you?" He looks at me. "Where the fuck were you when she got hit?"

Layla jumps to her feet, arms akimbo. "I don't need a nanny, thank you very much." She rolls her eyes at the skeptical look on Carlton's face. "I can take care of myself."

He cocks an eyebrow, taken aback by all her sass. "Feisty like her daddy. A bit of supervision won't do you any harm. You're in the middle of a war, Layla. It'll be best if someone's always watching over you."

We'll need to come back some other day for the contraceptive pill. I steer her out of the office before she starts hissing. Carlton will go down like a house of cards if he tries to argue. I pat his shoulder and close the door behind us.

"He didn't mean anything by it, Star."

"I know, but—"

"But you don't like it when people treat you like a clueless princess. I know, but sometimes it's better to let them say what they want."

She crosses her arms with a frown. I'm ready for a snarky remark, but instead of snapping, a satisfied grin twists her mouth. "So, you're jealous?"

She's so adorable, sexy, and fucking irresistible when she holds her bottom lip between her teeth. I push her against the wall, and my teeth replace hers. We've spent so much time together this past month that seven hours without her mouth, scent, and closeness are more than I can handle.

"I am a very territorial man, and you are the *most* prized of my possessions. *Jealous* doesn't begin to cover it." I kiss her forehead. "How sore is my pussy, baby?"

She rests the back of her head against the metal wall of the elevator. "Sore enough that you can forget about round two tonight, baby. I want a hot-water bottle and a big bucket of ice cream."

"Done. We'll stop at the store on the way home."

CHAPTER TWENTY

Dante

Spades waits in the car, with the engine running to keep the inside warm. He looks at me when Layla and I take the back seat. No words are needed. His expression paints the picture perfectly—someone's dead.

The only thing he overlooked tonight is that Layla's not some half-brained bimbo sitting by my side who can't figure out how to put an armrest down, let alone notice that something's wrong. This time, it's Layla.

Intelligent and perceptive Layla.

"Is everything okay?" she asks, sensing the heavy, ominous atmosphere.

"Who?" I counter, praying it's not one of my men.

Spades shakes his head, refusing to talk while Layla listens to our every word. Whatever happened is fucking *bad,* bad.

She rolls her eyes, silently stewing. "I'll wait outside," she clips, not passing on the chance to slam the door on her way out of the car.

"Jackson called," Spades says, forcing me to look away from my girl, who takes her phone out, pressing it to her ear. "Luca got a bit carried away. By *a bit,* I mean a whole fucking lot."

"What did he do?"

"He checked the security footage and found the guy who hit Layla. He split his skull open on the curb."

If there was a wall in front of me right now, my knuckles would bleed. I know the scene Luca based his act upon. Since he first saw *American History*, he wanted to kill someone that way. At the beginning of the movie, there's one of the most brutal scenes in modern cinematography. Luca's a bit psycho, but I didn't expect him to ever take it that far.

"He found him outside," Spades continues. "The guy stood with his friends, cleaning up his face. Jackson followed Luca but thought he was only trying to scare the guy. They argued for a moment before Luca rammed a baseball bat across his knees and made him bite the curb. Before Jackson realized he wasn't fucking around, Luca jumped on the guy's head."

I rub my face, trying to devise the most effective way out of this situation. I can't scold him for defending Layla, but he took it too fucking far. He executed a guy who hit her by accident. She was in the wrong place at the wrong time, and this guy has paid the ultimate price.

"I didn't want to bother you because I know you want to take Layla home, but we've got sixty witnesses. It's a matter of minutes before the cops raid the place."

A long conversation with the chief of police is unavoidable. If charged, Luca will get a life sentence for murdering the guy in cold blood. Twenty-five years if I bribe relevant people. The problem is that Luca is one of my most trusted men. Given their bumpy start, it's surprising he defended Layla to this extent, but I can't leave him alone in this shit.

I own the cops, but with sixty witnesses and the footage, there's no way of sweeping this under the carpet. The only light in the long, dark tunnel is Plan B.

Layla remains outside, talking over the phone, scraping her heel on the pavement. She makes her agitation known by sporting her signature calculated expression.

"I don't want Layla to see any of this," I say, determined to keep her in the dark. "You'll leave me on the corner of the street, and you'll take her back to my place."

Spades nods, glancing at Layla through the side window. "That's why I didn't want her to hear the news. She'll lose her shit if she finds out that guy is dead."

I open the door, bracing to feel her anger. "Come on, Star. We're leaving."

She turns on her heel, says one more word to whoever she's talking to, and gets in, slamming the door again. Spades performs an unintentional burnout on hospital grounds while Layla stares out the window, a fierce look on her perfect face. God, she's so deep under my skin I feel her everywhere. Everything I do is with her on my mind. Tonight's no exception. Covering up the murder and ensuring it never reaches her ears is my priority. She can't find out. She'd be devastated, and I can't fucking handle her tears.

I try taking her hand, but she jerks it away. "Don't get pissy with me. You can't hear or see it all."

"I *can't*? You don't make decisions for me. I already told you that you don't own me, Dante."

Her attitude is the sexiest thing about her. She's not scared and doesn't care how she'll come across, whether she'll vex me or anyone else. I love that she speaks her mind, but I want to strangle her right now.

"You shouldn't," I hiss, careful not to sound too demanding, or a shit storm will ensue. "I've got to get back to Delta, but it's no place for you to be right now. Spades will take you back to our house."

She clicks her tongue, looking away, her chin high, arms crossed. "Don't rush. Adam's picking me up from Delta. I'm going home."

I grit my teeth so hard they start to fucking crack. Adam informing Frank about the situation is the last thing I need. "Call him and tell him that you changed your mind."

"I haven't. He's on his way now. I'm going home."

I fall into the trap of my own rage. The confined space, Layla's attitude, the problems awaiting in Delta, and Luca's stunt all bubble in my mind like the reaction of sodium bicarbonate with acid. I just want to protect her, keep her safe, calm, and happy, but she makes it fucking impossible.

I grab her by the chin, turning her head my way, so she'll look me in the eye. "Spades will take you home. I don't want to see Adam outside the club, so either call him off or get the fuck out of the car. He can pick you up from here."

"Dante! Let her go, or I'll make you!" Spades snaps. His voice is muffled, like he's on the other side of a glass partition.

My gaze drops to my hand that's gripping Layla's face. I snap out of the haze, throwing myself back against the door. The look in her eyes makes my bones shiver... she's no longer angry, no longer determined to showcase her independence. She's upset. She's fucking *alarmed*.

I open my mouth, but she raises her hand to shut me up. She's not saying a word, staring at me with unseeing eyes.

We stop at the traffic lights by Lincoln Park, and Spades turns around, glaring at me. "Front seat. Right now, Dante!"

No fucking way. I stay where I am, with my back flush against the door as I try to make sense of what just happened. In some twisted, deranged way, my protectiveness of Layla turned against her. I wait for her to speak because I can't utter a single word, mayhem ruling my mind. Ten hours. Just ten fucking hours passed since she told me she loves me, but now she's looking at me with nothing but hatred.

It takes twenty seconds before she reacts. When she does, her small hand lands on my face. "That's strike one." Her voice is quiet but so powerful I feel her wrath as if it's my own. "And one is all you get."

"Fuck, Layla, I'm sorry, I—"

She shoots out of the car, cutting me off midsentence.

Spades locks the doors the second I twitch to follow her. "What the fuck is wrong with you?"

"Open the door." I yank the handle. "Open the door, or I'll break the window."

He glances to the right to check on Layla. She's walking in the opposite direction, a phone to her ear, her long navy dress brushing the sidewalk.

"I'll break your hands if you touch her like that again."

He should've done it just now. This is the first and last time I will ever vent my rage on Layla. The simple fact that she's not scared tells me it's not the first or even the tenth time she's been treated that way. She's immune to this shit. I don't want to be another violent guy in her life. There are enough of those already. I'm supposed to be the one she'll feel safe with, the one she'll trust.

Well, I fucked that up beautifully.

Layla rests by a streetlamp, pulling the coat tighter around her delicate frame as I approach.

"I'm sorry," I say. "Nothing justifies what I just did."

"You're right. Nothing does. I'm manhandled by Frank and his men all the time. There's nothing I can do to stop that; to rid them of my life. But this," she points between us. "This is different. I *can* rid you. I *don't* have to agree to this, and I *won't.*"

The meaning of her words hits me like a tsunami. The wave consumes everything in its path, killing thousands of people. It leaves nothing but destruction behind. Layla's words, the mere thought of losing her, have the same effect on me. It strips me of everything I care about, leaving nothing but emptiness behind.

She pushes away from the post when a car stops by the curb. She walks past me, and I turn around to see Adam. Layla motions for him to get back inside, taking the passenger seat, eyes on me as she holds the door open. "If you ever do that again, you can forget about me." With that, she slams the door, and Adam drives away, the tires squealing on the road.

A rush of adrenaline ignites my nerve endings, and my heart picks up its rhythm. She's livid, but she's still mine. That's all I need to know, not to lose my goddamn mind, but my fist lands on the metal of the streetlamp regardless.

I don't fucking deserve that girl. Not by a long shot.

Spades gets out of the car. "She dumped your sorry ass yet?" I shake my head. "She should've."

"Tell me something I don't know," I say, getting back in the car. "Come on. We've got shit to do."

Ten minutes later, a sea of red and blue lights greets us in front of the club. Six police cars are parked on the road, and two ambulances by the entrance. The only thing missing is the fucking SWAT team. I light a cigarette, walking up to the chief of police, Jeremy, who stands over a black bag. We're friends, for the lack of a better word. He charges a lot to make ninety-nine percent of my problems disappear, but one glance at his face is enough to know that the mess Luca created is not an easy fix.

"If it isn't the boss." He holds his hand out for me to shake, an ear-to-ear grin taking the width of his face as he bends down to unzip the body bag. "Awesome party!"

The guy's face is split wide open; his jaw is unnaturally twisted. He's missing eight, maybe ten teeth and a big chunk of his tongue. The skin from the broken nose lies on his cheek. The dirt mixes with dried blood that must've oozed from every hole, including his bloodshot eyes.

I let out all the air from my lungs, looking away, back at Jeremy. "Let's talk in my office."

He instructs his men to get rid of the onlookers before he follows me inside the empty club. The sound of our shoes tapping on the floor echoes throughout the place. Spades stops by the bar to grab a bottle of the most expensive bourbon.

Jeremy sits on the sofa with a loud sigh, wiping the non-existent sweat off his forehead with a silk handkerchief. "What a night," he chirps. "So? What's the story, Carrow? What happened?"

I rest against the desk. "No idea." Playing dumb is my part. Jeremy enjoys being in the know, and it's my goal to keep him happy. "I was at the hospital."

"Well then, I'll tell you what happened. One of your men, and I know which one because I've got the footage, executed the guy in the black bag, Alex Flemming. The only thing I don't know is why he did it and why here *in* front of so many witnesses. You're not usually this careless, gentlemen. What got into him?"

I offer Jeremy a Cuban cigar. "That'll be one of the first questions I'll ask him."

"You must know why Alex is dead. What did he do?"

"It's complicated," Spades interjects.

"Oh, come on!" Jeremy throws his hands in the air. "It's not like we just met. I'll find out sooner or later. If you start talking, I might be able to help."

I cross the room to sit in front of him. He's right. There's no hiding the reason. "He hit my girl."

"Layla Harston, right?" He claps, overly excited as if watching an episode of his favorite show. "Am I to expect more bodies soon? Is the war coming to an end? You hooked up with Frankie's daughter to get North under control?"

"Layla has nothing to do with what's going on between Frank and me." I'd give my right hand to make sure it stays that way.

Jeremy gestures for Spades to refill his glass. "That's not very exciting. Anyway, back to the murder mystery. You ordered your people to sort the guy out, right?"

"No. Layla found herself in the wrong place at the wrong time." I rest my back on the couch, taking a drag of the cigar. "She got hit by accident. The guy aimed at someone else. A misunderstanding is all it was."

Jeremy pouts, clearly unappeased. "So what? Luca killed Alex out of his own will? Without your order?"

"They don't follow my orders one hundred percent of the

time. You should know, some aren't prone to do as they're told."

He rubs his beard, resting his elbows on his knees. "There's not much I can do, Dante. Someone has to go down for murder. We've got a crowd of witnesses. To make matters worse, Luca's a very colorful character," he says, referring to his tattoos.

"Plan B?"

Plan B came into existence three years ago in similar circumstances. One of my men, Hue, killed a news stand owner at the Water Tower Place in broad daylight. Hue was young, stupid, and hot-headed. Not unlike Luca, he snapped like a dry twig. That's what happened that day—the poor man gave him different cigarettes than he asked for. A life sentence hung above his head when chief Jeremy Smith made an entrance. Aware of my dealings with four ambitious daughters, he was keen to help.

We couldn't pin it as an accident or an unfortunate event, but Jeremy came up with the idea of a look-alike doing time. He gave us a few hours to find the most suitable guy. A seemingly crazy idea, but Spades remembered about someone we met a few months earlier, Barry Baker. A miracle worker. He ran an institution for the worst kind of drug addicts, using them to do the dirty work for mafia bosses all over the US.

Hue had his whole life ahead of him. I couldn't just sentence him to rot in jail, so we made the call. Not long later, Barry entered Delta with Mick, a twenty-year-old junkie addicted to the heaviest drugs. Rehab wasn't helping. He battered his pregnant girlfriend and knew damn well he'd overdose or end up in jail. He chose option number two—voluntarily—for a high price. Including all the bribes, cuts, and money spent on lawyers, the total came close to two million dollars. A high price for one man's life. Especially for the life of a man who hung himself six months later when his girlfriend left him. I could've saved two million, but there's no foreseeing shit like that.

Jeremy clears his throat, rubbing his beard once more. "You've got three hours, Carrow. I want him at the station at six a.m."

Spades waits until the door closes behind Jeremy before he calls Barry to explain the situation and send him Luca's picture. The tattoos pose an issue, but I'll worry if Barry finds the right guy.

I take my phone out to call the idiot. "Get your ass down here *right* now." I let my anger show, hurling a crystal ashtray across the room. It flies an inch from Spades, earning me a *you're-fucking-insane* kind of look.

"I'll be there in twenty," Luca says, his tone like that of a child who broke grandma's tea set while playing soccer in the living room.

Spades finishes the last of his drink, refiling the glass. "What will you do with him?"

"I have no idea." I rest my head on the desk. "I'm tired, pissed off, and something just doesn't fucking fit."

"You mean that Luca argued with Layla every chance he got, but now he killed the guy who hit her?"

I nod, massaging my temples. "I'm missing something."

We sit in silence, buried in our thoughts, waiting for Luca to arrive. I'm also waiting for any sign from Layla. After my fuckup, it's in my best interest to call her, but it has to wait until the morning.

Luca arrives fifteen minutes later, looking like he fled the set of a lame horror movie. Blood covers his shirt, trousers, and shoes. "You want me at the police station?"

"Sit," I snap. "What the fuck happened?"

"I don't know. I watched the footage... I saw Layla trying to escape the brawl." He tugs at his hair. "The guy hit her so fucking hard her head turned." The torment in his eyes makes no fucking sense. He's protective, almost fucking possessive. "Something snapped inside me," he continues, glancing at the floor. "My mind switched off. I was on some kind of autopilot. I wasn't thinking straight."

"Damn right you weren't," Spades clips.

"*Sixty* witnesses!" I boom, and Luca, who's not easily scared, flinches in his seat. "CCTV, a crowd of people, and you *jumped* on his head!" I rest my hands on the side table by the sofa, looking him in the eyes, searching for any emotions; anything that'd prove Luca's still there, that he's not a psychopath. "You know it's a life for this, right?"

He draws his gun, toying with it and looking into the barrel. "I won't rot in jail. I'd rather pull the trigger."

"Put it away. We're waiting for Barry to call."

"Plan B?" Luca meets my eyes.

"Yes, but before I sentence another innocent person, explain why. Two weeks ago, you claimed she was Frankie's spy, but today you risked your freedom for a girl you fucking hate. Two plus two equals five here. Explain because I don't get it!" I say as I stand up.

He hides his face in his hands, motionless for a moment as if he's trying to make sense of it himself. "I don't know why. I can't explain it." He jumps to his feet, pacing the room. "I don't trust her, but it didn't mean shit when I saw that guy hit her. You know my past, Dante."

I move the weight of my body from one foot to the other, lighting a cigarette. I found Luca on the street when he was fourteen. His father beat his mother to death a few days earlier and was sent away, leaving Luca alone. He had nothing; no one to turn to, no house, no money, no hope.

"I used to be passive," Luca says, filling the glass Jeremy used with bourbon. "I couldn't protect my mom, but things are different now. Watching the footage, I remembered all of my mother's bruises."

"That doesn't explain why you took it upon yourself to protect the girl you hate."

He downs the drink, looking at his shoes. It takes a minute before he works up the courage to look at me again. It's unusual for him to cower, but tonight his hesitation is natural. "I didn't stop to think. I saw a woman being hurt, and I snapped. I don't hate her, Boss. I just don't trust her."

A phone halts our conversation.

Barry has found a guy.

CHAPTER
TWENTY-ONE

Layla

I'm tossing in bed as if I have an epileptic fit. Anger dissipated long ago, but sleep doesn't want to take me.

I don't care what happened at Delta and didn't expect details. Not even a summary. A simple *Layla, it'll be better if you don't hear this* would've been enough, but no. They treated me like an idiot, so I snapped.

Dante was right when he said nothing can justify his reaction, but truth be told, I had his outburst coming. When he called me back to the car, I knew something terrible had happened. The tone of his voice and the worry in his emerald-green eyes spoke volumes. My temper didn't help.

Getting me to boil over is easy. Calming me down takes much more effort. With each sentence pouring out of my mouth, I saw Dante's patience wearing thin, but I couldn't stop.

I sit up, rubbing my eyes. My guilty conscience won't let me sleep, so I get out of bed, determined to write my dissertation. Pulling my hair into a bun, I press double espresso on the touch screen of the coffee maker, my phone in hand in case Dante calls. Unlikely considering it's five in the morning, but I hope.

The fault is on both sides, but his sins are bigger.

He scared me enough to warrant a breakup, but the regret dancing in his eyes when he thought I'd leave him crushed me inside out. I'm starting to think clearly once caffeine filters through the noise of my thoughts. Instead of diving into the world of the insane, I grab my keys and leave.

Dante's charger is parked in the open garage when I pull up outside his house twenty minutes later. As I make my way upstairs, an ashtray sits on the countertop next to an empty glass. Clothes litter the bedroom floor, and Dante's asleep, lying on his back. I rest against the wall, watching his chest rise and fall steadily.

A few weeks is all it took for him to take my heart hostage. The one thing I promised myself not to do the day I entered Delta happened faster than I anticipated.

Careful not to wake him, I shimmy out of my clothes, leaving on my red lingerie. Dante wakes up as soon as the mattress dips under my weight.

He sits up, and his hand flies toward the gun on the bedside, but his features soften once he sees it's just me. "God, I'm so fucking glad you're here." He grabs my arm, falling back, cuddling me into his chest, lips on the crown of my head. "I'm sorry, baby. It won't happen again."

"I know. I'm sorry too. I overreacted."

He flips me, so I lay under him, letting out a shaky breath a second before he sinks into my lips, the kiss soft, slow, but full of something more profound than lust. "You've nothing to apologize for." He stamps a kiss on my forehead. "What time is it?"

"Almost six."

"Six? Why are you up already?"

"I couldn't sleep."

"You haven't slept at all?" He rests on his elbow, brushing my hair behind my ears.

"I hate it when we fight."

"That wasn't a fight. If we ever fight, sharp things will fly in my direction." He smirks, pushing his hand under my back to undo my bra.

"What are you doing?"

"Take it off. You'll be uncomfortable."

"No, I won't."

He dips his head to kiss a straight line from my neck to the soft spot between my breasts. "How's my pussy?"

God, that filthy mouth of his...

"Still sore." I squirm when his warm breath fans my abdomen as he hooks his finger under the elastic of my thong.

"I bet I can make it better." With methodical, slow moves, he slides my red lacy panties down my legs, throwing them on the floor. "You smell so fucking edible, baby."

He stares down for a moment, making me squirm. It's the

most intimate yet insanely erotic thing imaginable when he looks me over with hungry eyes, grazing his finger up the inside of my thigh.

He grips my hips, tugging me closer, and leans forward, his face moving between my thighs.

I whimper, weaving my fingers in his hair as his tongue drags over my folds before he latches onto my clit, drawing the sensitive flesh into his mouth.

"Oh God," I gasp, clawing at his shoulders.

I arch my back when he pushes one finger deep into my core, using it as he would his cock... or not. He curls his finger, stroking something deep inside me, and I cry out with full-blown need.

My hips buck, and thighs clench, locking his head in-between. He groans, prying my legs open with one hand, ensuring I'm spread wide for him.

I might be the one on the verge of a violent orgasm, but I know this is for his pleasure, too. I feel how hungry he is for me, lapping and laving my clit, drawing every slight tremor out of me when I start shaking, coming so hard I feel like I'll pass out.

My delirious moans bounce off the walls as Dante prolongs the high, his finger working inside me as he licks and sucks in a delicious, torturous rhythm.

This is addictive, the orgasm so intense and long, bordering on uncomfortable, that it's impossible to hold onto inhibitions. Impossible to care how loud I am or who could hear. I doubt I'd care if someone watched.

"You're so hot when you come," he says, close to my ear, his lips on my neck. "How's my pussy now?"

"Much better." I open my eyes to find him hovering over me with the most arrogant smile ever.

"Told you." He dips his head, kissing my forehead, before he moves over, wrapping his arms around me. "There was a problem at the club—"

"Um," I move away, rising on my elbow to look at him. "What are you... I mean, aren't we having sex?"

"Not until you're no longer sore."

"I'm not that sore. I'll be okay."

"Not until you're no longer sore," he repeats, pulling me back to his chest, his fingers in my hair, toying with a thick tangle. "About last night—"

"I don't want to know. I'm not mad that you didn't tell me. I'm mad because you treated me like someone who doesn't know better. Next time say it'll be better if I don't know, but don't act like I'm too stupid to understand."

"You're not stupid. You're smarter than all the girls of my people put together. I know you're made of a different cloth, but I'm a man. I'll always want to protect you. I always *will* protect you, baby."

I lift my head to peck his lips. "I'll try to tone down a bit."

"Don't. You drive me fucking insane with your godawful attitude, but it's part of your charm. Don't change it. Don't *ever* change, Star. You're exactly how I dreamt you." He kisses me again. "Now shut your beautiful mouth and get to sleep. I'm exhausted, and I need to be up at nine."

✦✧✦✧✦✧✦✧✦✧✦

"Coffee?" The maid asks when I come downstairs around noon.

I slept like a baby, didn't hear Dante's alarm, and didn't feel him wriggle out of my embrace. "Yes. Cappuccino. "

She bobs her head without a smile and retreats to the kitchen. I braid my wet hair into two braids and check the phone to find a voicemail from Frank.

*Nikolaj is coming over for an early dinner. I want you back home
before three.*

The maid enters the room with a silver tray in hand.
"Would you like breakfast?"

"Yes." Dante enters the living room. "Pancakes with honey
for Layla, eggs benedict for me." He leans over the back of
the couch to kiss my head. "Morning. Sleep well?"

"Yes, but looking at your energy, I'm starting to doubt it.
You hardly slept; how can you be so cheerful?"

He shakes his jacket off, throwing the car keys on the
table. "Two coffees, some good news, and my girl waiting at
home might have something to do with it."

"Your girl needs to go home after breakfast. the Capones
are joining us for dinner today." I sigh, rolling my eyes.
"Frank's trying to impress Julij so he doesn't cut him out when
he takes over New York."

Dante sits, creases on his forehead. "Is Nikolaj retiring?"

"He doesn't have much choice. He's got cancer. From what
I gather, it's bad. He's not long left. That's why they flew over,
to tell Frank that Julij's taking over."

Dante seems lost in thought for a moment but snaps out
of it quickly, pointing to something behind me. I look over my
shoulder, and when I turn back around, he's sipping my coffee.

"I don't like that you're spending time with Julij, but at least
you won't be here alone. I have to leave again in an hour."

"Will you be disappearing like this all week? If you will,
can I sneak in here to work on my dissertation?"

"Yes, this is your house. You've got the keys."

"It isn't but thank you. I'd love to return the favor, but you'd leave in a body bag if Frank found you wandering around his house."

A shadow sweeps across Dante's face, forcing the fine hairs on the back of my neck to stand on ends. "Yeah, that's not the best idea."

"Did you know him?"

"Be precise, Star. Who is *him*?"

"The one who ended up in a body bag last night."

A small smile curves his lips. "Clever girl. How did you know? No, I didn't know him."

"I suspected it yesterday, but I wasn't sure, but your body language betrayed you just now." I scoot closer to him, weaving my hand through his hair. "I wanted to know if it was one of your people."

"Don't worry about it. It's been taken care of."

I bob my head, and moments later, we sit at the table to eat breakfast.

CHAPTER TWENTY-TWO

Dante

It nears eight in the evening when I exit the police station. Along with a couple of bribed officers and the chief himself, we schooled Luca's look-alike. He has to know the fabricated story of last night's events by heart.

According to the revised version, Jonathan, the look-alike, walked into Delta around midnight high as a kite. Forged blood results are already on the prosecutor's desk.

He started the brawl, and once security kicked him out, he took his anger out on Alex—the jaw-split-open guy.

Jonathan repeated the story for four hours straight while the chief, police officers, and I corrected the statement so it sounded more believable. The hearing's set for Tuesday, so there's not much time to perfect his testimony.

Getting in my car, I light a cigarette, dialing Spades.

"How did it work out?" he asks.

"If he doesn't change his mind at the last minute, he's going down. He wants McDonald's for dinner. Get it sorted."

"Seriously? He can have caviar, lobster, or the most expensive steak money can buy, but he wants burgers?"

"Get him whiskey and heroin while you're at it."

"Heroin? Fuck. He'll be dead in three months."

I can't disagree. Heroin addicts don't last long in prison. Most overdose in their first year. Jonathan has nothing to lose or gain, no motivation to crawl up from the bottom. "Take it over to him today and another package tomorrow. I want you in court on Tuesday. And call Luca. Tell him to lay his fucking head low until this blows over."

"No problem. I'll make the delivery and call the dumbass."

I make a U-turn in the middle of the road, heading back the way I came. "Did the load from Detroit arrive?"

"We're at the warehouse, waiting. The driver called to say he'll be here in ten. Go home, Dante. I'll take care of it."

Thank fuck. I don't feel like checking the load despite doing so every time since I started working with the V brothers. I'm barely able to keep my eyes open as it is. The only thing on my mind now is a drink, a couch, and Layla whining in my ear that she's bored because there's no fucking way that girl can focus on a movie for longer than five minutes. Sex would be better, but I bet she's still sore, so it'll have to wait.

Half an hour later, after speeding down the interstate, it's time to head home. I call my girl, hoping she has said her goodbyes to Julij and Nikolaj by now.

"Hello?" she shouts over the background noise.

"Where are you?"

"We're bowling, or rather finishing up now. We've got three shots left each. I'm losing! Julij's plane leaves in an hour, so he needs to go soon. Can you pick me up? Can we watch a movie? Or not. Let's go to bed. I'm sleepy."

I rest my forehead on the steering wheel, closing my eyes. She's a little chatterbox when she's tipsy, and I'm too tired to get annoyed. "How much did you drink?"

"Not much, just a glass of wine and two small drinks, but I haven't eaten since breakfast. Cream of mushroom with wet bread was served for dinner... *eww.*"

At least she's in a good mood.

"Where are you? I'll pick you up."

"Oh, okay. Tenpin on State Street."

"I'm on my way. And baby? No more drinking."

"I promise."

Twenty minutes later, I enter the bowling alley. The stench of burnt fries, burgers, and beer hangs in the air. Layla's at the back of the room in a snow-white girly dress. Loose hair frames her glowing face as she laughs, holding an orange bowling ball. She pushes her shoulders back, taking a firm stance, turning to face the lane. Instead of putting her fingers in the holes, she throws the ball as if playing basketball. No wonder she's losing. I want to take her home but can't let her fail like that. She needs to learn how to play properly. I pay for a few more games, ready to save my girl from embarrassing herself. Repeatedly.

"You came!" Layla jumps, wrapping her hands around my neck, her sweet lips on mine for a hot kiss.

Good thing Julij stands nearby and takes the tray of drinks from me in time, or it'd end up on my shirt.

"How are you getting on, Star?"

"Great! I knocked over three pins!"

A guy from the other lane looks at her with a frown. "Too bad they weren't yours."

"Yeah, sorry about that," I throw two tokens for two more games for him to catch.

He mumbles something that must be *thanks*, turning back to his friends.

"I'm out." Julij motions to the screen when I start a new game, adding my name to the list. "I've got a plane to catch, but I want to talk to you."

That I didn't expect. Nikolaj and Frank go back years. I thought Julij would want to maintain their working relationship once Nikolaj dies, but the look on his face says something entirely different.

"Layla told me things are changing in New York."

He nods, glancing at her with a fond smile I want to wipe off with my fist. I don't like the guy, but if working with him means stealing the last ally from Frank, then I'm game. Frank is too weak to handle things on his own. He has no authority left in the world. He won't be able to hold on for long if he part ways with New York.

Entering a business partnership with Julij will prove impossible if I start off by battering his face. Besides, Julij might not be the brightest bulb in the box, but he won't touch Layla, knowing she's mine. He knows it'll end in his fucking funeral.

"I'm glad she didn't keep the news to herself. New York will soon be under my command. I'll decide who I'm doing business with. I hope in Chicago it won't be Frank." Julij is acting differently from six months ago. He's being respectful and humble, as if he realized I'm superior.

"I'll be in New York soon with Layla. We can talk over the details then."

"Layla shouldn't be involved in any of this."

"That's one thing we agree on. Not bad for a start." I smirk, handing him my business card. "She's got things to do in New York. She won't be in the way."

He shakes my hand and then walks over to Layla to kiss her cheek. With one last fond look at her, he leaves.

"So?" Layla grabs a bowling ball. "Shall we?"

Instead of the lighter ball she holds, I hand her the heaviest. "Put your fingers here."

"I don't want to. Those holes are too big."

I drape my hand around her waist, pulling her flush to my chest. "Do as I say, Star." With a pout, she puts her fingers in the holes, letting me move her hand back and forth. "Let go."

The ball rolls down the lane at a turtle's pace before hitting the middle pin that tumbles over, knocking one more on the way down. Two is better than zero.

"It's too heavy!"

"Exactly. You won't throw it far. Focus on the floor, not the pins, Layla. Don't twist your wrist."

She holds the ball in both hands, but after another pout, she slides her fingers in the holes. Eight pins fall, and Layla jumps around me, beaming. There is nothing more peaceful than seeing her happy.

"Can we go home now?" she asks, pressing herself into my chest as she rises on her toes to speak in my ear. "I want you to take me to bed."

I gather the white fabric of her dress in a tight fist on her lower back. "Are you still sore?"

She smiles against my skin, tracing open-mouthed kisses below my earlobe. "No, but I am very, *very* wet."

I exhale a shaky breath, my mind swimming with the images of last night, the way she looked when she came. "Good girl. Always tell me when you want me." I grab her hand, taking her back to my car, eager to hear her moans.

I want to see her hooded eyes, enlarged pupils, and rosy cheeks. Her lips on my skin, nails digging into my back. I want to inhale the scent of her perfume, have her sweet breath on my cheek, and feel her fingers in my hair... the warmth of her hot, petite body, hissing, shivering and moaning. I want her to tell me she loves me.

Twenty minutes later, we're home. The second we step through the threshold, I lift her into my arms, my mouth on hers as I climb the stairs. My shirt lands on the bedroom floor, and seconds later, it turns into a pile of clothes.

She's so fucking beautiful naked on the bed, her face framed by a veil of dark hair. I take her hard, candy-pink nipple between my lips, my hands on her sides. I'm high on the scent of her skin and the sound of her breathless moans. Everything I feel for her rushes to the surface, boiling beneath my skin, overwhelming my mind. I'm never letting her go.

"It'll only feel good now, Star," I say, feeling her tense when I glide my hand lower between her legs to circle her clit with two fingers. "I'll show you just how good sex can be. You'll learn how to enjoy your body."

She bites her lower lip, ghosting her fingertips over my jaw when I push two fingers deep inside, making her gasp. She was too anxious last night to enjoy sex. Time to fix that.

I curl my fingers, stroking her G-spot, watching her pleasure build higher. She gets to the edge so fucking fast... I may already be addicted to feeling her walls spasm.

"I love you," she moans, throwing her head back as the orgasm rumbles through her in a series of intense vibrations.

"You're so sensitive." I bring her down slowly, pumping my fingers slower every time, and I move away to stare at her blissful, glowing face. "Get on your hands and knees."

She cocks an eyebrow but obeys, rolling onto her stomach before she gets onto all fours, her hair draped over one shoulder, exposing the nape of her neck. I lean over, my cheek against hers, one hand snaked around collarbones, the other on the mattress, supporting my weight.

I bite her earlobe, slipping inside slowly, dizzy with the heat radiating from her body. Layla arches back, touching her head to my shoulder, her lips parted, eyes closed, hands fisting the sheets.

The most arousing sight of all—my girl in my arms, in ecstasy, in *love*. I let the primal hunger have its way, driving into her like I'm on a fucking mission. I am. On a mission to see her lose herself time and time again. It doesn't take a lot to have her writhing with my name on her lips. I already know I'll be spending a lot of time making her come on my fingers in the most unusual places just to see how fast I can get her there under pressure.

"Oh, God," she gasps, clawing at my hand when I knot our fingers. "Don't stop, I'm-I'm..."

"You're almost there. Let go, Layla. Don't hold back. Let yourself feel."

She bites the pillow, coming so hard her knees buckle. Her orgasm triggers mine, exploding from the base of my spine, through my shaft, and into Layla. We're both breathless when I collapse beside her, resting on my elbow to kiss her nose. She smiles, cuddling into the pillow with a soft sigh.

"You've got to be kidding me." I tug on the sheets when she covers herself up. "You think I'm done with you? I'm not. You're in for the most exhausting night of your life. You'll be too fucking weak to crawl out of bed tomorrow."

"I need to be at college by ten."

"You need to open your legs for me, baby. You've got a lot to learn tonight." I move to the edge of the bed, hooking my elbows under her knees. "Lesson one: in bed, I make the rules." I lick her, bottom to top. "Lesson two: when I want this sweet pussy... you better give it to me."

CHAPTER TWENTY-

Dante

I stopped at nothing for two weeks to make sure Layla didn't find out about what happened at Delta. I bribed people daily, isolated her from the news, and broke a few jaws. Just when I thought the whole thing had blown over, and she'd long forgotten about it, a bold title appeared on the first page of the newspaper—*A mob hit gets out of control.*

Fucking assholes printed it on the day we're supposed

to fly to New York. As if they couldn't have waited one day extra. On Fridays, the newspaper is handed out for free everywhere in the city—including Layla's college. There's no way she missed the article written by Max Grover, who relayed the statement presented in court. Then, he spewed his own truth, relying on anonymous sources as he speculated that the dead man was the same one who hit Layla.

It doesn't matter who helped him write the article. The article itself doesn't fucking matter. Johnathan's been locked up for over a week. The case is closed. The problem is that the only person who wasn't supposed to know a thing now knows everything. I'm faced with a massive moral dilemma: to lie or not to lie.

It's almost five o'clock, and Layla's due home any minute. I didn't have time to take her to college this morning, so she took her car instead. The flight to New York leaves in three hours, and I wonder if I'll be boarding the plane alone.

The sound of the alarm being disarmed rumbles through the quiet house like a clap of thunder when Layla enters the room. She rounds the bar in silence, a folded newspaper in hand. I watch her every move, muscles in my neck and shoulders painfully tense. The ringing silence doesn't bode well. I'm growing painfully aware that she's fucking brainwashed me. Before I met her, I would've screamed at or dismissed a girl who'd dare question my ways, but I can't yell at Layla. I'm physically incapable of raising my voice after the outburst two weeks ago that almost cost me our relationship.

Now, she's upset again. Guilt prickles at my eyes like an allergy. I should've seen the article coming. I should've known someone would try to uncover the truth, and I should've stopped it before it saw daylight. But I failed.

I failed to protect my star.

She places the paper on the countertop, letting it roll out, the bold title like a slap on my cheek. Layla turns to fill a glass with wine and swallows half in one go.

Not good.

She turns my way again, her eyes glistening with fresh tears, chin quivering as she holds her finger up, refusing to admit her weaknesses. Despite having a valid reason to be upset, she's embarrassed about not handling the news better, making me realize once again that she's too strong for her own good. Stronger than she fucking should be.

She wasn't able to be weak around Frank. He doesn't respect that. Layla's one of the toughest people I know, but it fucking kills me that standing three feet from me, someone she should feel one hundred percent comfortable with, she fights to prove she's tough.

"Is it true?" she asks, wiping the tears away.

There's only so much a person can take... Layla can't take much more, but it doesn't stop her from trying. A rush of inordinate protectiveness spreads inside me like a contusion below the skin. I round the bar to pull her into my arms, but she steps back.

I expected many things: screaming, arguing, and punching, to name a few, but not this. I fist my hands, unsure if she's afraid or just angry. Her sadness, coupled with not knowing, shatters my composure.

"Layla..."

"Don't lie." It sounds like a plea, but her attitude changes, anger replaces sadness as if it's easier to control. "You had him *killed?* He didn't do anything..." She's not shouting, not raising her voice, but I feel her rage. "How could you?"

"I didn't have him killed, star. I didn't even want to punch him." My teeth clench because that's a fucking lie... I won't do it to Layla. "Okay, I did, but I wasn't going to look for him." of course, I wanted to punch the fucker. I wanted to break his hands ten different ways.

"So what happened to him? Why is he dead?" Fresh tears dance in her gray eyes. "He's dead because of me."

I catch her hand, ignoring the weak protest, and pull her into my arms. "It's not your fault."

She presses her face to my shirt, tears staining the fabric. "It is. If I weren't there, if I stayed home, if—"

"If you weren't mine?"

She jerks away, shoving her finger in my chest. "If you didn't love me, nothing would've happened!"

If I didn't love her... Is that possible? I crossed a line at some point, and I don't know when.

This is it.

She is *it* for me.

I'm over my head in love with her. I'm fucking terminal, and I won't make it without her.

"Promise that you didn't have him killed," she whispers, drinking the rest of her wine.

"I swear." I cup her face, wiping her cheeks with my thumbs. "If anyone ever hurts you and I decide they should die, I'll kill them myself. Understood?"

It's not a confession she wants to hear, but like a good girl, she nods, biting her lip, and sits at the bar. I stand behind her, one arm snaked around her collarbones as I kiss the crown of her head. It's supposed to calm *her*, but it does more to calm me.

She has the right to know what happened, but the truth will only cause more trouble. The guy who's in jail isn't the one who killed. All Layla will see is that another innocent person's life was ruined because of her.

I sit beside her, taking a cigarette out of the packet. "Do you want to know what happened?"

"No. I know it's my fault. I know you didn't kill him... I don't need more." She slides off the stool. "I'll go and pack."

I catch her hand. "I hate seeing your tears, but I'd rather see you cry than see you try to hide how you really feel. Don't ever do that around me again. You don't have to pretend when you're with me."

She leans down to kiss me with a small, sad smile.

We arrive at 165 East 72nd Street just before midnight. Isla greets us as soon as the elevator doors open in the living room of her apartment on the top floor. She embraces Layla, kissing her cheeks, excited beyond reason. She's loved my girl ever since I mentioned she existed. She's probably chosen the church, the wedding dress, and the names of her future grandkids.

Layla would start interrogating my mother if it weren't that late, but she had to settle for a good night's sleep in my arms. I lie awake most of the night, wondering about the future. Nikolaj's death will be the beginning of an end.

With Julij refusing to work with Frank, and Nikolaj's protection dying with him, Frank will be left with nothing. Chicago is too small for us both. One has to bow out, but neither of us will do so voluntarily.

It's almost four in the morning when I last check the time. I'm not surprised I don't find Layla beside me when the alarm rings at nine.

"What time did you get up?" I ask, finding her at the dining room table with my mother. A tape recorder is next to her coffee, and Isla watches us from above her rimless glasses, a full-blown smile stretching her thin lips.

"About two hours ago. I wanted to go over my notes, but your mom was up, so we got straight to work."

Isla twitches in her seat, running her long fingers through her short hair. "She's amazing, Dante... so intelligent."

"That she is." I snatch Layla's coffee, stepping away when she frowns. "I'm glad you're getting along because I need to leave for a while."

"You're leaving? Without breakfast?" Isla scowls. "I'll get Marie to fix something for you in no time."

I'm nearing my thirties, but she still treats me like a five-year-old. "I don't have time for breakfast, Mom." Ignoring the disapproving look, I crouch by Layla, resting my hands on her thighs. "I need to take care of something. I won't be long."

"I'll be fine." She kisses my forehead. "I doubt you'd find this interesting, so go ahead."

I hand her the half-empty cup back, grab the keys to a rental Camaro, throwing my jacket on.

"Baby?" Layla stops me as I leave the room. "Say *hi to* him for me."

I'm either getting worse at hiding things from her, or she's too perceptive. Probably the latter. I enter the elevator but march back into the dining room before pressing any buttons.

"Did you forget something?"

"Yes." I stop in the doorway. "Don't leave the penthouse without me, Star. Call me if you need me."

"Was he always so bossy?" she asks my mother.

"Layla, I mean it."

The sleepless night and the possible scenarios that played in my head turned my protectiveness up a notch. It's irrational, but I can't do much about it.

She gets up, resting her hands on my chest, and pecks my cheek, too polite to kiss my lips in front of Isla. "I'll be here. Bye, bye for now. I'm busy."

I smirk, remembering she used those words to get rid of Adam when he rang her the first night she came to Delta.

Julij texted me earlier with the address for what turns out to be a restaurant when I park by the curb outside of the modern building in the heart of New York. One of Julij's henchmen mans the door, standing still like a Grenadier Guard outside Buckingham Palace.

"Take the stairs," he says, with a harsh accent.

All of Nikolaj's men are Russian. It looks like Julij decided to uphold the tradition and surround himself with his fellow countrymen. I walk past a long bar and row of tables by the wall, then climb the stairs.

Out of the corner of my eye, I notice two more henchmen standing in front of the emergency exit. The décor upstairs matches downstairs—dark brown tables, navy chairs, and bricks on the walls.

Julij sits by a large window overlooking the main street. "I'm glad you're here," he says, shaking my hand. "How was the flight? What did you do with your beauty?"

"Layla's at my mother's."

Julij sheds his suit jacket, hanging it over the back of his chair. "Excuse the time, but we can talk without witnesses while the place is closed. Coffee?"

"Yeah, black, one sugar. Is this your place?"

"It is. You like it?"

"Looks good..." One of his henchmen sets down a small tray in front of me and moves away, taking his colleague with him. They descend the stairs, leaving us alone to talk. "You mentioned working together. I'm open to offers."

Julij gets up to fetch us an ashtray. "I've been keeping an eye on you for a while. You've got a knack for business, Dante. You gained powerful allies despite not having Nikolaj's protection. It's one hell of an accomplishment to go from nothing to building the largest network in the country."

Smuggling drugs with the V brothers from Detroit is the most profitable part of business, but apart from drugs, I smuggle alcohol, tobacco, and, recently, petroleum.

People approach me daily, offering their services, but I can't stretch my wings because of Frank and his involvement with Nikolaj. Some of the most influential bosses in the US are Nikolaj's puppets. It wouldn't end well if I tried to undermine their activities.

"You deal under Frank's nose, often with his people, but he has no idea."

"Frank's business is failing because he is too focused on getting rid of me."

"Nikolaj suffers the consequences now, but soon, it'll be me," Julij clips. "He protects Frank because of their past. Otherwise, someone would have killed him by now."

Frank and Nikolaj's story began twenty years ago. Their lives intertwined during those years in many ways. Frankie used to tell me stories about how Nikolaj arrived in Chicago from Russia with his brother, wife, and Julij. He opened a restaurant in the city where, weeks later, Frank met both him and Jess. He was starting his career in the mob at the time, working for Dino,

Nikolaj didn't care about the mafia until the restaurant went bust ten years ago. Frank convinced Dino to help Nikolaj get back on his feet. At Dino's request, Nikolaj moved to New York and started working for the old boss. It quickly became apparent that Nikolaj is much better at cooking meth than stroganoff. He took over the city two years later. It wouldn't be a lie to say that Nikolaj made his fortune thanks to Frank.

Then the tables turned. After Dino's death, everyone put a cross on Frank. He was Dino's right-hand man, yet he killed him. Everyone who ever dealt with Dino moved to work with the boss from New York—Nikolaj; it was his turn to take Frank under his wings and offer protection.

"Whatever happened to your uncle?" I ask. "Frankie told me years ago that Nikolaj came here with his brother, but I never met him."

"Anatolij? He wasn't here long. Less than a year, I think. I don't know what happened, but he and Nikolaj fell out. They're still not talking."

"What does he do now?"

"I don't know who to compare him to..." He pauses for a minute, then bursts out laughing. "Too bad Layla's not here. She'd enjoy this. Anatolij is in Russia like Al Capone was in America. He lives in Moscow. There isn't anyone in the whole country who could mess him about. Anyway, while Nikolaj's alive, Frank rules Chicago, but in a few months, the city will be yours. The *whole* city."

"So, what's your plan? You want to kill Frank?"

"Only if everything else fails." Julij surrounds himself with a cloud of smoke. "I simply won't do business with him when Nikolaj dies. If he steps aside, he'll be safe. But even if I let him live, he won't last six months unless he flees the country. He turned many people into enemies. Very unforgiving enemies."

That's not surprising. For six years, instead of taking advantage of the help offered, rebuilding his name, and creating the network he used to crave, Frank has tried everything to regain the South. I heard about deals gone wrong, FBI raids, and blatant murders. And that's just a drop in the ocean. Like a racing horse, Frank wears blinders, scheming to eliminate me from the picture. The only thing he won't do is put a bullet through my head.

Not without reason.

Eight years ago, we did our weekly rounds collecting money from the brothels that paid Dino for drugs and protection. One of the owners refused to pay. Marcus was a gambler; he used to lose a lot in the casinos, but that night he lost half a million dollars. He was high, probably drunk too, and when we walked into his office, he greeted us with a .44 Magnum. He aimed the gun at Frank's head... I did the first thing that sprung to mind—I shoved Frank aside when Marcus slid his finger to the trigger, drew my gun, and shot him just as he fired his gun. The bullet intended for Frank hit the door.

He can't kill me. He owes me his fucking life.

Julij's smarter than I give him credit for. Working with me once he is in charge is one of the more prudent strategic moves he can make. He's new in our world. He doesn't know people or the rules. Nobody respects or trusts him yet. Nikolaj kept him in the shadows too long, and now Julij needs a way in. He needs *me*. He needs someone who's respected, trusted, and feared. In return, he can give me something I crave: cut Frank out of the picture; stop doing business with him, and consequently rob him of protection.

"Frank won't step down voluntarily." I light a cigarette, throwing the packet on the table.

"I'd be surprised if he did, but he knows his protection dies with Nikolaj. I hoped Layla would force the two of you to forget about your differences, but after my chat with

Frank, I realized he'll never forgive you. You have to stay safe, Dante. Keep Layla safe too."

I shake my head. "That's a miss. Frank won't kill me. If he could, he would've tried a long time ago, and Layla's his daughter. He's one evil fucker, but he won't hurt her."

"Do you really think he won't kill you when it comes down to you or him?" He puts the cigar out, resting his elbows on the table. "I hear he's looking for a hitman."

"Let him look." I brush it off despite the news coming as a surprise. "Don't worry about Layla or me."

I don't like the idea of Layla under someone's watchful eye at all times. She hates being controlled, and I really can't see Frank hurting his own daughter.

Julij's jaw works furiously. "Don't be careless. Are you honestly one hundred percent certain Frank won't use Layla? Maybe he won't hurt her, but when he finds himself against a wall, she'll be his only way out of this shit, and he *will* use her. If I know you'll give up everything for her, then Frank knows it too."

Maybe he has a point. Desperate men do desperate things. Frank is desperate. The ground is slipping from under his feet, and he'll soon be buried alive.

"You have someone you can trust, or should I send my people to Chicago to watch over your girl?"

"I don't surround myself with people I don't trust."

I don't have to think about who Layla's bodyguard will be. She won't be pleased, but recent events prove that Luca's perfect for the job. He'll stop at nothing to keep her safe, and *safe* is all I need her to be if I'm to function like any other sane person.

CHAPTER
TWENTY-FOUR
Layla

Isla's a remarkable woman. Positive, warm, and cheerful. She never stops smiling. Everything brings her joy. Since I woke up, she must've hugged me a dozen times. It'd take Jess ten years to top that, which makes spending time with Dante's mother rather difficult. She appreciates me for who I am, making me painfully aware of how much I crave the same from my parents.

Expecting them to hug me daily is out of the question—miracles don't happen—but if they'd take an interest in my life, I'd be the happiest person alive.

"What are you thinking about, sweetie?" Isla's melodic voice erases my troubles as if she wiped a whiteboard clean.

"It's nothing... could you play something for me?"

"I'm mainly a composer, but I'll take out my violin for you, sweetie." She squeezes my hand with a fond smile. "I want you to know I'm thrilled that my son fell in love with you, Layla. He's different around you. Happy, relaxed. And the way he looks at you? I've never seen him care so much."

I force a smile while my heart breaks bit by bit. I love him more than I ever thought possible and hate myself for it. I hate myself for trusting Frank and following his orders.

"I care about him too. More than he'll ever know."

I lose my boots, getting comfortable on the cream couch decorated with green pillows as I wait for Isla to come back with her violin. The maid brings over a stool, leaving it in the doorway leading to the dining room. Isla climbs onto it, readjusts the elegant dress, and places the violin between her chin and left shoulder, holding the bow in her right hand.

"My father used to listen to your music all the time. I loved one piece the most. It was a slow melody. Like a lullaby."

Isla's eyes stop glowing with the contagious positivity, her smile slips, and tears dance in the corners of her eyes.

I pluck the courage to ask about something I've suspected since Dante told me who his mother is. "There was something between you, wasn't there?"

"Dante's right. You're very clever."

"I can add two and two together."

"It was a short affair. A misunderstanding," she says, repentant. "A stupid mistake."

"You don't have to explain." I sit up, tugging on the sleeves of my sweater. "I don't blame you. My parents' marriage is a farce. They're together only because of Frank's image. I assume Dante doesn't know about this?"

She shakes her head. "He doesn't. I'd appreciate it if it stayed that way." She puts the violin on her knees, her shoulders tense. "Dante's father passed away when he was fifteen. I didn't handle it well. Dante ran to his uncle in Chicago soon after that, and a few months later, I found out what career my son chose." She wrinkles her nose, visibly burdened by the past. "I flew over there to change his mind and met your father. It was the wrong time. I was mourning my husband, and—" She blushes, shaking her head.

"And you need a distraction," I finish for her. "He loved you, didn't he?"

"Very much. We were only seeing each other for two months, but your father was ready to divorce your mother. I broke him when I left, but he took it like a man. He mentored Dante for years. He always had his best interests at heart. I think that deep down, he hoped I'd change my mind."

I can't help but wonder how different my life would've turned out if Isla had stayed with Frank. She couldn't have known, but their short affair had indescribable repercussions. Frank's broken heart changed him forever, and Dante's betrayal was the last nail in the coffin.

"I think he stopped hoping a long time ago," I say, offering Isla a small, sympathetic smile.

Isla picks the violin up, inhaling deeply as she touches the bow to the violin's strings. The soft, familiar melody brings back memories of all the evenings I sat in the living room with Frank, surrounded by darkness and this masterpiece. Instead of watching cartoons, I listened to classical music because it meant spending time with my Dad. He was happy back then, peaceful. I miss him. I miss the person he was before he killed Dino, and Chicago was split in half.

Frank was never a great father, but back then, he was *present*. Six years ago, he became uncatchable like smoke.

Isla finishes playing, but I remain curled in a ball, buried under an avalanche of memories. It's not until she pulls me into a tight hug that I snap out of it.

The characteristic sound of the elevator doors sliding open resonates throughout the penthouse. Dante walks in, eyes on me, his muscles instantly tense.

"What's wrong?"

"Nothing. Your mom played the violin for me."

"You're just in time," she points toward the dining room. "Lunch will be ready in ten."

"Give us a minute, Mom." He helps me up when she leaves. "I'll ask again, Star. This time I expect you not to lie." He curls his finger under my chin. "What's wrong?"

"Your mom's amazing." I rest my forehead on his chest. "She's been lovely all morning, kept calling me *sweetie*, and hugged me every few minutes as if I'm her daughter. She even played the violin when I asked, and I realized how awful my parents really are."

He kisses the top of my head, but I turn toward the dining room, not letting him speak. There's nothing he can say to change reality.

The flight back home and the thirty minutes we spent in the cab were unnaturally silent. On our way to the airport in New York, Dante picked up a call, and after twenty seconds, during which he said three words, his good mood evaporated.

Three hours of silence is long enough.

"What do you feel like doing?" I ask, watching him drop our bags by the staircase. "Should I pick a movie?"

He doesn't answer, rounding the bar as if he hadn't heard me to pour himself a drink, staring at the glass.

I hug his back when he sits at the bar. "You're not here, baby. Is everything okay? Did something happen?"

He presses his lips to my wrist, mindlessly spinning the glass. "It's nothing, Star. Pick a movie. I'll grab a shower."

I collapse on the couch, taking the remote control with me. Dante's distraught. I want to distract him, but I don't know how... I turn the TV on, then switch it off when a thought flashes in my mind. I follow him upstairs, stripping off my clothes in the bedroom, and tiptoe to the bathroom wearing nothing but white lingerie. Clouds of steam, thick like cigar smoke, hang in the air.

Dante stands motionless with his back to me, his head under the stream of hot water, hands resting on the wall. My heart slams against my ribs, and my hands feel damp. He hasn't touched me yet, but it doesn't stop my breath from slowing or my lungs not filling to capacity.

He turns around as if he can sense my presence, his eyes roving my body before meeting my gaze.

The muscles in my abdomen contract when he parts his lips. Water trickles down his tattooed arms and broad chest. Worry disappears from his face when I slide my thumbs under the fabric of my panties, pulling them down until they fall to the ground.

Dante's eyes turn darker with intense desire. Hot, misty air fans my face, sending chills down my spine when he slides the shower door open.

He doesn't wait longer. He grabs my waist and breathes out, sinking into my lips like a starving man, but this is not what I had in mind. We've been in bed two, sometimes three times a day during the last two weeks. He taught me many different things, but there's one thing we haven't got to yet. One thing that I'm eager to try.

I drop to my knees, wrapping my hand around his stiff, long cock, and close my lips on the swollen head.

"Fuck," he growls, fisting my hair. "Layla..."

I take him deeper, cutting his incoming protest short, and glance up at his aroused face. The fire dancing in his eyes eradicates my unease, the irrational worry that I won't do a good job. I twirl my tongue, licking off the first salty drop, exhilarated by his taste.

The control I have while my hand pumps in sync with my mouth makes me press my hips together in desperate need of friction. Every one of his hastened breaths, every growl, and tug on my hair fuel my desire.

"That's it, good girl," he mutters. "Faster, baby."

Muscles in my abdomen spasm when he grips my head, adjusting my moves to his preference. I let him because, in bed, he makes the rules. He's in control.

He holds me still, moving his hips, filling my mouth with more inches, and the head of his cock hits the back of my throat. "Ready for me, Star?" he rasps. "In or out?"

I claw at his thighs, holding him in place. The low, satisfied growl rumbling deep within his chest sends a jolt of electricity zapping through my body. Two more moves, and he comes, spilling in my mouth, his body rigid for a few intense seconds before he slides out with a soft pop.

He's breathing faster as he looks down at me, wiping a trickle of his cum from the corner of my lips. "You've no idea how beautiful you are when you're on your knees for me." He hauls me up, pinning me against the tiles. "My turn."

CHAPTER TWENTY-FIVE

Dante

"You've got a snitch among your people."

My informant's words echo in the depths of my mind. If Layla hadn't barged into the bathroom, willingly dropping to her knees for me last night, I would've left her to meet up with Spades and Nate.

Finding the rat is a priority.

Obviously not that fucking big, considering I preferred a surprisingly good blowjob and an hour-long session in bed with my girl over preparing a plan of action to find the mole.

My priorities have been in the drain since she came along. It'll fucking get me killed if I don't cap the crazy.

Just like I have someone among Frank's men, Frank has a snitch among mine. Until recently, I knew who the double agent was—James. He became a part of my crew by accident, stumbling upon a business meeting gone bad. He witnessed Spades torturing a scumbag who owed me half a million dollars. I had two choices: kill him or employ him. I chose the latter. My bad. Three weeks later, Nate discovered that James was working for *Daddy dearest.*

Frank's not as lucky. I didn't plant a new guy among his people. No, I recruited someone who has worked with him for years. Someone he trusts—Kyle Shaner, first cousin of Frank's great uncle's daughter. Or something along those lines.

Kyle rang when Layla and I were on our way to the airport, heading home. He hadn't yet found the identity of the snitch but said that Frankie knew about my meeting with Julij, which narrows down the list of suspects.

If not for the difficult choice, sex with Layla or chit-chat with Spades, I would've dragged my most trusted people out of bed to form a plan of action and find the fucking snitch. Knowing *who* means I get to control what he reports back to Frank. Not long before I met Layla, James vanished. The coincidence didn't strike me as odd until now. My natural suspiciousness takes over, posing irrational questions and making me wonder if Layla walking into my life was just luck. Not many people knew about my meeting with Julij. My main entourage, Julij's people, and *Layla.*

I squeeze the bridge of my nose. Nikolaj's imminent death, and the long-awaited changes it foreshadows, I doubt everyone for no good reason. Layla can't be a spy. She stays out of my work at all costs, so she has nothing to tell Frank. And it's not like she's fond of the guy.

She loves me.

She said it more times than I can fucking count.

The snitch could be anyone, really; someone smart enough to connect my visit to New York with the brief time Nikolaj has left, one of my guys' girls, or even Frank himself. He's a manipulative bastard, after all. He could've guessed I met with Julij and fed the idea to his people to catch the mole he knows I have up North.

It's eight in the morning, but Layla's no longer in bed. Naughty girl. She shouldn't have left before I could eat her pussy for breakfast.

I reach for my phone to call Spades, ignoring the hour.

"It better be important," he mutters, half asleep.

"Kyle called; we've got a new snitch. Get yourself together, pick up Nate, and I want you at my house in two hours."

"Lucky bastard," he says more to himself than to me. "We'll be there at ten."

"You and Nate, keep it to yourself for now."

They're the only two who know about Kyle, and it needs to stay that way. The more people who know, the greater the risk of exposing Kyle. He has to maintain his position until Chicago falls into my hands.

"Sure. We'll be there."

"And get someone to always watch Luca. I want to know his every move."

I find Layla in the kitchen still in a black see-through nightdress, a focused expression on her doll-like face as she looks at the screen, biting her cheek. A pile of open books and the tape recorder she used while interrogating my mother litter the table.

"Who gave you permission to leave our bed?"

She jumps, looking over her shoulder. "Why are you sneaking up? You scared me."

I move closer to kiss the top of her head. "I ask you a question." Pushing her laptop aside, I catch her hand and don't let go until she sits on the table.

"I didn't want to wake you."

The nightdress hugs her frame, highlighting her boobs— the one part of her body she's self-conscious about for no apparent reason. They're not the largest but fit perfectly in my hands. I don't need more than that. In fact, if I could change one thing about Layla, it wouldn't be her looks or her personality. It'd be her surname. Apart from this easily fixable detail, she's a dream.

My dream come true.

"You're not allowed to leave the bed until I let you." I bite on her ear and take her upstairs, determined to fill the two hours before Spades and Nate arrive with nothing but her moans.

Layla point-blank refused to skip classes all week in favor of sex, but I'm all over her the minute she gets home every day. Sex has always been my go-to tension reducer, and with all the problems hanging over my head, I can't get enough of Layla no matter how long we're in bed. How she managed to finish her dissertation on time is beyond me. We have sex at least three times a day. We've christened the bath, shower, kitchen, and living room. We tried every position I could think of to find those she enjoys most, but I can't get enough of her. The sweet, breathless moans, the way she tastes and looks when she comes.

I gave the maid a few days off so she couldn't listen to Layla's moans, my growls, the bed slamming against the wall, or witness us on the couch while Layla rides me, with her mouth on my neck, my hands on her back. She enjoys dominating and is getting good at maintaining a demanding pace.

"You'll be late," I say when she walks out of the bathroom, her hair wet, eyes gleaming, legs weak after the intense orgasm she had while I held her pinned to the wall under the stream of hot water, driving into her from behind.

I do my utmost to make her writhe, squirm and beg for release. Knowing that she needs it so much, that she needs *me* so much is empowering.

"It's the last day before Christmas break. Newson can handle me being late for a change," she says, struggling with the zipper on her back.

It starts too low for her to reach, but she'd rather dislocate her shoulder than give up. I drape her hair over her shoulder, zip her up, and kiss the nape of her neck. "Can he? Good, because I'm fucking starving." I throw her on the bed, yanking the dress up and panties down. "Open."

"We *just* had sex!" she chuckles.

"Don't deny me my pussy. Open, Layla. Nice and wide."

She lets her legs fall apart, her smile morphing into parted lips and hooded eyes when I latch onto her clit like a starving man, slipping two fingers inside.

She had an orgasm ten minutes ago, but she's fucking soaking wet, already on the brink of another violent release within minutes.

"There it is... good girl, don't hold back," I say against her when she writhes, pressing her sweet pussy to my lips as she comes, flooding the house with her moans. I love that she's so fucking vocal, letting me hear how good it feels when I make her come. There's nothing more arousing than seeing her ripped to shreds by an intense orgasm.

My plan for the day consists of dropping her off and picking her up from college and hours of catching up with paperwork in-between, but it all goes to shit five minutes later when I ascend the stairs to find Spades on the sofa with a take-out cup in hand, two more on the table.

"Morning," he says. "It might be a wise idea to change the alarm code, Dante, so no one can barge in here unannounced now that Layla lives here, and..." he trails off, cocking an eyebrow to non-verbally finish the sentence.

"Are you blushing?" I smirk, plopping down on the sofa. "My house, my girl. If you don't want to hear her come, don't arrive unannounced."

He swallows hard, rubbing his hands on his trousers. "I'll remember that."

"Get on with the show, Spades. You found the snitch?"

"Not yet. There are more pressing matters to attend to right now. Caro rang earlier. The V brothers are flying in this afternoon. They want to meet up at the club."

The V brothers are my closest business partners. We've worked together for five years, and they're a pleasure to deal with. Always well prepared, organized, and informed. They're eloquent and well-put-together, but only while we talk business. Once we start drinking, their facade brakes—they're out of control, hitting on everything that moves.

Spades glances over my head when soft footsteps reach my ears. Layla joins us with a bag full of books on her shoulder, a printed and bound copy of her dissertation in hand.

"I guess I'm driving myself today?" She takes the cup, sending Spades a grateful smile.

"I can call Rookie—"

"I'm already late. I can manage on my own." She pecks my lips, waves at Spades, and leaves the house within thirty seconds of arriving downstairs, her steps still a little off as she saunters away on weak legs.

"What do they want?" I ask Sapdes once the door closes behind Layla.

"Caro says they know about Nikolaj. I guess they want to talk plans for the future."

"I want everyone at the club by half seven. Order the girls from Tony. Eight should do it. You got anything on Luca?"

"Nope. He's as clean as they get, Dante. Nothing out of the ordinary. He's been keeping his head low like you ordered. I really don't think he's the snitch."

Neither do I, but his conflicting behavior toward Layla has me thinking. "Then I should call him."

"You want him there tonight?"

"No. I want him here."

He barks out a short laugh. "Luca's supposed to look after your star? I assume it's because of the talks that Frank's looking for a hitman?"

"Better safe than sorry."

"I get that. It's not like I doubt Luca's competence. He won't let anything happen to her. Just tell me one thing." He stretches his hands over the back of the couch. "How will you keep her safe from him?"

I finish my coffee, placing the cup back on the table. "He's the one who'll need protection. Layla mops the floors with him. Luca knows if he lets a hair fall off her head, a chalk outline of his body will be all that's left of him."

Thirty minutes later, Luca takes Spades' place on the sofa. We've worked together for almost six years now. He was never the most obedient person, but he never cowered until now.

"What's going on?" he asks.

"I have a job for you. The V brothers are flying in tonight. I need to leave, but I'm not leaving Layla alone. You'll be watching over her until further notice."

I accommodated his wishes for years. I turned a blind eye to his short temper because of his past, but the special treatment has expired. It's time to teach him a lesson. He has to take responsibility for his actions just like the rest of my men; otherwise, he'll never learn.

"Aren't you overacting? No one will touch her down South because she's with you and up North because she's Frankie's daughter. Why does she need security?"

"Frankie's looking for a hit man." I light a cigarette, and Luca follows my lead. "I'm not risking some nutcase hurting her to get to me. I won't need you often for now. Layla will be with me most of the time, but I expect you here tonight at seven. If I'm not with her, you need to be. Understood?"

"Why me? Spades, Rookie, Nate. They like her. They won't strangle her by accident when she starts bitching."

Watching over Layla is a far worse punishment than if I'd tell him to cover the cost of plan B. This time we closed the bill at one million. He'd be paying it back for a year, but he'd take the deal with open arms over babysitting my star.

"Don't get on her nerves, and you'll be fine. You killed a man for her, Luca. I trust you with her."

Putting my most skilled fighter on the sidelines to become a nanny is a low blow, but I have two reasons for doing so. It's not just about trusting his viciousness. There's also the laying-low business. He needs to stay out of the spotlight until the press forgets about the mayhem in Delta.

"Where is she now?" he asks. "I guess she's not pleased with this either."

"She's in college. Don't get in her way, and I'll make sure she won't give you a reason to strangle her."

He leaves a few minutes later, performing a burnout on the white gravel to let off some steam.

CHAPTER
TWENTY-SIX
Layla

Aaron grabs my hand when I'm getting in my car after the last lecture. "Don't run," he pleads, glancing over his shoulder. "Please, Layla. I won't hurt you. I swear."

When he meets my gaze, the thought of locking myself inside the car vanishes. He's scared, petrified almost. His muscles disappeared over the last two months, and worry replaced the smile he wore on our date.

I grip my phone, ready to call Dante the second I'll feel threatened. "What do you want?"

"Don't call him," he pleads, scanning the parking lot quickly, his hands shaking. "I won't touch you. I swear." He lets go of the door and crouches down, pulling his hood up. "I'm so fucking sorry, Layla... for everything. For that evening, for not warning you, for following his orders, but... I had no choice. He kidnapped my fiancée. I had to do it!"

I don't understand much, but his behavior erases my anxiety. He's afraid of his own shadow, and his nails are bitten so short it looks painful.

"You need to be more precise." I place my phone on the passenger seat. "Who made you do it? What did they make you do? What fiancée?"

Aaron tilts his head, glancing over his shoulder again. "Your father. He made me..." He turns back to me but refuses to meet my gaze. "He told me to scare you. He had my fiancée, threatening to hurt her if I didn't do what he wanted."

My body turns cold. Time slows down for a moment. I watch Aaron with unseeing eyes; his words looped in my head. I don't want to understand, know, or feel.

My father asked him to rape me.

Everything Frank did made sense. His moves were well planned and thought through. I understood why he told me to stay away from Dante and treated me like an enemy since I started dating him. It made sense. It had an explanation.

But not this time.

There's no rational explanation this time, not a single reason that'd justify rape. What was Frank trying to achieve? The last few months were like puzzles turned upside down. Every day a new piece was uncovered. I knew what the final picture would look like. It was just a matter of putting the pieces together. Aaron is a piece that doesn't fit.

"Layla, I'm sorry." He inches closer but seeing me flinch, he jerks away. "I've no idea why Frank wanted me to hurt you, but please stay away from him. He's a sick man."

Tears sting my eyes. "Why are you telling me this now?"

He sighs, looking behind him for the nth time as if scared that Frank, or worse—Dante—will jump out of the bushes any second. "We ran when Frank let my fiancée out. We moved back to California, but I couldn't just leave you like that. I couldn't sleep knowing you're oblivious. That night, God, it was the most horrible thing I ever did to a woman. I've been trying to talk to you all week, but you're never alone."

He didn't have to risk his safety to warn me. He could have stayed in California, but he took a risk.

"Thank you," I reply, not knowing what else to say. The irony doesn't slip my attention. I'm thanking a guy who tried to rape me acting on my father's orders.

I need to talk to Frankie. He's taken it too far.

"Look out for yourself, Layla." With that, he walks away, leaving me scared, furious, and confused.

Tears fall down my cheeks. I cry, banging my fist at the steering wheel, defeated. Frank's vicious when he's out to get what he wants, but I wouldn't have thought he'd sacrifice so much. My heart cracks in half as pain soars through me, cutting deep.

I can't believe what I was willing to do for someone who doesn't care about me. I lived in a fantasy land, *praying* that Frank would love me the way a father should. I fulfilled his every order and followed him blindly because I wanted him to appreciate me. But no matter how hard I try, his walls are impenetrable. He keeps finding new ways to hurt me. I should've given up a long time ago, sparing myself the pain I've endured over the years and the pain I still face.

My phone snaps me out of my pity party. Dante's face flashes on the screen, amplifying the turmoil of emotions inside me. Tears threaten to choke me when I wipe my face, starting the engine. I inhale deeply to get a hold of myself before answering his call.

"Where are you?"

The conversation with Aaron and my shameful sobbing took twenty minutes—five more than it usually takes me to arrive at his house after college whenever I drive myself. *Five* minutes and he's already worried. My heart swells, and the cracks heal for a short time before they re-open. He loves me more than I ever thought possible.

And I don't deserve it.

"I was about to call you," I say, trying not to sound upset. "I need to go home to pick up some things if I'm supposed to stay with you until Christmas. Don't sound the alarm. I'll be back soon."

"Come home, Star. I'll take you shopping." He aims at casual, but the tension in his voice ruins the effect.

"I've got two exams in January. I need my notes to study. I'll be back in an hour." It's not a lie, but not the truth either.

He exhales loudly. "I don't trust Frank, Layla. Frank knows Julij won't work with him when Nikolaj dies."

"You think he'll hold me hostage, until you give him South in return? Should I remind you that he thought the exact same thing not so long ago about you?"

"Layla, you're the most important thing in my life." The power of his words could annihilate the whole city. "If Julij sees it, so does Frank. He's losing, and he'll stop at nothing to stay afloat."

I turn left to avoid traffic. "Frank's unpredictable, but not to that extent."

That's not part of the plan.

"Fine. I'll meet you there." Keys rattle in the background, cutting the time I hoped to have with Frank in half.

"You're overreacting. I'll be okay."

"I'm not leaving you there alone, Layla."

Before I could persuade him, he cut the call. Frank's car sits outside the garage, but Jess's pink Escalade is gone. Nerves rage in me like a hurricane as I storm inside the house, the heels of my boots clicking on the marble floor. I march straight into his office, ready to scream and call him names. Ready to pack my bags and never set foot in this house again.

Frank sits by the desk, a cigar in one hand and a half-empty glass of whiskey in the other. One look at him, and my battle-ready mind crumbles. Courage fades, leaving just fear.

"Is it true?" I ask, my throat closing in. "You told him to *rape* me?"

Frank looks up, eyes narrowed. He doesn't have to answer. It's in his face: guilty as charged.

"Why?! How could you?! What did I do wrong? I did everything you told me to!"

"Calm down," he snaps, tearing himself out of the chair without glancing in my direction. This conversation can't take place inside. Frank's too afraid the house might be wired. I follow him outside and join him when he stops under an old cherry tree. "The plan was falling apart," he says, his voice full of something much more sinister than the remorse I hoped to hear.

CHAPTER TWENTY-

Layla

EIGHT MONTHS EARLIER

The hotel bellboy leaves my suitcase by the bed and pro-
ceeds to unload my ski gear off the trolley. I take my thick
winter coat off, heading straight to the bathroom to take
a hot shower. Frank offered to spend a few days alone with
me for the first time since I turned six. If there was anything

else I wanted more than his attention, I wouldn't have agreed to a weekend in Aspen.

Just the thought of all the snow and freezing temperatures is enough to scare me away, but I agreed because spending time with Frank compensates for the inconveniences. Skiing and talking took up most of our time. Each time he asks a question, I feel happier. He wants to know my plans, how my Italian is coming along, and whether I've made friends with Allie.

He's cheerful for the first time in years. He even smiles, watching my clumsiness stop me from mastering the art of not falling down every ten seconds.

After dinner, we sit in the corner of the room, Frank with a glass of bourbon and me with a glass of mulled wine. It has been a while since I've felt so blissfully happy.

"It was a pleasant day, don't you think?" Frank stretches out in his chair.

"Yes. We should do it more often. I'm willing to endure the cold and a sore butt."

"Yes, it'd be nice if we could do it more often and build our relations without anything standing in our way." His tone changes. He's still friendly but nervous, too.

"What stands in the way?"

"Me... my business." He waits for a moment as if deciding whether to keep talking. "I need your help."

An unexpected shot of adrenaline jolts my body. I've never heard Frank Harston ask for help before. He's too proud, too self-sufficient to seek help. I know that him asking and asking *me of* all people is significant.

I jitter in my seat, growing impatient. Maybe if I help him, I'll earn his acceptance. for five years now, he's been treating me like a stranger. He was never a loving, caring father, we were never close, but five years ago, an invisible, impenetrable wall grew between us.

"Of course. What do you want me to do?"

Frank smiles, pleased with my eagerness. "I want you to help me regain South."

My eyebrows form one line. That's the last thing I expected to hear. "I don't understand... how?"

"Five years ago, Dante Carrow took South of Chicago away from me." His expression turns serious. "He was like my brother, Layla. I taught him *everything*. I showed him this way of life and introduced him to the right people." He scoffs, anger tainting his features. "There was a time when I'd give my right hand for him. I trusted him, and he put a knife in my back. He betrayed me." He lowers his voice. "The time has come for revenge. I want to destroy him. I want to take away everything he holds dear, but I can't do it alone, and there's no one I trust more than *you*."

A wonderful warmth washes over me. "But how am I supposed to help you? What do you want me to do?"

Frank strokes his beard, staring at me. "Make him fall in love with you."

I choke on the wine and start coughing, glaring at him wide-eyed. This has to be some sort of cruel, sick joke. It makes no sense. It sounds absurd, but Frank is very serious. "Make him fall in love with me?" I drink more wine to moisten my dry, sore throat. "You're joking, right? I don't understand. How will it help you?"

"Two birds with one stone," he says, not explaining anything. "I want him to feel what I felt when he betrayed me. I want him to know what it's like to lose something that means the world."

I consider laughing. This is... *absurd*. Incomprehensible, but I know better than to question or—God forbid—disregard my father, so I tread lightly. "Why don't you just kill him?"

Frank chuckles as if I'm the one to say something funny. Did he hear himself? "I will. Of course, I'll kill him, but that's not enough. I want him to trust someone as much as I trusted him back in the day. I want him to love and not be able to function without love, and then I want him to lose it all. I want him to suffer the same way I suffered."

He's serious. Until now, I thought, I *hoped* he was making fun of me. I try to understand his reasoning despite it making no sense, but I don't know why he thinks I'm the person for the job. I know next to nothing about Dante Carrow. The fact he's nine years older than me makes the task ahead even harder.

"Daddy, I'd love to help you. I really would, but I don't know how. You know I'm the worst actress. I have no experience with men."

"Exactly!" He claps once. "And that's your biggest advantage." He waves the waiter over to order more drinks.

I didn't notice when my glass emptied. "My lack of acting skills is my biggest advantage?"

"No, your lack of experience is. *I* introduced Michael and Sam to you. You think I didn't realize they weren't straight? I've been thinking about all this for a long time, Layla. I know Dante better than anyone. I know what he's looking for in a woman. I know what he's attracted to, so I know he won't be able to resist your innocence."

I fold my arms over my chest, narrowing my eyes at him. "You knew about Sam and Michael? I wasted a year of my life with those two!"

"Calm down." He takes my hand, squeezing lightly. "I had to. I trusted that when the time came, you'd help me, but before I could talk to you, I had to make sure you were growing up to be a woman Dante couldn't resist."

I can't decide if I'm ashamed, sickened, or angry. My own father turned me into a freak show. He raised me like a pig for slaughter; controlled every aspect of my life to take revenge on a man who took half of the city from him.

Half.

Dante didn't hurt him; he didn't kill his family. He just works the territory that used to be under Frank's command for a short while. A few square miles of land are enough for my father to sacrifice my best years for an abstract plan.

"I know you're mad, baby girl, but I need your help." He strokes the back of my hand with his thumb, staring into my eyes, sincerity shining in his. "I'm tired of this. I want to get rid of Dante and get to know *you*, but with Carrow in the picture, I can't think about anything other than revenge."

I glance at his hand resting on mine, trying to remember the last time he touched me. It's been years. I miss the father he once was—never perfect, never acting like a regular dad, but present in my life. When Chicago split in half, he disappeared without a trace. He became distant.

Now he's offering me a chance to get back what I had and maybe earn more. Maybe without Dante in the picture, with the whole of Chicago under Frank's belt, he'll be able to muster a little love for me.

I sigh but nod in agreement. If he believes this will work, he must have a reason. I don't need to understand to follow his orders.

"I don't know how to do it. He'll see right through me."

Frank rests against his chair with a fond smile. "Be yourself, Layla. You're perfect. Sassy, intelligent, feisty. Don't change. Don't pretend to be someone you're not."

"How can you be sure he'll like me? that he'll look at me?"

"I've known him since he was fifteen. I know everything about him."

I'm not convinced, but I'm ready to trust him. Fear mixes with excitement inside my head, filling me with stomach-churning anticipation. I want to do well. The prize is too tempting to pass on the opportunity. A few months with Frank's enemy, a few months of pretending to love him isn't a high price to pay if Frank is to be my father again for the rest of my life.

CHAPTER TWENTY-EIGHT

Layla

PRESENT

Now that I've uncovered more of the puzzle met Dante, and more importantly—Isla, I know Frank's taking revenge on them both. Isla tore his heart out when she rejected him. Now, he wants me to do the same to Dante.

Frank takes my hand, pulling me back into reality. "I had to act before it all fell apart, Layla. Aaron was just that—a tool, a trigger."

"You ordered him to rape me!"

He dismisses me with a wave of his hand. "Stop being so fucking dramatic. Do you think I don't know what you're capable of? I knew you wouldn't let him take it that far. He was supposed to scare you, nothing more. It was all about an impulse... *Dante* needed an impulse to act."

"An impulse?!" I throw my hands in the air, my chest heaving, anger retaking the stage. "Where do you get these ideas from? You're negating yourself! Everything was moving along well until *you* told me to cut him loose! So, I did, and when he left me alone, you hired a guy to *rape* me so Dante would come back?! It doesn't make sense!"

Frank clutches my arm hard enough to leave a bruise. "Don't act like a dumb tramp." He shoves me back, and I stumble over my own feet. "I told you to get rid of him because you acted like a lovesick puppy two days in! It wasn't believable."

"I'm not the only one who acted that way from the start."

Frank smirks, nodding his head. "Yes, it turned out just as I anticipated."

I hug myself protectively. "Dad..." My eyes travel from the ground to his face, and my shoulders sag with the weight of the confession. "I'm in love with him."

"No, you're not," he replies, not missing a beat.

Frank always has it his way. Always the smartest, always the boss. He thinks denying my confession will make it go away, but I won't let him dismiss me today. Julij's words echo in my head, pushing me to act, to at least *try*.

"There are hundreds of examples in history where women saved the day."

I'm lost in Dante, in love and being loved and cared for the way I've craved my whole life. I owe it to myself to at least try to end their war, to be the bridge that brings them back together.

"You just think you love him, Layla," he clips, his tone condescending. "He's the first man to touch, kiss, and fuck you. of course, you *think* you love him, but the truth is you're young. You're naïve, Layla. He's manipulating you, and he's fucking good at it. Don't be stupid. You're a tool in his hands."

My chest squeezes, pain radiating all over my body. Frank's right. I am a tool in the hands of a man who wants to gain half of Chicago. But Dante isn't that man.

Frank is.

"Dante's charming, but he's still our enemy, sweet girl. Yours and mine," he says, his voice softer, filled with remorse. "You've got to remember that because he's the only thing standing in our way. He's the only thing stopping us from building the family you want."

The idealistic image of a family tempts me as much as Dante. Giving up on either is impossible and unavoidable at the same time. Desertion is not a part of the plan. I'm not supposed to care about Dante. I'm not supposed to love him.

"Can't you just leave the past where it belongs?" I beg, my voice barely a whisper as tears pool in my eyes. "For me? Can't you work together?"

My head turns to the side when Frank backhands me hard, his face bright red with barely controlled fury. The urge to touch the burning skin disappears when the metallic taste of blood fills my mouth. My lungs shrink in half, eyes fall shut. I fight the panic, pushing away the image of blood trickling down my chin.

Frank's impulsiveness terrifies me just as much as blood. He's short-tempered and cruel, but he's never hit me before. My heart races, but I remain glued to the spot, watching him, the image distorted by tears. For the first time in a while, I have a chance to take a good, hard look at him. We didn't spend much time together these past years, so I hadn't noticed how gray he turned despite only being thirty-five. He's tired, his eyes a sea of regret and disdain.

"Layla," he whispers, touching my shoulder. "You have to trust me. It'll all be over soon. With Nikolaj's death approaching, I had to alter the plan. This won't last much longer, I promise. Just stay strong. When it's over, I'll finally be able to give you everything you want. I won't focus on Dante anymore. I'll be the father you deserve. I promise. I *swear,* sweet girl."

He wraps his arm around me, the height of his ability to show feelings. I soak up his closeness like a sponge. It's so rare to have him close. Even when I was a little girl, he used to hug me as a last resort and only when I came over to him.

"You always wanted to go to Europe," he says, pushing me away. "France, Italy, Portugal. I'll take you wherever you want when this is over. "I'll have time to make up for all those years I wasn't there for you." He starts walking again, this time towards the house. "Your relationship has no future, Layla. Sooner or later, Dante will hurt you, or worse—he'll find out that you willingly participated in this."

I stop in my tracks, and a cold sweat breaks out on my neck as I read between the lines. He's not saying that to tell me that Dante might *accidentally* find out. He's informing me that if I don't hold up my end of the deal, he'll do everything in his power to make Dante aware.

And if he finds out, he won't just hate me.

He'll *kill* me.

I'm fighting a losing battle. My feelings don't matter. It doesn't matter how much I want the ending to look different. One of them will end up in a coffin. I need to fulfill my duty, or I'll be the one to end up six feet under. When I agreed to help Frank, I never imagined that Dante would be everything I ever wanted. I didn't think he'd give me everything, expecting little in return.

If I could, I'd turn back time and never agree to help Frank, sparing myself the most challenging choice of my life. I'd still have no father, but I wouldn't have Dante...

I wouldn't love a man I have to betray.

CHAPTER
TWENTY-NINE
Dante

Eyeing the door to Frank's house as if I can summon Layla telepathically, I wait outside, counting seconds and smoking like a chimney. It takes ten minutes before she emerges with a bag hanging over her shoulder. She stops at the top of the concrete steps, half of her face covered with a scarf, the other half hidden under the hood of her jacket. I don't need to see tears to know they're there. The way she hugs herself paints the picture.

My instincts kick in before a single rational thought penetrates the growing madness. I shove my hand under my jacket, grabbing the gun. No thinking, no rationalizing. My body flips into battle mode, and my reaction is both natural and worrying simultaneously. I don't know what happened. Whether Frank had anything to do with her tears, I'm ready to make a sieve out of him regardless.

Layla drops her hands, descending the steps. "I'm fine."

"Then why were you crying?"

She hides in my arms, inhaling my scent. "We had a fight. Can we go? Please, I don't want to stay here any longer."

The plea in her voice stops me from asking another question. I grit my teeth, kiss her head, and give her the helmet. "Put it on. You ever rode a bike?" She shakes her head, watching me mount the Ducati. "Hold on to me. Don't lean over to the sides."

"Where are all your cars?"

"This is faster than any car in my garage."

The engine springs to life, and its roar drowns out my racing thoughts. I look over my shoulder and grab Layla's thighs to slide her closer to me. She rests against my back, arms around my stomach, cold hands under my jacket.

I miss the adrenaline of speeding through the city at a hundred miles an hour on a bike. With Layla clinging to me like a child, I watch the speed, but I'm eager to get home, so I double the limits a few times.

Layla jumps off when we park in the garage. I take my helmet off and watch her do the same. She turns to go upstairs, but my pulse speeds up faster than the Ducati ever could. Her scarf slides, revealing a crimson trickle of dry blood that marks a line from her mouth down her chin. Seeing the swollen, cut lip freezes my blood.

"It's nothing," she says, her eyes red from crying. "Frank's impulsive, I said too much, and—"

"Stop," I seethe, reaching for my helmet. "Stop making excuses for him."

She tears the keys out of my hand, backing away. "Don't go there. It won't change anything. You'll just fight for no reason."

"*No reason*?! Give me the fucking keys!"

Her back rests against the wall. I'm right there, towering over her, the muscles on my back like stone, the need to break Frank's neck so powerful it threatens to bring me to my knees.

Layla hides the hand that holds my keys behind her back. "Please, let it go. I'm fine, really. It's my fault... I angered him."

I grip her shoulders. "He hit you. I don't care what you said or did. He fucking *hit* you, Layla. Nothing justifies this."

I can't believe the fucker.

He hit his own daughter.

He hit *my* girl.

How can any man hurt a woman in the first place? I'd fucking skin him alive if I saw him right now.

A single tear rolls down Layla's cheek, changing my attitude. I never could handle the sight... I pull her into my arms and kiss her temple. It's been years since I wanted to kill someone as much as I want to kill Frank, but it has to wait. Layla needs me to calm her down. She needs me to clean her up.

My hands still shake when I search the kitchen cabinets for a first-aid kit.

"I was scared to look in the mirror," she admits, her cheeks pink. "That's why I didn't clean it up." She cringes when I part her lips with my thumb to clean the cut.

The grimace on her pretty face pushes me to grab a gun

and a shovel and bury the fucker, but killing Frank means hurting Layla, and that's the one thing I refuse to do. I remember when she saw blood on my fingers, and I don't want to think how scared she must've been when she tasted it in her mouth.

"I know, baby. You're not going back there again." I throw the towel aside. "You live here."

"Isn't this quick? We've been dating for—"

"Why? Why does it matter how long we've been together? We're not standard, so don't expect us to follow some socially acceptable relationship timetable."

She sits on top of me, her fingers weaving into my hair. "Frankie's my father, Dante. I know you hate him, but I won't cut him out of my life."

My hands rest on her hips, and she cuddles into me, resting her head on my shoulder, pecking my neck. Everything I want is right here in my arms, but I'm painfully aware that once the war ends, Layla might not want to be a part of my life anymore. If Frank doesn't bow out, if he insists on being the last one standing, I'll have no choice but to kill him. Layla loves me, but the strength of her feelings is a mystery. Challenging times await us both.

"I don't want you anywhere near him alone. If you want to see him, I'm coming with you."

"Yes, of course." Irony coats her words. "Because that won't end in a blood bath." She wriggles out of my arms. "Don't blow this out of proportion. I'm fine, baby, but I do need a hot bath. I'm freezing." She leans over to kiss my forehead.

"Tell me you're okay, Star."

"It's not my first rodeo with Frank. He's never hit me before, but it didn't surprise me. I'm immune."

That calms me down a little bit. Until now, I wondered if he had hit her before or if she hid bruises under make-up. I wondered if she suffered many panic attacks at the sight of her own blood. Knowing this was the first time stops the tormenting line of questions but doesn't ease my rage.

"I'm fine. Really."

I let her go and almost call Spades to cancel the meeting with the V brothers, but I can't. There's too much to discuss, and the clock is ticking. Nikolaj might die any minute. I need to be prepared for any outcome or move on Frank's part.

I get ready in one of the guest bathrooms, and forty minutes later, I enter the ensuite to inform my star that Luca's due in fifteen minutes to keep her safe.

She lays in the bubbly bath immersed up to her nose, cheeks pink. "You look nice."

"I have to leave." I sit on the edge of the tub. "My business partners from Detroit flew in this afternoon. They didn't announce it sooner."

Layla smiles, so I stop talking. "You don't have to explain. If you have to go, you have to go. The amount of time you've been spending with me is quite impressive." She slides underwater and resurfaces a few seconds later, wiping her face, then grabs a bottle of shampoo, glancing at me as if surprised to see I hadn't moved. "Go. I'll be okay. I'll go to bed early."

I developed a compulsive need to quadruple-check if she'll manage as if she has two left hands. She proved many times she's different from the women I dated in the past. Maybe because of her upbringing, or perhaps she's reasonable, and all my exes were spoiled brats. Either way, I bite my tongue before another *will you be okay?* leaves my lips, but there's one more thing to discuss.

"You're not staying here alone. Frank's looking for a hit-man, and I won't risk some nutcase hurting you."

"So, you found me a bodyguard?"

"Luca will be here soon."

"Luca?" She sits up, testing my concentration, when her beautiful boobs covered in soap bubbles come into view. "You've got so many people working for you! Why him?"

At least she's not trying to talk me out of the security-detail idea. "Because I trust him. I know he gets on your nerves, but he won't let anyone touch you. You can ignore him or argue with him if it helps you cope, but he's watching over you tonight."

She crosses her arms, pushing those perky boobs higher. "I'm trying," she says, eyeing a large, round glass bowl filled with colorful bath bombs. I half expect her to smack my head with it. "I'm really trying to understand your reasoning. I mean, okay, you're worried, I get it. Nikolaj's dying, and Frank feels threatened. I get it. He might do something stupid, so it'll be better if someone keeps an eye on me. I get that too. What I don't get is why you chose Luca. The one I hate." She bites her lip, smiling. "Okay. I do get it. You really are crazy jealous."

I open my mouth to object but think better of it. Explaining why I chose Luca requires informing her he was the one who killed the guy at the club, and I don't want to go there.

I peck her lips. "Don't wait up."

She brings her hands up to hold my head in place and sinks into my lips, the kiss slow, full of lust. She sighs, grazing her nose along my cheek.

"Damn you, Star," I whisper. "Wait for me. Naked."

CHAPTER THIRTY

Layla

For the first time since I started dating Dante, I'm relieved when he leaves me alone. I need time to come to terms with everything Frank said. for weeks now, I hoped the plan could be altered, that nothing was set in stone. The deeper I fell in love, the more I believed Frank would let go of his animosity. How naïve of me.

Frank is not the type to let things slide.

He's dreamt of revenge for years, and my feelings for Dante are merely an inconvenience. Frank doesn't care that the second his heart stops beating, mine will shatter, and no one will be able to put it back together. I tell myself off for allowing my feelings to trap me. Now, the only way out is through. I have to finish what I started eight months ago. I was thrilled back then to help my father triumph. Now, I want to stop feeling. I want to fall asleep and wake up when the pain subsides.

Dante said Luca's due any minute and closed the door behind him. I pour myself a glass of wine, sitting at the bar, my head hanging low. I don't want to cry. Tears won't help, but there's no stopping them. I take a deep breath when the alarm disarms, closing my lips on the glass. Luca would've noticed my red eyes the second he walked in if not for the dimmed lights.

"The TV is there." I wave my hand in the correct direction, swallowing to rid the lump in my throat. "Pretend I'm not here, and I'll return the favor."

He rounds the bar to grab a bottle of water from the mini-fridge. All of Dante's men usually wear suits, but tonight Luca's in skinny jeans, the sleeves of his sweater rolled up, showing off the many colorful tattoos marking his body. I make out roses on both palms, letters on his knuckles, a diamond, a serpent, and a forest on his arm. My favorite one, the Phoenix on his neck with wings spreading to his ears, is exposed by the V-neckline.

He eyes me up, thin lips part as if to voice a snarky comment, but his expression changes in a blink of an eye. His jaw clenches, eyes narrow. He closes the distance between us, leans over the bar, and grips my face, his eyes on my lips. "Who the fuck did that to you?"

I jerk away. "That's none of your business."

He fists his palms, closing his eyes briefly. When he looks at me again, my body feels cold. He breathes out through his nose as if doing all in his power to keep it together. He doesn't... he lands his fist on the wall to his left. "Did Dante hit you?" He glares at the wall. "Layla! Was it Dante?"

"No! of course not."

"Then who was it? Who the fuck hit you, Layla?" He runs his hand through his short hair, still shaken.

"Frankie," I say, too stunned by the anger in his eyes to argue. "Daddy hit me. Happy?"

"Do I look happy? Get dressed."

No, he doesn't look happy. Ever. But he does relax a bit.

I cross my arms over my chest. "Why?"

"Have you ever held a gun?"

It seems that not all wires are connected to the right places in his head.

"A gun? You do remember who my father is, don't you? of course, I've held a gun. What's your point?"

"But you can't shoot, can you?"

The sudden change in his behavior takes me aback. He's no longer furious but not an ass either. He prods at me on purpose as if he wants me to use him as a punching bag.

"I can shut your face."

The corners of his mouth twitch. "You will be a self-serving bitch your whole life. Take a day off and get dressed. I'll teach you how to fire a gun."

If he's trying to lift my spirits, then good job. I asked Frank to take me to a shooting range a thousand times, but he always answered with a harsh *no* but wouldn't explain why. I dreamt of shooting paper targets since I found a gun in his desk drawer when I was eight. It wasn't loaded, but I played with it for an hour, pretending to shoot different objects until Frank came home and locked me in my room.

"Aren't you scared I'll *accidentally* shoot you?" The delight in my voice is almost tangible.

"I bet you won't hit the target the first time around. Fuck that, the first *ten* times."

I stop on the stairs, glancing at him over my shoulder. "Don't hold your breath."

Not waiting for a change of heart, I rush upstairs to change my outfit in record time. Three minutes later, with boots in hand and a hair tie in my mouth, I stop in the living room. Luca hands me a full glass of wine, waiting until I drink half before he takes me outside to his Dodge.

The shooting range looks like nothing much from the outside. An old building not far from the port, in one of the most dangerous neighborhoods. I'd think the building was abandoned if not for the modern reception desk inside. The paint peels off the walls, dirt marks the concrete floor, and most windows are boarded-up.

An older gentleman sits behind the tall, metal countertop, motioning his head in greeting at Luca, seemingly oblivious to my presence. Luca shoves big, black earmuffs over my head. Once he makes sure they're on correctly, he opens the door to a large, long room. The wall on my right is covered with different kinds of guns. Hundreds of pistols, revolvers, and rifles hang on large hooks with ammunition littering a metal table. To my left, in the distance, are the paper cut-outs of people. The smell of gunpowder irritates my nose, but a smile tugs at my lips when every shot fired by various men at the stations vibrates through me.

Luca points me toward a distant station, grabbing a medium-sized pistol along with the clip. "Think, Layla," he hisses when I try to load the gun. "You said you held a gun before. No one told you to aim it at the floor when you're not shooting? Guns like to fire on their own. If you keep looking into the barrel, you'll shoot yourself." He waits until I put the clip in before standing behind me, his hands on my shoulders. "Outstretch your hands." He explains how to stand and corrects me a few times. "Now, for the most important part." His knee digs into the back of mine, and I bend my legs, almost kneeling on the dirty floor.

I turn to face him, remembering to aim down so he can't scold me. "Are you nuts?"

"You're petite. You have to stand firm, or the recoil will hurt you. If I give you a more powerful gun, you'll dislocate your shoulder, and Dante will disembowel me." He turns me toward the target, helping me stand properly. He grips me in a few places, showing me where to tense up, then moves his hands to my arms to see if I'll bend my elbows. "Here," he pats my shoulders. "This is where you have to be tense. Your arms and shoulders are the most critical part of your stance."

I nod, eyeing the center of the target. "May I?"

Butterflies swarm in my stomach, making me feverish. Trying to remember everything Luca said, I slide my finger to the trigger. The recoil shakes my body, and the bullet hits the wall next to the target. I don't care that I missed. Adrenaline throbs in my veins, erasing my problems.

"Go on," Luca says. "Knock yourself out. Don't focus on hitting the target. Learn how to control the gun first."

The recoil isn't significant, but enough to make hitting the target tricky. At least with the first clip. With the next one, I start hitting the right spot, and with the last bullet, I manage to hold my hands still.

Luca approaches the wall and brings back something bigger. "This is Dante's favorite pistol, 92 Beretta."

"I thought he liked his gold revolver best."

"Out of all the revolvers, yes, but if you give him a choice, he'll always take this."

The recoil on the 92 is significant, but because the pistol is heavier, I find it easier to shoot straight. A few times, I see Dante's or Frank's head instead of the target. I put the gun down immediately. My mind tricks me, urging me to choose even though I have no choice.

I'm not sure how much time has passed. I'm too engrossed in the task at hand to check my phone. Luca keeps bringing different guns for me to try, and fires a few rounds at the next station making a sieve out of the target. It's Dante who stops the fun when he calls.

I take my earmuffs off to answer. "Yes?"

"Are you fucking stupid?! You wanna be deaf?" Luca drags me out through the emergency exit.

"Where are you?" Dante asks, his tone clipped.

"At a shooting range. Luca's teaching me," I can't contain my excitement.

"People I work with want to meet you. Can you come over? I'll tell Luca to bring you here."

I glance at Luca, then back at the emergency exit. I'd much rather keep shooting, taking my contradicting feelings out on the paper targets, but no matter how many holes I make, there's no changing the facts. No altering the past, present, or future. All I have left with Dante are a few weeks, months at the most. "Yes, but I need to change. I'll let Luca know. We should be there in an hour."

Luca clenches his jaw, kicking the trash can. "They're fucking idiots, Layla. Don't go there."

"Let me talk to him," Dante says. "And baby, just so you know, we've got eight hookers here. The V brothers..."

"Don't worry. I don't think you're cheating on me with hookers. Frank makes his money the same way you do. You think I don't realize what your business meetings look like? I'll be there soon."

I hand the phone to Luca, watching his jaw work. "Why the fuck do you want her there? They'll holler every time she snaps!" He kicks the trash can again while listening to Dante. "Fine. Suit yourself."

An hour later, Luca parks the car in the underground parking lot, taking his phone out to call Dante. For the twentieth time, I check in the rear-view mirror whether the red lipstick covers the cut on my lip. The club is mainly lit by strobe lights cutting through the darkness, but dimmed halogens hang above the booth. I don't want to explain to Dante's people who hit me.

Lipstick and concealer hide the cut well, so no explanation is necessary. I run my fingers through my hair, draping it over one shoulder, then leave the car, straightening out the canary-yellow dress.

"If they start fucking with you, I'll take you home." Luca joins me with a cigarette in his lips. "Vince is bearable, but Vinn is an idiot. More so when he's drunk."

I smile, seeing Dante walk out of the elevator. "Three... two..." I count, looking into Luca's dark eyes, "...one." The smile on my lips grows wider. "It's break time, Luca. Thank you for tonight. I expected us to kill each other, but when you're not on your period, you're bearable yourself."

Dante's arms wrap around my stomach. "How are you feeling, Star?"

I turn to kiss him. "Good. Luca helped a lot. I let it all

out at the shooting range. How are you? You look like you need caffeine."

He nods, glancing at Luca. "You can head back home, but if you want to stay, stay here."

"I'll stay. I'll take her home when Vinn gets out of hand."

Dante laces our fingers, pulling me toward the elevator. "They promised to behave. I can vouch for Vince, but not for Vinn. He's unpredictable, young, and never filters his words. He wants to see you in action, so feel free to show him his place. Spades told him I'm hiding you because you're sassy."

"You wanted me here, so I'll argue with him?" My good mood evaporates in a flash. "I'm not a circus monkey!" I storm out of the elevator.

"I wanted you to come because I wanted you close, Layla," he says, stopping behind me when I'm already at the bar. "I thought you enjoy shooting guys down."

"No, I don't. I shouldn't have to fight for respect. I've been doing it all my life. How could you think I'd enjoy arguing with some dimwit for his entertainment?!" I drop my clutch bag on the bar, waving the bartender over.

"Hey Layla, the usual, is it?" he asks, beaming.

"Yeah, but make it stronger."

Dante rests his hand on my waist, pulling me to his side. "I'm sorry. I didn't think you'd mind, you know I like it when you get so feisty." He tries to kiss my cheek, but I turn my head the other way, too enraged to be appeased.

"When should I send another one, dolly?" The bartender hands me a drink.

Dante lunges over the bar, grabbing the bartender by his tie. "*Dolly?*" he snaps, yanking him even closer. "Who the fuck do you think you're talking to?" He shoves him back, looking at me just in time to catch me roll my eyes.

Knowing full well how childish it is, I smile at the bartender. "Next one in five. Thank you."

"C'mon, I'll sort them out," Dante says.

"Forget it. They'll think I'm afraid of them. I have to earn their respect now. I sure hope they work for you and not the other way around because if they take it too far, I'll fucking destroy them."

Two wrinkles crease his forehead, and he grips my hand, yanking me closer. "Don't *ever* swear again. It doesn't fucking suit you."

I'm just as surprised as him that *fuck* came out of my mouth, but rage chews at my brain, and my filter went to hell. Everyone at the table looks up when I approach.

"Finally! I've been waiting for three hours, girl!" A blond guy in the middle yells, shaking a hooker off his lap.

"That's Vinn, the one next to him is Vince, and that's their right hand, Caro," Dante says, then snaps his fingers, ordering two hookers to get out of our space.

I keep my mouth shut, scooting closer to Spades to give Dante a little room. There's no way I'll start the show, but I threw my inhibitions out the window, so God help them.

Vinn rests his elbows on the table like a CEO of a fancy organization. "So, you're Layla." He sizes me up. "You got me on my knees."

Not only is he brusque, but so unoriginal. Half of the people who meet me for the first-time quote Clapton's song.

"Don't get up."

Vince chuckles under his breath, looking me over before turning to Dante. "She's young."

"Perfect for me," Vinn clips, a self-indulgent smirk on his thin lips. "You even look like my future girl."

"And you look like rejection."

"If I didn't respect your man like I do, I'd take you out the back so you could put that filthy mouth to good use."

Dante tenses beside me, but I open my mouth before he can cut in. "Doesn't it say 'warning: small parts; potential choking hazard' down there?"

Spades bursts out laughing. I feel as if tickets should be available for my performance.

"You were fucking right to keep her away, man," Vinn tells Dante. "I'll fall in love, and you'll have an opponent."

I scoff, rolling my eyes. It's incredible how little it takes to hate someone. "Sorry to clip your wings, but I don't date men who attack women to inflate their egos."

Nate looks at me from behind Spades' back. "He's just messing around. He wanted to check if you're really that feisty."

I get up, squeezing in-between Dante and the table, then bow as low as Adam often does in front of my father. "Next time, get a magician to entertain your guests, *baby*. Good-night." I turn on my heel, storming off, not daring to look behind me or wait for more insults.

"Layla, wait." Dante catches up to me in the elevator and shoves his hand in-between the closing doors.

"Leave me alone. I'm not going back there. I lived through enough humiliation for one day. I'm going home! You can call me in the morning."

"You're not going to Frank's."

"You won't tell me what I can or can't do!"

"You don't get it!" He grabs my waist and pins me to the wall, his face inches from mine, anger in his green eyes, but his voice steady. "I'll lose my fucking mind if something happens to you."

"Let me go... I want to fall asleep and pretend that today never happened. Frank, Luca, you, and the high-maintenance idiot upstairs!" Tears betray me rolling down my cheeks to fuel the fire inside my head. "Enough!"

Dante hushes me with a kiss. His lips battle with mine, his hands in my hair, his body pressing hard against mine. I'm grateful for the distraction, for his possessiveness, because all I need to get a hold of myself is him. I kiss him back, fisting his leather jacket when he moves his hands to cup my face. It's just us, lost in each other, the moment, and all the conflicting emotions running through us.

"I'm sorry I asked you to come." He brushes his lips over my nose and takes my hand, intertwining our fingers. "We're going home. I want to watch you fall asleep."

CHAPTER THIRTY-ONE

Dante

Layla wakes me up, jumping on the bed. I can't complain, she wears my shirt and white panties.

Her messy hair fans her too-breezy-for-seven-thirty-in-the-morning face. Her hands, in which she must hold a gift, are tucked behind her back as she rocks from left to right.

"Merry Christmas!" She gives me enough time to rub the sleep away from my eyes before she shoves a small box into my hand. "Open it!"

"Good morning to you too." I go about untying the white bow while her face fills with frustration. She lasts ten seconds, then tears the paper, tossing it on the floor. "Why did you bother wrapping it?" I open the lid on a brown leather box to find a watch inside.

The same one I wanted to buy but had no time for shopping. The Christmas schedule is filled to the brim. Demand is through the roof. Lonely people search for a brief high to forget about reality, regular customers stock up to save themselves supply trips while the streets fill with joy and clubs order double the usual amounts expecting higher traffic.

Three trucks a week are now six. Drugs are being delivered hidden everywhere, even in the fuel tanks. The more courageous drivers stuff their mattresses to earn extra cash. As fate would have it, the last two deliveries came hidden in tires. Twelve of my men emptied the trailers for eight hours straight while I checked that the quantities delivered matched what the V brothers sent. I haven't had much time for Layla, let alone shopping.

Good thing I had her gift ready last month.

"Thank you." I clasp the watch on my wrist and lean over the bed to open the drawer. Layla eyes the small, red box with a faint blush on her cheeks. "It's not what you think," I say, amused by the mortified look on her pretty face. "Well, yes, it's a ring, but not an engagement ring." I pull her into my arms, her back to my chest. "Remember what you told me the first night in Delta when I asked what you dreamed of?"

"A little shooting star." She imitates the mocking tone she used then.

My chin rests on her shoulder as I open the box.

"A little shooting star?" she asks quietly.

I put the ring on her finger, pleased that it fits perfectly. "This," I point to the star made out of platinum, "is the little star, and this," I touch the black stone in the middle, "is a real star."

"I don't understand." She moves to the side to look at me. "What do you mean?"

"It's a shooting star, baby."

"Are you saying this is a meteorite? Where did you get it?"

"They're not that rare. There's a lot of jewelry with meteorites, but this was made to order. It took the jeweler a while to locate the right stone."

Layla pushes me flat on my back and straddles me, leaning over to kiss my lips. "Thank you. It's beautiful."

"And what do you dream of now?"

"I dream things won't change and that you'll always be mine. I want you to remember that I love you so much that it hurts. It's not possible to love more."

I think the same, but my mind and heart prove me wrong each day. "Consider me yours as long as you want me."

She arches back, resting on the pillows with a content smile. "Stop the time."

"I got you a shooting star, but this... you'll need to ask Santa."

"Okay, fine. I want a cat. A ginger one with a flat nose."

I catch her legs, slide her closer and throw her over my shoulder. "You're not getting a cat. Now, show me what you bought yesterday."

I arrived home late last night, too exhausted to check the state of the house. It probably resembles Santa's Grotto. Layla asked if she could buy a Christmas tree and some decorations, so I sent her shopping with my black Amex card, Luca, and two other guys to keep her safe.

Julij rang on Monday to say that Nikolaj was rushed to the hospital in critical condition. There's nothing left for the doctors to try. They stopped the chemo and put Nikolaj on morphine to alleviate the pain.

He had a few months to live not long ago. Now, he has days left. Every time my phone rings, I'm sure it's Julij calling to say his father has passed away, but Nikolaj's hanging in there so far. My protectiveness has kicked into overdrive, and I tripled Layla's security.

I enter the living room, setting Layla down on her feet, soaking up the view. A ten-foot-tall tree stands by the glass wall overlooking Lake Michigan. Tinsel is wrapped around the bar, and the stair rail and a large glass vase filled with gold baubles of different sizes stand on the coffee table.

"Is this it?" I ask.

"*Is this it?* Is it not enough? You don't like it?"

"I do, but I thought you'd buy more. I told you to reach the daily card limit. I doubt this cost twenty grand."

She drags me toward the door, yanks her warm boots on, and runs outside, not waiting for me. "Tah-dah!" She stops in the middle of the front garden wearing just my shirt.

I drape a coat over her shoulders, looking at the house. A giant sleigh with six reindeer is parked by the garage while Santa climbs the gutter on his way to the roof. Hundreds of colorful lights hang around the windows, doors, and under the eave. They must've been switched off last night because there's no way anyone could miss them.

"Please tell me you made Luca run up and down the ladder like the good boy he is to hang it all."

"I tried, but he's not that stupid. He hired a team. The house was decorated within three hours."

We retreat to the kitchen for our morning caffeine fix. The maid busies herself preparing Christmas dinner for us. Over the past week, Isla rang every day to invite us to spend Christmas in New York, but due to Nikolaj's worsening state, I can't leave Chicago. Instead of flying over here, she decided that we'd face time at dinner and spend Christmas together that way. Watching my mother and her friends smiling from the screen of my laptop doesn't sit high on my list, but Layla and I both need a breather. A moment to forget about the approaching finale.

Isla helps a lot with her babbling.

We spend two hours at the table. During that time, I joined the conversation no more than four times because my mother and her friends preferred to talk to Layla about her dissertation. We say goodbye at seven o'clock, and Layla hauls herself onto the table.

"You need to change," I say, standing between her leg, my lips on her neck.

In the fitted evening dress with a slit that reaches all the way to her hip, she looks sexy, but without that dress, she looks even better. I slide it off her shoulders. It takes thirty seconds before she sits before me in nothing but black lingerie. Her hot body reacts to every touch of my lips.

I switch off when she's close. Money, problems, the end of the war... all cease to exist. She's the center of my world. My focus point. "What have you done to me?" I lift her into my arms. "All I see is you, baby."

She runs her fingers through my hair, kissing my neck while I carry her upstairs. I lay her on the bed, unclasp her bra, and lean over her, pushing her legs apart with my knee. Goosebumps appear everywhere I touch while she battles with the tiny buttons on my shirt.

When I drive into her warm, tight pussy, a breathless, audible gasp fills the room.

"I love you," she whispers, and for an hour, she repeats the words over and over like a prayer.

My heart swells every time she says that, but there's something other than love hiding behind her words tonight. Something worrying. The way she says it, how she looks at me, how she craves my closeness... something's wrong, but not one rational explanation springs to mind.

I lay next to her an hour later, a mist of sweat on my back. Layla immediately presses her cheek to my chest, wrapping her arms around me as she listens to my racing heart. She taps its rhythm on my ribs with her small finger.

"Tell me what's wrong." I press my lips to her head.

She stops tapping, lifting her head. "Nothing. Why?"

"You're shaken up, Star."

She sighs, holding onto me for dear life. "Let's run away somewhere where no one will ever find us."

"Why do you want to run? Aren't you happy here?"

She sits up, pulling the covers to her chin to cover her boobs. "Frank called. Nikolaj's at the hospital... the doctors aren't giving him much time."

"I know." I brush my fingers down her spine. "Why does it worry you so much? You knew that he's dying."

She shrugs, avoiding my gaze. "I thought we had more time before everything would change. You and Frank... Julij wants to work with you, meaning he'll cut out Frank."

"No one wants to do business with Frank anymore. He messed up too much over the years. The only reason he's still breathing is Nikolaj's protection. The minute Nikolaj dies, Frank will try to kill me because if I'm not here, people will have no choice but to work with him."

"Let's run away... please."

"Baby, I know you're worried about him—"

"It's not just him I'm worried about." She turns to look at me. "I wish you could work things out, stop fighting, stop this madness! Frank is vicious and blinded by revenge, but maybe... maybe you could somehow make him forgive you?" She shakes her head because she knows reconciliation isn't possible.

Frank's been fueled by hatred for years, and now he's also driven by fear of losing everything he's worked for since he was a teenager.

"I'll do what I can to make sure Frank doesn't get hurt."

"Make sure *you* don't get hurt."

There, the worried tone again, the sincerity and firmness that feels like an iron fist clamped around my throat.

"I'll be fine, Layla. I've got *you*. I won't leave you here alone. There's a line of men waiting to take my place. No way in hell I'll let that happen."

She chuckles as she drapes her hands over my neck. "There's no one I'd rather be with. You make me the happiest I've ever been. I mean it, Dante. I love you so much. I *really* love you. More than you can imagine."

"I know, baby," I press my lips to her forehead.

My phone rings on the nightstand. From the corner of my eye, I see *Spades* on the screen. I'm supposed to see him soon, and that's why I answer. He'd wait to tell me in person if it wasn't important.

"Fire!" he screams. "Get down here right now!"

I pull my eyebrows together. "What?"

"Delta's on fire!"

Deafening ringing reverberates through my head. My reactions slow down for a short moment before adrenaline rushes through my veins like a bolt of lightning. My mind is focused, ready for hell. I jump out of bed, throwing a t-shirt over my head. "Where's Luca?"

"He's here. Frank sent his guys to do the dirty work. We killed two. The third one is alive. Luca's torturing him."

"Send him over here right now. Tell him to bring someone to help. Someone with a good shot."

If Frank is taking radical steps, it means Nikolaj is dead. Every muscle in my body turns to stone when I realize this is it. The finale, the six-year-long war over territory is at my fingertips. Before the end of the night, only one boss will be left standing.

Spades cuts the call and grab my holster out of the drawer, strapping it to my belt.

Layla sits on the bed, pale, eyes following my every move. "What's wrong?"

"Delta's on fire." I take a black leather jacket out of the wardrobe. "Luca will be here in ten minutes. He'll watch over you until I come back." I open the drawer to my bedside table and pull out another gun. "You know what to do with this. You *won't* need it, baby, but I'll feel better knowing you have it. No one can get in without the code, all windows are bulletproof, and Luca will tear apart anyone who tries to touch you." I say it out loud for my peace of mind as if listing the reasons why she's safe here will make it easier to leave. I rest my fists on the mattress, leaning over to kiss her. "Sleep, Star. You're safe here but if anything happens, call me straight away. Don't wait for Luca to take care of it. Understood?"

She cups my face, kissing me deeply. "I'll be fine."

For the first time in my life, I'm cold at the thought of possibly not coming home. I have to come home. I have Layla, and I'll walk through hell to get back to her.

CHAPTER THIRTY-TWO

Layla

Moonlight slips inside the bedroom through the cracks between the burgundy curtains. It travels across the ceiling above the bed, dancing on the walls and shining in my face. Silence rings in my ears, amplifying my screaming thoughts to the point of madness. Time moves like something old and crippled; each second stretches and the ticking reverberates through the room like the lowest 'A' note on the piano.

I lay under the sheets, a war of my own raging in my head. Which one do I love more?

Frank is my father. I need him; I crave his attention because I've never had it.

And Dante... he gave me all I ever wanted and more, without asking for anything in return. He's here when I need him, always ready to help, calm me down, and make my dreams come true. He's a man I should run away from, but deep in my heart, I know I won't get far.

Frantic, silent helplessness invades my mind, sucking out the will to live. I don't know what to do. My heart coos at me to stay, wait and hope. My mind roars at me to flee and never look back. I want to fall asleep and wake up in an alternate reality. One where Dante and Frank's war never started, one where they'd rule Chicago side by side.

Why, instead of choosing the one who gives me everything, I fight for the one who gives me nothing? Because I want to prove I can earn Frank's love, that I deserve the family I dream of.

I can't make a conscious decision. I shouldn't even try because the fire at Delta is the beginning of an end. Over the next few hours, Chicago will see its new boss.

And it won't be Dante.

My cell phone screen lights up with an incoming call from Frank. Immediately, fear wraps around me like a quilt fashioned out of many cold, wet hands. My vocal cords stick together like strands of overcooked spaghetti when I flip the nightlight on.

"Run," he barks. "Layla! Run! Dante *knows*. You're not safe. Run. Now!"

As if electrified, all my senses come back, working better than ever. I jump to my feet, throw on a hoodie and sweatpants, and run out of the bedroom with the phone to my ear despite Frank cutting the call. I'm not thinking straight. I'm detached from reality as if watching myself from the sidelines.

I take two steps at a time, visualizing the garage. Dante's custom-tuned orange Camaro is the most powerful car there, maybe even powerful enough to break through the bulletproof garage door.

The light's on in the living room.

My concentration slips, brows furrow, and feet hesitate. I miss the last step, falling face down, extending my hands at the last moment to brace.

And then I realize why the lights are on.

Lifting my head from the polished, wooden floor, I see two pairs of elegant shoes, legs, chests, and faces. Luca stands six feet away, a phone to his ear, disdain on his face. His friend stands behind him, tilting his head as if unable to comprehend how I found myself flat on the floor.

"She just flew downstairs," Luca says, crouching beside me. "I'll take care of it, Boss."

A nerve-shaking, blood-curdling sense of horror consumes my mind. I can tell by the disgust in Luca's eyes he knows I work with Frank. I spring to my feet and bolt toward the garage but only manage a few steps. Luca's friend grasps a handful of my hair, pulling me back. I cry out in pain, landing with my ass hard on the floor.

"What's the hurry?" Luca smirks, looking down at me. He unzips his jacket, revealing two guns. "Can I convince you to stay?" Cold fear slithers in the pit of my stomach. I've seen Luca with a gun... he has the best shot I've ever seen.

"Tie her up," he says to the guy who still holds my hair.

He yanks hard until I lay on the floor, tears in my eyes. A knee digs into my back, and a thick rope bruises my wrists.

"Let me go!" I scream, tossing and turning. Shock laced with fear rules my mind. "Let me go!"

I'm not thinking; I'm not comprehending that because of the restraints and the advantage they have over me, I won't make it half a step. The basic survival instinct won't let me give up. I swear in my mind thinking about the gun Dante gave me before he left. It's upstairs on the nightstand. The initial frenzy caused by Frank's words made me forget all about it.

"Shut up, Layla. Screaming won't help you." Luca kneels on one knee. His wild smile disappears when I spit in his face. I regret the decision when he backhands me, glaring at the other guy. "Get me the cigar cutter."

"No," I squeal, terror rising up my throat like hot oil. "Luca, please... please..."

"I've waited for this far too long," he hisses, amused. "Try not to scream."

He turns me around to grab my left hand. I feel the cold steel around my small finger. Tears trickle down my face when he presses harder on the cutter. My whimpers grow louder, a solid rock of pain in my chest.

Luca's breath fans my neck. "Be a doll and shut your fucking mouth," he whispers, closing the cutter.

A spine-chilling, escalating scream cuts the air like a scalpel.

CHAPTER THIRTY-THREE

Dante

The stench of burnt plastic fills the air. Two fire trucks are parked outside Delta, and the firefighters rush around, collecting equipment. The captain stands beside me, eyeing the open doors to the club as if expecting to see more flames.

"You should call the police," he says, watching his crew finish up. "*I* should call the police," he corrects, meeting my gaze, his eyes hesitant as if he's not sure how to go about asking for money in exchange for keeping his mouth shut. "It's not a joke, Mr. Carrow. If not for the quick reaction of your men, someone could've died."

Someone died. Two someone's, to be precise, but thankfully none of my people are hurt. Three of Frank's men barged inside the club with canisters of petrol. Instead of keeping their heads down, they made a lot of noise, lighting the first room with a gun instead of matches.

All of my men rushed to check what had happened. They killed two of Frank's pawns, and Jackson overpowered the third one, leaving him alive.

Thank fuck for that.

I need to talk to him. None of this makes any sense. Frank sent three newbies and ordered larceny despite knowing my men would be there tonight, and his people wouldn't come out alive. A strange feeling that something's once again slipping my attention squeezed my throat when I arrived, and it won't let go.

I motion to Spades, so he'll take care of the captain. My head is too preoccupied with figuring out what is going on to hand out bribes. Involving the police will only waste too much time. Time I don't have. I've already wasted an hour.

Vinn takes the captain's place at my side. He invited himself over to the party with his brother because he's crawling out of his skin trying to apologize to Layla. The morning after he made an enemy of her, two and a half thousand red roses were delivered to my house. Fifty bouquets of fifty flowers. Six flower shops. Almost four thousand dollars to apologize to my girl for being an asshole.

It didn't work. Layla threw out the flowers and refused to talk to him despite his persistent phone calls. I guess Vinn decided he'd have a better chance of earning her forgiveness face to face at the Christmas party at Delta that was supposed to start half an hour ago.

"What's the plan?" Vinn opens a packet of Marlboro. "Get your people together, and let's go finish this." He offers me a cigarette.

I want to kill Frank.

Until Spades called to say that Delta was on fire, I thought someone would do it for me or—wishful thinking—that Frank would step aside.

Now, I know there's no chance of that ever happening. By setting my club on fire, he sent a message. Either he dies, or I die. Once again, I face a moral dilemma. Killing Frank equals hurting the one person I care about.

Spades joins us as the fire trucks drive away. "Everyone's waiting for orders."

I flip the cigarette on the pavement, taking my phone out of my pocket when I feel a short vibration.

Luca: Shall we play hide and seek?

Luca: Or would you rather have it the easy way?

Luca: Step aside, and your star will get out of this almost untouched.

I can't process the information fast enough.

Layla—in danger.

Luca—the snitch.

And Frank laughing in my fucking face.

The ground shakes beneath my feet. The chain unfolds in my head slowly, relentlessly like a snake coming alive in the heat. A blizzard of confusion. Pure, frantic anarchy seizes my mind.

Luca: Eenie, meenie, miny... one. I'll count to ten.

The phone vibrates again: a picture of Layla on the living room floor, face down in a pool of blood, hands, and legs tied. A cigar cutter glistens beside her head, and right next to it... a *finger*.

The cell phone slips out of my hand. My blood turns to ice, and my heart reaches cardiac arrest range, beating its way out of my chest like a trapped, wild animal. Fear consumes me whole. It starts in my heart, spreading to my lungs, legs, and the deepest recesses *of* my fucking soul.

I'm losing my grip on reality.

My vision blurs. Within seconds all I see are dark spots. Someone grabs my shoulders. Sounds distort, and voices blend together into incomprehensible gibberish. My legs, like two tubs of water, are fucking useless. I try to move but only manage a few awkward steps before, incapable of anything else, I double over, throwing up.

I'm shaking so violently it feels as if I'm standing through an earthquake. I clasp my hands over the unrestrained thunder of my own pulse ringing in my ears, fighting to distance myself from my delirious mind. My thoughts lose their form. Logic is absent. I fist my hands and close my eyes but regret it immediately when the image of Layla covered in blood flashes before my eyes.

I throw up again.

The ability to control my emotions went to shit. I'm losing my fucking mind. In a mechanical reflex, I reach for my gun, point it at the sky and press the trigger.

Bullet follows after bullet.

The smell of gunpowder, the deafening noise, the recoil—it all helps me regain the ability to think straight, to re-emerge from the helpless madness. With every shot fired, an ounce of fear morphs into a hot, white rage.

That's better.

I can't fucking cope with fear. I've never felt anything close to the madness seizing my mind. I've no idea how to come out on the other side.

But I have to.

I have to get a fucking grip. I can't fall apart. There's no time. I need to act fast before that fucking psycho sends another picture.

"Pull it together," Spades says, squeezing my arm. "She needs you, Dante. Pull it together."

He helps me up from where I'm kneeling on the ground, making sure I can hold my weight before he hands me my phone and a full clip. I reload the gun to feel like I'm in control. Like I'm still capable of functioning while my world splinters apart.

My hands ball into fists, and my jaw locks, muscles so tense it's fucking painful. Three deep breaths, and I turn around, a mask of confidence back in place.

My people stand in a group, waiting for orders. Twenty men in front of Delta, thirty more a phone call away.

"What the fuck are you waiting for?!" I bellow. "Find her!"

Nate, Jackson, and Rookie divide people into smaller groups shouting orders. Next to me, Vince is on the phone using his contacts to find Layla. Vinn does the same thing, standing a few feet away, holding a machine gun.

"I want Luca alive!" I yell when everybody rushes to their cars. "Kill everyone else."

Thirty seconds later, the street fills with the roar of a dozen V8 engines cutting through the peaceful, quiet night. V brothers and Spades stay behind to help me beat the information out of Frank's pawn.

"Where's the last of Frank's men?" I ask.

"In the basement. Luca fucked him up bad."

The sound of his name boils my blood all over again. I want to kill him with my bare hands, inflicting as much pain as possible. I want to hear him beg for mercy. He better have dug his grave before laying a finger on my girl because that's where he'll end up before sunrise.

"I wouldn't count on him telling us much tonight," Spades adds. "If I hadn't dragged Luca out of there when you told me to, he would've fucking killed the guy, and now I know why."

"He'll talk." I dial Carlton's number. "I need you. Right now." The distraught tone of my voice lets on more about my mental state than I wish to share.

"What the fuck happened?"

"I'll explain when you get here. Bring something to keep the fucker conscious. Meet me at the club."

Spades pours a bucket of water over Jack's head. He chokes and coughs, thrashing in the chair like a retard. Blood trickles down his wrists where the ropes cut through the skin. His used-to-be white t-shirt turned crimson and now lays on the floor, drenched in blood. I've been torturing him for an hour. Vinn interjected a few times, using his face for a punching bag. Jack can no longer see. His eyes are swollen shut, and his cheekbones and nose are all broken in at least a few places.

Carlton emptied a syringe into his neck as soon as he arrived. Whatever he gave him worked a treat, stopping Jack from taking the easy way out and fainting. Unfortunately, he's not eager to talk, testing my already questionable patience. I've reached for my gun a few times, but Spades stopped me before I pulled the trigger. Dead, he's useless.

"I think you're too delicate," Vince says. Until now, he stood by the wall, a silent observer.

I glance at him, toying with a long knife. "Be my guest."

He crosses the room toward a row of cabinets at the back of the basement.

"I'll wait outside," Vinn mutters, his face a faint shade of green as he turns to leave.

His brother joins me, armed with a spoon, and my expression probably matches Vinn's. "Give him another dose," he tells Carlton.

"His heart will burst."

Vince rolls his eyes, snatching a syringe out of Carlton's bag. "He only got twenty milligrams before. He'd need three times that to die." He shoves the needle into Jack's neck, tosses the empty syringe, and shimmies out of his suit jacket. He rolls up the sleeves of his white shirt, taking off a gold watch, before gripping a fistful of Jack's hair and tugging hard, forcing his neck to rest on the back of the chair. "You got a girl?" he asks, sliding the spoon down his forehead. "You remember what she looks like? Of course, you do. Think about her for a minute. Try to remember her smile. Memorize it because you won't see it again."

Without warning, asking, or ordering Jack to talk, Vince slides the edge of the spoon under his eye. A horror movie kind of scream—loud, long, blood curdling high-pitched scream fills the room. Vince holds him in place, and a chill runs down my spine when Jack realizes the slightest move will make things worse. He sits there, still as a statue, screaming.

"Stop!" His nails crack when he digs them into the wooden chair. "Stop! Layla's in the warehouse!"

Vince stops but doesn't pull the spoon out. Almost half of it has disappeared under Jack's eye already. "Which warehouse, Jack? I'm going to need an address."

"S Kreiter Avenue. NASC warehouse," he pants.

"And I should believe you because...?"

"Because it's time for the finale." The tone of his voice changes; fear evaporates, leaving no trace.

Vince pulls the spoon out, as surprised as I am. "Finale?"

Jack sits up as much as the ropes allow. "In an hour, you'll wish you were dead, Dante. I promise. Frank made sure of it."

Frank will die tonight. I don't fucking care who kills him. I want him and all his people dead because all of them, knowingly or not, contributed to hurting the only person that matters to me.

"I can promise you something too," I say, taking my gun out. "If I don't find her there, I'll gouge your girlfriend's eyes."

"You'll find her, and you'll regret you ever did."

Never.

I pull the trigger silencing Jack forever. "Get everyone to that warehouse," I tell Spades. "Now."

Vinn joins us when we walk out of Delta, and we all jump into our respective cars. I put my foot down, the tires screeching. Every mile closer to Layla makes it easier to control my emotions. I know where my star is. God be my witness, I'll obliterate the whole fucking state to get to her.

CHAPTER
THIRTY-FOUR
Layla

A line of light entering the claustrophobic cell through a slit under the door is my focus point. Curling in the corner, I hug my knees, rocking back and forth. The room is cold, the floor damp. The stifling stench of wet concrete and mold makes me nauseous.

A tray with food Luca brought when he threw me in here sits where he left it, untouched. A cockroach swims in the watery oatmeal, struggling to escape the confinement of a metal bowl. His attempts are desperate, as if he mocks me for giving up. I accepted my destiny. I'm waiting for death to arrive, the Grim Reaper in a black leather jacket with Dante's face, a gun in his hand instead of a scythe. He has every right to kill me. My father won't come to my rescue; his triumph is the only acceptable outcome. Saving me means defeat, and Frank is too proud to go down without a fight.

The surrounding four walls will be my prison until my body gives up from tiredness, thirst, or hunger. Or until a bullet penetrates my head or heart. Frank won't give Dante the North regardless of how much hurt Dante can bring upon him. Even if he kills me, Jess, and his men. Until Frank is no longer breathing, North will remain under his command.

I rest my forehead on my knees. There's no sleeping in this place. I'm exhausted, but fear keeps me alert. Unwanted pictures of the moments I spent with Dante flood my mind whenever I close my eyes. I remember every touch of his lips, every night spent in his arms, every look of his green eyes, and I loathe myself more with every second.

Heavy footsteps echo outside the door, clapping loudly in the still, silent space. My heart tries to make a run for it, climbing to my throat. I squeeze into the corner, trembling and hiding the bandaged hand to protect my remaining fingers. I jump, startled by the sound of keys hitting the concrete floor.

"Fuck," Luca clips.

Apart from the bowl, the cockroach, and the tray, nothing around could be used as a weapon. No hole to hide in. The door swings open with a loud creak letting bright light filter inside the room. My fear threatens to turn into a full-blown panic attack at the sight of the cigar cutter in Luca's hand.

"Eenie, meenie, miny, mo. Which finger will you give up voluntarily, Layla?" He basks in his power, smiling maniacally.

I can't speak, move, or force my eyes shut.

I don't want to see or feel, and I no longer want to live.

"I'm kidding. You can keep your fingers."

My eyes dart to his face. He'd only spare me if Frank surrendered to Dante. That's not possible.

Had Dante changed his mind? Is he allowing me to leave? Or maybe he wants to talk before he decides what to do? Or maybe Frank is dead...

Luca crouches beside me, tearing my hand from behind my back. "The dressing needs changing, but it'll have to wait. Boss wants to talk to you. I'll go get him. Make yourself presentable." He turns to leave when a gun goes off in the distance. "Shit." He looks into the corridor, a gun in hand.

The acoustic warehouse fills with screams. More shots are fired, the noise ricocheting off the walls.

Luca grabs my arm and drags me in front of him like a human shield, one hand across my stomach. He presses the cool gun to my temple, pushing me out of the room. We turn left, and the subsequent shots seem to come from different directions as if we're in the middle of the shootout.

"Luca!" Dante booms far behind us.

And instead of fear, I feel *relieved*.

Something in the tone of his voice doesn't match the situation. He doesn't sound as if he's calling him over. He sounds as if he wants to tear him apart.

I stop in my tracks, watching the pieces fall into place before my eyes. "Dante didn't tell you to bring me here," I mumble to myself, "This place, my finger... it wasn't Dante's orders! He doesn't know."

Luca shoves at me, so I'll move, but my legs are glued to the spot. "No, he doesn't. Not yet, but he'll find out soon enough. Get moving. It's almost over."

I spin to look at him, ignoring the gun pointed at my head. "You work for Frank!" I yell, and Luca covers my mouth.

"Luca!" Dante booms again, closer this time.

"Yes, I work for Frank, you dumb bitch. Now *move!*"

I shove his hand away from my mouth. "That's why you watched over me," I mutter. Swelling at the thought that Frank had gone to extreme lengths to keep me safe while I fulfilled the plan. "You were supposed to keep me safe."

"Blah, blah, blah," Luca snaps. "I was supposed to make you more believable and help if you started screwing up. And fuck if I didn't. You got any idea how hard I worked to keep this plan from falling apart?" he scoffs, running his hand through his short hair. "Aaron was first, then the brawl at Delta, then I killed that moron who hit you... all so Dante would trust me with you, so I could be at his house tonight to take you away instead of putting the fire out in Delta."

"Aaron was your idea?!"

Luca grits his teeth and grabs me in the middle, throwing me over his shoulder. "Dante's got a savior complex." He ignores my fists, ramming his back. "Aaron was a trigger. Dante respected your wish. He left you alone, but that wasn't part of the plan. *Obviously.* We had to improvise." He stands me up, turning me toward the metal emergency door. "Open it."

"Luca!" Dante booms again, closing in on us.

"Open it!" He taps the gun against my temple. "He can't catch us inside."

I pull on the handle. It's still dark outside. The area doesn't look familiar but brings to mind a closed factory. Old machinery with flat tires stands scattered around next to a few rusty containers.

"Why not tell me you work for Frank? Why maim me? Why bring me here?" I'm stalling, asking every question that springs to mind to keep Luca occupied, to make him slip, so that I can run or Dante can catch up to us. "Why did you kidnap me from Dante's house?"

"Stop talking!" he snaps. "Where the fuck does Dante get his patience from? Everything we did was to lure him here." A sinister laugh escapes his lips. "Straight into the trap."

We walk toward a white van parked by one of the containers. Luca's pace slows, and I swear in my head. This is where he wanted Dante all along; out in the open, where he's ready for him. I look around, searching for silhouettes hiding in the shadows, but see no one. The emergency exit door flies open, hitting the wall with a bang. We turn around, face to face with Dante. His eyes are on me, scrutinizing my body, searching for cuts or bruises, his gun aimed at Luca, who hides behind me, his gun to my head.

"Let. Her. *Go*." Dante's voice is stoic, cold, and terrifying.

"He'll kill you," I whisper to Luca.

"Frankie won't let him."

Nate runs outside through the open door, followed by Jackson, Spades, and the rest of Dante's men. Everyone aims at Luca, who tenses behind me. Neither my father nor his pawns are within eyesight. Maybe they're all dead by now.

Dante waits a few seconds for Luca to obey the order, but when that doesn't happen, he looks at me, and his eyes dart to the ground. I catch it just in time. Trusting my instincts, I bend my knees, sliding down Luca's body while Dante pulls the trigger. The bullet wooshes above my head, hitting its target. Luca's lifeless body hits the ground with a thud.

Dante takes one step toward me, worry etched in his expression, but he stops at the sound of quiet, rhythmic clapping. Frank emerges from the side of the building along with Adam, Burly, and a whole army of men. Each one aims at a different member of Dante's crew. Frank takes his time, approaching with a revolver pointed at the back of Dante's head, a triumphant smile on his lips.

I stare into the green eyes of the man I love but have to learn to let go of within the next few minutes, or my heart will give out. Somewhere along the way, I forgot there would be no happily-ever-after. I fell in love, ignoring the consequences.

A single tear slips down my cheek.

Frank stops a few steps behind Dante, taking a second gun out of his pocket. "I've been waiting too long for this moment, my friend." He's not shouting, but the power of his voice makes him heard by everyone. He moves his eyes to me as he breathes a theatrical sigh of relief. "I'm so proud of you, baby girl."

He throws the spare gun my way, and I catch it with trembling hands.

Dante's face turns white.

His eyes stop shining.

And his heart stops beating for me.

"Yes," Frank says, smiling as if this is the best day of his life. "I'm taking away what you hold, dearest, Dante. I'm taking away what you love most. Now you know what it feels like to be betrayed by the person you trust with your life." He looks at me again, and his smile grows wider. "Do the honors. It's your prize for the time you spent with him."

It never crossed my mind that Frank might want *me to* kill Dante. He calls it a prize, but he means punishment for my insubordination, for loving his enemy. The last test of loyalty. I can't fail now, not after all I've done, not when the finish line is so close. I have to do it, or else nothing will change. Tomorrow I'll still be a stranger to my own father... I won't get another chance to earn his love.

"Why didn't you tell me about Luca?" I ask, stalling again.

"You're more believable when you don't know the details."

Anger bubbles inside me like boiling water. "You told him to cut off my finger!"

Dante shudders but remains silent, standing there with his gun pointed at the ground, his stance poised, eyes not veering off my face for one second.

"You think Dante would come to your rescue if I locked you in a hotel with a bottle of champagne and a butler?"

"He'd come for me everywhere."

I'm as sure of it as I'm sure that either I kill him or Frank does. I squeeze the gun and raise it, tasting the salty tears on my lips. I aim at the man who trusted and loved me the way I always wanted to be loved—unconditionally.

"I really do love you," I whisper, looking into his eyes, my voice defeated. I don't want him to die thinking he never knew true love or that the time we shared was worthless.

I found peace where there should be fear, happiness where there should be disappointment, and love where nothing but death should await.

"I know, Star." Not a hint of doubt on his face or in his voice. He knows me well enough to understand my reasons.

My hand is shaking, but I slide my finger to the trigger. "I'm sorry," I mutter, my heart no longer beating as powerful sobs tear me apart.

"Do you need me to count down from five for you, Layla?" Frank growls, disdain in his voice like a low blow to my stomach. "We don't have all fucking night. Get it over with."

I let the air out of my lungs, blink the tears away and pull the trigger. The recoil throws my hand back. At the shooting range, guns were loaded with blanks and seemed weaker than the .44 that falls to the ground.

The bullet pierces his heart, but it's not the precision that surprises me most.

It's relief.

I feel *free*.

Silence falls upon the scene. Frank's gray eyes remain open as his motionless, lifeless body lies on the gravel, blood seeping from the wound in his chest.

Dante stares at him for a few seconds before he spins around, his back to me. Frank's men kneel before him in surrender, dropping their weapons, heads hanging low.

Adam dies first.

A bullet from Dante's Beretta strikes Adam's head, and he falls as if in slow motion. Allie's face flashes before my eyes, and fear grips me by the throat.

The second bullet is for Burly.

I force my legs to move, painfully aware that one of those bullets is destined for me. I drop to my knees by Luca's body, frantically searching his pockets for the keys to the white van. My hands are covered in blood when I pull them out of his jacket. Adrenaline keeps me moving, my senses agile, though exhausted; my mind focused, though hesitant.

Panic is pushed back by survival instinct.

Gunshots tear through the otherwise silent night as I run toward the van, not daring to check how many people died. The engine springs to life seconds later. My foot hard on the pedal, I make a sharp turn, burning out of there, praying to get as far away as possible. I tremble like a leaf, ignoring blood and the piercing pain in my left.

Tears are absent.

I don't regret killing my father. Hearing the disdain in his voice helped me realize he was rotten to his core. There was no saving him, no gaining his love or acceptance. Nothing would've changed if I'd kill Dante. Frank would find a different thing to obsess over, a different reason to keep me at a distance.

He didn't deserve me, my love, or my allegiance.

I risk my life when I park the van outside Frank's house. I need money, documents, and clothes to start over somewhere far away from the man I love.

"What are you doing?" Jess enters my bedroom while I'm throwing things into two large travel bags. "What happened?" She points at the crimson bandage on my hand, her eyes wide.

"Frank is dead," I say, rushing from the wardrobe to the bathroom and back, packing everything I can get my hands on. "Dante's taking over Chicago. I'm leaving." I grip her by her frail shoulders. "You shouldn't stay, Jess. Run as soon as you can."

Her chin quivers, eyes pooling with tears. "He's dead? Frankie's *dead*?" She covers her mouth. "How? What happened? Why are you running?!"

I zip the bags, shoving Jess aside to throw them down the stairs. "I have to go. I can't stay, Mom..." Words stick in my throat, so I simply hug her and leave.

I burst into Frank's office. The only safe in the house I know the combination to is in his desk. I load a bag with as much cash as I can fit in there, then fill my coat pockets. I load the trunk of my BMW and start the engine, but Jess stops me, opening the driver's side door.

"Why are you running?!" she sobs, taking my hand. "Where are you going?!"

"I don't know, but I need to leave." I push her away, grabbing the door handle. "Stay safe. I'll call you soon."

She nods, mascara-stained tears rolling down her cheeks. I don't look back when I drive through the gate and onto the road. I won't miss this place. No happy memories exist in my mind of Frank or Jess. All the best moments of my life I spent in a different house, with a man who hates me more than he ever loved me.

I don't know where I'm going or if I'll ever be safe again. I only know that my life has changed forever.

TO BE CONTINUED...

Let's connect! Join my reader group and newsletter for exclusive news, content and giveaways

Instagram
Facebook
Reader Group

Layla and Dante's story continues in

BROKEN
promises

I. A. DICE

Printed in Great Britain
by Amazon